CONTACT

ALSO BY JONATHAN BUCKLEY

The Biography of Thomas Lang

Xerxes

Ghost MacIndoe

Invisible

So He Takes the Dog

Published in 2010 by
Sort Of Books
PO Box 18678, London NW3 2FL
www.sortof.co.uk

Distributed by
Profile Books
3a Exmouth House, Pine Street,
London EC1R OJH

10 9 8 7 6 5 4 3 2 1

Typeset in Melior to a design by Henry Iles

272pp.

A CIP catalogue record for this book is available from the British Library

ISBN 978 095600 386 7

CONTACT

JONATHAN BUCKLEY

Sort Of
BOOKS

for Susanne Hillen and Bruno Buckley

1

My life began to veer badly off-course on a Tuesday morning in May. I had been to my company's Guildford branch, in North Street, and was on my way back to the car when my phone rang: it was Kirsten, a researcher from a TV production company that was putting together a programme on British designers. She'd contacted me a week earlier, to ask if I'd be able to give them an interview, and now she was ringing to talk about the schedule, and to tell me a little about the presenter: Otis Mizrahi was his name, and he was, Kirsten told me, totally brilliant – a star in the making. Seconds after this conversation had ended, the phone rang again.

This call was from Alan Stirling, the manager of our Tottenham Court Road showroom. He told me that a young man had turned up, asking to see me. Or rather, demanding to see me – this character had been aggressive from the outset. When Alan had explained that I wouldn't be at the showroom today and didn't know when I'd next be in, the man had made it clear that he thought he was being given the brush-off, and more or less called Alan a liar. For a second or two it had seemed that things might turn nasty, but Alan had eventually managed to convince him that he really didn't know the details of his employer's timetable. 'When you see him, give him this,' the man had said, scrawling a number on the back of a catalogue, then he'd left in a hurry, barging a customer out of the way. Alan read out the number and I made a note of it, but no sooner had I written it down than Kirsten was on the phone again, and in the course of the drive back home I had another call from my office at Tottenham Court Road – we had a problem with one of our suppliers. The problem turned out to be a major one. So, within an hour, Alan's troublesome young man had been shunted into a remote siding of my mind. Consequently, I didn't get round to calling the number that evening.

The next day I reached Tottenham Court Road at about ten o'clock. Alan had news: yesterday's visitor had been waiting at the door when he'd arrived, and had been even more unpleasant than previously. Straight away he'd accused Alan of having failed to pass on the message. 'This is important,' he'd said, talking over Alan's reply and giving him a hard stare. He'd written down the number again. 'This is what you're gonna do,' he'd said. 'You're gonna ring your boss and I'm gonna come back this afternoon to check you've done it. And if you don't do it, I'll be a very unhappy bunny.' Alan had asked if he could tell Mr Pattison what this was about. 'It's personal,' he'd said, with a smile that was worse than his stare.

'What age was this chap?' I asked. He was in his mid-twenties, Alan guessed. He described him: a little over six feet tall, short dark hair, muscular, grey eyes, a scar – a burn, he thought – on one forearm. Tattoos as well. The description brought no one to mind.

I rang the number, and the person who answered was disconcertingly polite. 'Thank you for calling, Mr Pattison,' he said. There was a trace of East End in the voice, a trace that became more prominent, erratically, in the exchange that followed. He denied having used threatening behaviour with my manager – he'd simply wanted to impress upon him (his words exactly) that this was an extremely important matter. 'I didn't care for his attitude, I have to say,' he said. 'He wasn't very accommodating. Off-hand. Like he couldn't be arsed. Couldn't be bothered, I mean. But if I put the wind up him, I'm sorry. I just thought he'd binned my number, and I wanted to make sure he understood the situation.'

I wanted to know what this important matter might be.

'Nothing bad,' the man replied. 'Opposite of bad, in fact, so don't worry yourself on that score.'

I assured him that I was not worrying myself and was rather busy, so would he please get to the point.

'Oh, right. Sure. OK,' he said, like a schoolboy called to order. 'Thing is, this has to be face to face. Not like this. It's not something I can do over the phone. When you see me, you'll understand. Believe me. I'm not taking the piss. I mean, this isn't a wind-up,' he said.

There was no possibility, I replied, of my scheduling a meeting with someone whose name I didn't know, for purposes equally unknown.

'Sam,' said the man. 'My name's Sam and this really is worth your while, believe me. All I need is five minutes, no more than that. Any place, any time. Straight up: five minutes is all, and you'll thank me for it. Name the place. Give me five minutes, that's all I'm asking.' I hesitated. 'You think I got heavy with your manager and you're thinking I'll get heavy with you. Is that it? Is that the problem?'

This wasn't the problem, I told him, untruthfully.

'Look,' he went on, 'the bloke was nervous. OK. I accept I made him nervous. Wasn't my intention, but there you

go. He's a little geezer. I'm not. The place was empty. Just
the two of us. He felt he was at a disadvantage. So you
and me, we'll meet where there's a crowd, OK? Kind of
insurance policy, if you like. We meet in the shop, go for a
coffee and a chat. A quick chat. Whenever you like. What
do you say? Not a lot to ask, is it? Come on. Believe me,
I'm not having you on. It'll be worth your while. What do
you say?' he repeated, and then he said 'Please,' with so
strange an intonation – almost as though we were long-
standing friends who had fallen out and he was pleading
for a reconciliation – that I found myself saying that I'd
think about it.

'What's there to think about?' he said. 'Name a day, I'll
be there. You're not going to get any trouble from me, I
guarantee. But I do need to see you. So, give me a day.
Any day. Any time. But soon.' I said I'd give him a call
in a day or two. This was not acceptable: 'No,' he said
emphatically. 'Don't give me that. Come on. This is important.'

I told him I'd be free the following Thursday, around
lunchtime. 'That's good for me,' he replied instantly.
'What's lunchtime in your world? One? Let's say one, at
the shop.'

Not wanting him in the showroom, I suggested instead
a café on Warren Street.

'Great. Cool. I'll be there. But you're a busy guy. I know
that. So if something comes up, give me a bell. OK? You've
got my number. If you're held up for some reason, we'll
fix another time. OK?' I agreed that I would do that. 'Nice
to talk to you. Thanks for this. I appreciate it,' he said,
as if deeply touched by something unusually considerate
that I'd done for him.

The following Thursday, at 1 p.m., I walked into the
café. It was busy and I couldn't at first see anyone who

was unaccompanied. Then I saw, in the furthest corner of the room, a man sitting at a small table; he was the only solitary person in the room. His head was lowered, presenting a crop of black hair in which three or four scars stood out like ticks of chalk. He was wearing a black sweatshirt that was flecked with paint of various colours, and as I approached he was picking a scab of paint or plaster off the back of a finger. Glancing up, he seemed to recognise me instantly and stood up with such urgency he almost toppled his chair. He offered a hand, smiling as though meeting a celebrity; the hand was as rough as a dry old glove, and his grip would have shattered a mug. 'Very pleased to meet you,' he said. 'Really pleased. Thanks for giving up your time.' And before I could say a word he went on, having sat down: 'Look, I think, on second thoughts, this isn't the best place. Didn't think we'd have such a crowd. I mean, I can hear every word of what's going on next door,' he said, blatantly aiming a dismissive look at the two women seated to his left. 'Don't want to feel like we're being bugged, do we? We don't want an audience.'

'An audience wouldn't bother me,' I said.

'I think it could do,' he answered, with a smile that hinted momentarily at intimidation, then seemed to be promising me a pleasant surprise. 'But we can stay here if you like,' he said, raising his hands. A tattoo of red and blue Gothic script appeared, running under the sleeve from the inside of the wrist of his right arm. 'If you insist. But I really do think it'd be better outside. Let's take a stroll. Down towards Goodge Street. By the time we get there I'll be done. Ten minutes, tops,' he said, standing up. A waitress, hurrying to our table, slowed down and gave me a questioning tilt of the head. 'It's all right, babe. We're leaving,' he told her loudly, adding a wink, plus another for the two women alongside. He held the door open and swept an arm outward with overdone courtesy.

'So what's this all about?' I began, once we had turned the corner. 'Let's start with who you are.'

'I'm Sam. Sam Williams,' was the reply. This was answer enough, he clearly believed. He looked me in the eyes, to ascertain that his name had tripped the right circuits.

In my mind, however, very little was happening. Only two connections suggested themselves. 'As in Clive?' I asked. 'You're related to Clive?'

'Who?'

'Clive Williams. Used to work for me.'

'No. Try again.' We had come to a pedestrian crossing. Sam Williams turned his face towards me, to offer a clue that surely could not be misread.

'Simon Williams?'

'And who might he be?'

'A neighbour, years ago.'

'Cold. Very cold,' he replied, with a frowning smile, surprised at how badly I was doing.

At this point my patience expired. 'Look, just tell me—'

Irked by this rebuke, he interrupted me with: 'That's Williams as in Sarah Williams. I'm her son.'

The meaning of the name took a second or two to arrive. Sarah, absent from my mind for years, was now there; for now, however, she brought no association of guilt. Ignoring the signal to cross, Sam kept his face in front of mine, allowing me to examine his features for a few seconds longer. In the set of the mouth there was, perhaps, a slight similarity to Sarah's; nothing more.

'We'd better get moving,' he said. 'People will think we're a pair of queers.' He stepped out into the road, forcing a taxi to brake; the driver snarled at him, and received from Sam a savage stare and 'Go fuck yourself.'

At the kerb he touched me on the elbow, lightly, yet impelling me to keep pace; it was as though we had a pressing appointment and were running late. 'You see the resemblance?' he asked.

'Possibly,' I said.

'Possibly?' he cocked his head back, startled. 'You're having me on. You must be. It's totally obvious.' Putting fingertips to his chin, he presented his profile to me.

'Maybe,' I said, observing nothing familiar.

'OK. OK,' he muttered, coming to terms with the disappointment of this response. 'It's been a long time, I suppose. You haven't got a clear picture any more. That's understandable. But believe me, I look like her. I really do.' He tugged a flattened packet of cigarettes from the back pocket of his jeans, lit one, and went through the motions of offering one to me.

'So—' I said, inviting an interruption.

'Yes?'

'How is she? What's she doing nowadays?'

Sam took a long drag and expelled a strong jet of smoke. His lips tightened; his gaze turned penetratingly downward, as if he were considering a question of great difficulty; and then he laughed. 'Not a lot,' he said. 'Not a lot. Nothing at all, in fact. The thing is, she's dead.'

The impact of this announcement was not especially strong, and there was no element of grief in what I now experienced. The emotion that prevailed, for the first few moments, was something like relief that the purpose of this meeting had now been declared. 'I'm very sorry to hear that,' I said.

He nodded but did not look at me. His next drag consumed a quarter of the cigarette.

'When did she die?' I asked.

'Four months ago. Five.'

'What happened?'

'Brain haemorrhage.'

Again I expressed sympathy.

'Getting a meal ready, she was,' he went on. 'Opened a cupboard door and – pumpfff!' He brought a forearm down from the vertical to the horizontal, shaking his head – not so much upset by the manner of her death, it seemed, as amazed at the immediacy of it.

'I'm very sorry,' I repeated; the only response from Sam was a shrug. Still we were walking rapidly towards Goodge Street. 'Thank you for telling me,' I said, slowing.

Sam halted, turned to face me, and squinted as if he suspected that my remark had carried a subtle meaning. 'So?' he said.

I had no idea what he required me to say. 'Is there any other family, apart from you?' I asked.

'Just me,' he said, maintaining the squint.

Evidently a particular question was expected of me, but I couldn't think what it might be. 'Do you live in London?' I asked, finding nothing better.

'For the time being.'

'Whereabouts?'

'South,' he replied, with a small quick smirk, then his scrutiny relaxed and he exhaled the sigh of a man giving up. 'Fuck me,' he whispered. 'You're slow, old chap, you know that? Really slow. You're not getting it, are you?' He scanned the street to right and left, put a hand to my back, and propelled me twenty paces along the pavement, until we were standing by a van that had silvered windows at the back. He stepped down into the gutter, pulling me with him. 'Look,' he ordered, pointing to the images of ourselves in the glass. His reflection regarded me incredulously. 'Come on, Mr Pattison. For God's sake. It's obvious. Look. Look,' he whined, passing a hand in front of the adjacent faces, back and forth, back and forth. 'Sarah was my mother. You're my father. Look.'

All I saw was a grin on the face of Sam, and my own flabby stupefaction. A weakness struck me; I felt the ground lurch. 'That's not possible,' I said.

He was smiling at me with the happiness of accomplishment. 'Not just possible, Mr Pattison,' he said. 'True. Totally true. Your son – here I am.' He clapped a hand to my shoulder in congratulation, then hooked a hand under my armpit to hoist me out of the gutter.

'She said nothing,' I objected. 'She'd have told me.'

In a gesture of powerless sympathy his arms rose and fell. 'What can I say? She didn't like you. She didn't like me. There you go. We're in the same boat.'

As I regarded my supposed son, I was seized by the courage of a timid man who instantly decides that he refuses to be mugged. 'I don't believe it,' I stated. 'It's impossible.'

'You've already said that,' he replied. 'It's a lot more than possible. It's a fact.'

'You're nothing like me.'

'I can't believe you don't see it. I just can't.'

'There's nothing to see.'

'Maybe it's your eyes,' he suggested. 'I'm not being funny, but do you normally wear glasses?

'My eyes are fine. There's nothing to see.'

He put out a hand to take my arm. 'Let's walk,' he said.

'Let's not,' I said, stepping out of reach.

He withdrew his hand, as if from a small dog that had snapped, but he was smiling. 'It's a shock for you. A big shock. I understand,' he said.

The smile became patronising; there was nothing in it of the emotion that a man would surely feel upon being united with his father after more than a quarter of a century apart. 'Who are you, really?' I said. 'What do you want?'

Sam wrenched his face into an expression of wounded perplexity. 'What do you mean, what do I want? You're my father. A few months ago I'd never heard of you. Then I found out who you were, and I thought I should meet you. Natural, isn't it?' Taking my bemused nod as assent, he went on: 'It's a story. I'll tell you everything. Anything you want to know, I'll tell you. But this isn't the place. Not the place, not the time. I know how you feel. It's unreal. It's a bit unreal for me, to be frank, but for you it must be weirder. I understand. I do. You need time to get used to the idea. We both have to take our time. This is just the start. We'll build on this. We'll—'

He might have gone on for minutes like this, had I not murmured: 'It's simply not possible.'

This made him pause, but only for a few seconds. 'Proof,' he resumed. 'You want proof, don't you? I can tell that's what you're thinking. It is, isn't it? That's OK. No offence taken. You won't believe it until you see it in black and white.' The tone was that of an adult addressing a child who required a demonstration of the bizarre notion that something made of metal could float on water. 'It's fine. I'll give you proof. When you're ready, we'll meet again. Give me a call. Or I'll give you a call. Let's have your number.'

'I'll give you a call,' I said.

'Sure. Sure. Whatever you like. You've got my number, yeah?'

'I have it.'

'OK. Good. OK.' He was shifting from foot to foot now, rubbing his hands together. 'Well, we've started. You're a busy man. I'll not keep you. A week, say? We'll get together in a week. Call me,' he said, shoving a hand into mine. As he sauntered away he had the swagger of a lout strolling away from a man he'd just punched unconscious for insulting him. When he was a hundred yards off, however, he turned and waved to me, and he was more like a boy walking down the garden path, waving goodbye to his parents.

2

Aileen was in the kitchen when I got home; she'd been up in London, to meet a couple of clients and to help her sister choose an outfit for a friend's silver wedding anniversary party. She was at the sink, preparing a salad, with her back to me. I walked up to her and put my arms around her waist. A scent of chamomile rose from her hair, a perfume so comforting that it made me put a kiss there, lightly. Then it struck me that this kiss was an unusual thing for me to do, and I let go. She didn't turn round, of which I was glad – I was sure my face would show her that something was amiss. I started to set the table.

'How was your day?' she asked me, over her shoulder. I told her about the football player who'd walked into the showroom and within half an hour had bought the best part of twenty thousand pounds' worth of furniture, most of it red. He'd had his girlfriend with him, who'd carried on as if the CCTV cameras were the lenses of the paparazzi, and kept shielding her face from them while doing little twirls that made her skirt fly up. Alan had felt obliged to make out that he knew who she was, but he didn't have a clue; he wouldn't have known who the footballer was if a courier hadn't told him. The footballer had seemed like a nice enough lad, I told her, then I realised I was talking too much. The pedal bin needed emptying, so I busied myself with that. 'And how was Eleanor?' I asked.

She gave me a clenched-teeth smile and rolled her eyes. For two hours they had trawled Oxford Street and Regent Street, looking for a dress that was stylish and expensive-looking without actually being expensive; having tried on more than twenty, and become increasingly dismayed by what the changing-room mirrors were showing her, she'd opted for a dress she'd picked out right at the start of the expedition. 'Not sure my presence was necessary,' said Aileen. But Cerys had met them for a coffee, and she was on great form, she told me with a smile, a particular smile that her niece often brings out in her. Cerys was in a semi-professional production of *Anything Goes*, and rehearsals were going well: the director, it appeared, was quite taken with her. She had a new boyfriend as well: Simon, a trainee vet, who also had a part in the show. 'It's always good to see her,' said Aileen. A pause followed, in which Sam – having been held at bay for a while – sprang forcefully back into my mind. I took the bin-bag outside.

Over the meal we talked about my conversation with Kirsten, and what I was going to say on the programme, and various trivialities, then we watched TV for a while. Aileen went to bed early, halfway through a film. 'Sorry,' she said, giving my hand a squeeze as she rose from the sofa. 'Oxford Street has caught up with me.' I stayed downstairs for another hour, perhaps wanting to be sure that Aileen would be asleep when I went up.

I kept the TV on, but I wasn't really watching it. I wasn't really thinking, either – it was as though I had mild concussion. I looked around the room. The things that it contained – the furniture, the pictures, the souvenirs – were evidence not just of the years that Aileen and I had spent together: they signified a deep accord, an enduring like-mindedness, and in the act of looking at them I seemed to be reminding myself of the contentment of that like-mindedness. I found my attention returning to the objects that were ranged on a shelf behind the television, and I took some of them down, as if I needed to touch them to get the full meaning out of them. I picked up a glass paperweight; I had no idea where it had come from. Ditto a small brass urn with a lid that didn't open. A figurine of a morose clog-wearing boy sitting on a tree stump, however, I knew to be a gift to Aileen from Eleanor, but why or where it had been bought, I couldn't recall. But next to the boy stood something – a little basalt cow – that instantly raised a full-bodied memory: Aileen had bought it about fifteen years earlier, in a village in the Massif Central, near the place where a lunatic called Raël claimed to have been taken to a planet where he'd met Muhammad, Buddha, Moses and Jesus; there was picture of crazy Raël in the shop, which was run by a huge woman with violet hair and beads the size and colour of satsumas round her neck; the day was so hot that the soles of our shoes stuck to the road and Aileen burned her hand on the car door. A portable sundial, made in 1900 by the Ansonia Clock Company of Brooklyn, likewise brought back the occasion of its acquisition: we'd found it amid a pile of junk at a market in Canterbury, soon after we'd moved into the flat in Chatham Road. And at this point, finally, inevitably, Sarah re-entered my thoughts, as though she'd been waiting for the right moment to come in.

It was while Aileen and I were living in Chatham Road that I'd become involved with Sarah. The circumstances in which it had begun were fairly clear: she had been a customer; she'd bought a small table from me, and later a bowl, a cherrywood bowl; she came to the shop quite frequently, perhaps as often as a dozen times in the space of half a year, but, as I remembered it, I never realised how keenly she was interested in me until the day of the photographs. She'd recently come back from a holiday in Morocco, and her tan was accentuated by the white shirt – a man's white shirt – that she was wearing, under a scuffed leather jacket, blouson style, soft, sandy in colour. Remembering that afternoon, I saw this quite distinctly. In the pocket of the jacket she had some holiday snaps, which she showed me. It was the usual stuff: beaches, mountains, gangs of smiling children, a huge lizard on a wall, dazzling fabrics. Then there was Sarah on a motorbike, Sarah haggling at a market stall, Sarah in hiking boots, and lastly Sarah lying belly-down in shallow water, topless. I was holding the picture, and she made no attempt to hurry me along; she laughed, but there was no embarrassment in the laugh; she gave me a look. Remembering this moment, I couldn't recall precisely what this look had been. Perhaps it was like the look she'd directed at the camera? I didn't know. But I remembered that there was a look, and that it surprised me as much as the photo itself. And I surprised myself by feeling a momentary envy of the man – obviously it had been a man – who had taken the shot. The shirt that she was wearing was his, I decided. It's possible, even, that I actually said that I envied him.

I sat in front of the TV, staring at the wall, trying to picture the scene, to hear what I'd said to her, to reconstruct what had followed. We'd met late one afternoon, near the castle; the light was extraordinary – the walls were apricot in the sun, but the sky above them was dark purple; this, I was almost certain, had been our first rendezvous. But when I tried to dredge from my mind some remnants of the first time I'd gone to her flat, I found that those hours were wholly lost to me. Instead what came to the surface were moments from one of our last arguments: Sarah screaming at me, wanting me to believe that she was heartbroken by my decision to move to London, that she hated me for it, when in fact we'd both known for a while that we were at the end. Now I came to think of it, I was sure that I'd told her that I was going to London only after (some time after) a row in which she'd ridiculed the very idea that she might have loved me, as if the notion of her having any serious attachment to me were nothing but a product of my vanity. I could picture her sitting on the windowsill of her bedroom, arms crossed, glaring; I saw the dismissive quick uplift of her chin, the disdainful slow lowering of her eyelids, and I could hear her telling me that I was running away. That was why I was going to London – to get away from her. This wasn't true, I said.

There might, however, have been some justice to the accusation. Aileen and I had been talking about moving to London before I met Sarah, but it was not unlikely that Sarah had been a factor in the timing of it. An opportunity had arisen for Aileen, and I had an offer of work as well, but would I have hesitated more than I did, had the circumstances been different? 'Why is this the first I've heard of it?' Sarah had demanded. I couldn't recall what I'd answered, and I didn't have an answer now. Had I embarked on the affair knowing that it would necessarily be ended soon, when Aileen and I left for London? Or had I thought, at some point, that the relationship with Sarah might turn into something more than an affair? Was that why I hadn't said anything to her – because I'd not been entirely certain that I would be leaving? I found it hard to believe that this might have been what had been going through my mind. Then again, it was hard to believe that the affair had happened at all.

I couldn't answer my own questions, and from the meagre material of my memories I couldn't make a story that I knew to be true. I had always told myself that I had learned truly to love Aileen after the affair with Sarah, that I had appreciated her properly only after it was over, that having indulged in that meaningless excitement I had made a new and genuine commitment to the woman I now knew I would stay with for the rest of my life. But perhaps, rather than seeing Aileen more clearly, I had been motivated by remorse more than anything else? Had I married Aileen to atone for my betrayal of her? And perhaps, though Sarah had told me 'I don't want to know where you're going', as if my treachery had merited perfect oblivion, she had in fact been as distraught by my departure as she had sometimes said she was. And maybe she simply hadn't been able to find me again, after I'd left? No – this idea was implausible. If she'd been expecting a child, I convinced myself, she would have found me.

It was long past midnight when I went up to bed. I tried not to wake Aileen, but as I lay down she smiled without opening her eyes. 'I was dreaming of the biggest department store in the universe,' she said, with her eyes still shut. 'I was on the escalators with Eleanor. You couldn't see where they ended. They went on forever.' A minute later she was asleep again.

I lay beside her, thinking of Sarah, trying to see her clearly, and failing. When I pictured her sitting on the sill in her bedroom, telling me what a creep I was, I saw a figure that I knew to be Sarah: this figure spoke some words that I knew she had spoken, and the figure had attributes that had been hers – she was slim, her hair was auburn and piled up messily, the tone of the voice was Sarah's. She gestured as Sarah used to gesture. But this imagined figure wasn't fully in focus – it was as though I were seeing her with my peripheral vision. When I tried to make her face appear, I only glimpsed her as she sped out of sight too quickly for me to fix the image in my mind. Were she still alive, I told myself, I could have walked past her in the street without recognising her.

A week after my first encounter with Sam, I rang him to suggest that we meet the following week. 'I appreciate it,' he kept saying, as if deferring to a magistrate who had shown him leniency. We arranged to meet in Russell Square Gardens, at midday.

3

A hazy drizzle had begun a few minutes before I reached the gardens, yet Sam was slouched on a bench, with his head lolling against the upper slat and his eyes closed, as though enjoying a dose of sunshine instead of getting a faceful of light rain. A cigarette drooped from the corner of his mouth. A hand came up to the cigarette, removed it for a second while he exhaled, replaced it and went up to tug at the edge of his black woollen cap, and all the time his eyes remained closed, even though he must have heard my footsteps coming closer. From a distance it had appeared that he was wearing gloves, but it was a piece of sky-blue cloth that was wrapped around his hand. Several brown stains blotched it.

When I stopped, a couple of yards from the bench, he finally opened his eyes and removed the cigarette with his bandaged hand, slowly and delicately, spilling no ash. 'Good day to you, sir,' he said, flexing his legs. He grimaced at the sky, before swiping the dots of rainwater off the sleeves of his sweatshirt, the same black sweatshirt as before. 'I've got an hour,' he said. 'How about you?' The way he said it, it was as if we had a job to get done. I told him I could manage thirty minutes, at the most. 'Right then,' he said, slapping his legs as he stood up, 'where do you want to go? There's the Crown, that's nearest. Five minutes from here.' He gave me a look, the sort of look a shop assistant might give you when you've put on a jacket that doesn't quite suit you. 'No,' he said, 'not a pub. OK. You don't want to go to your office, do you? Not a good idea, I can see that. Right. OK. I'm out of ideas. Does the rain bother you?' I had my umbrella; it wasn't cold; I was happy to stroll, I told him. We set off, walking on opposite sides of the path.

'So how are you?' he asked, lighting another cigarette.

'I'm well,' I answered.

'Good,' he said.

'And how are you?'

'Good. I'm good,' he said, nodding. 'I'm good. Really good. Never better.' The nodding became more vigorous as he spoke, as if he were coming to agree with himself that he had indeed never been better. 'Business doing well?' he asked.

'Thank you,' I replied.

'That's good. Opened a place up in Leeds, haven't you?' he asked.

Clearly he expected me to ask him how he knew this. Instead I merely answered 'Yes.'

'Saw a thing about it in a magazine,' he said.

I cut the subject short with a question of my own. 'What have you done to your hand?' I asked.

'Take a look if you like,' he said, unwinding the cloth. He extended his fist towards me, at eye-level. The knuckles were swollen and pink and wet, with clots of near-black blood and grime all over them; on the outside of the little finger a piece of flesh had been snipped off, leaving a cut that looked like the open beak of a small bird. My grimace amused him. 'It's nothing,' he said. 'Give it a couple of days and it'll mend.'

'You should clean it,' I told him.

He turned his hand this way and that, inspecting the damage. 'You're right,' he said, then he rewrapped the hand. The inside of the strip of cloth was as filthy as the wounds were. 'I will. As soon as I get back I'll give it a dip.'

'What happened?' I asked him.

'Some twat dropped a joist on it,' he said. 'Then he went and stood on the fucking joist. He won't be doing that again in a hurry, I can tell you.' He threw a couple of punches at the air; the punches were fast and purposeful.

'So,' I said, 'you're a builder?'

He snorted and did a slack-jawed face. 'Well, yeah,' he said, holding up his hands to make the point that only an idiot could look at these and not see immediately that their owner was a builder.

'That wasn't necessary,' I told him, and at this he shut his eyes tightly and pressed his mouth shut, silently cursing himself.

'Fuck. Yes,' he said. 'I know. Sorry. Fuck.'

'And that's not necessary either.'

'Yes, but I can't help it,' he said.

'Well, try,' I requested.

'OK. I'll do my best.'

'Thank you.'

'Not at all,' he said, smiling as though to say: 'You see how well we're getting along already?'

I asked him where he was working. It was a good job, he told me. He spent a lot of his time doing stupid little jobs – a bit of plastering, a bit of painting, a bit of repointing. But this was a big one: the 'mother of all sheds', an architect-designed music room for a banker up in Highgate. They were building it in his garden, and the thing was going to be the size of a bungalow, he said.

'Triple-glazing, foundations you could bury a tank in, oak doors, oak panelling. Sound-proofing that's going to cost an absolute fucking fortune. Stuff they use in recording studios. A two-hundred-pound bomb could go off outside and you wouldn't hear anything. Fittings coming in from Finland or somewhere. The door handles – they're like a hundred quid each. Straight up – a hundred quid for a fucking doorknob. This bloke's got money coming out of his arsehole. Sorry. But it does your head in. His wife's piano is going in there, and it's not just any old piano – it's this fucking great thing from Italy that costs the same as a Ferrari. It's in the living room at the moment. Fills the whole fucking room. A beautiful thing. Really beautiful. Took a year to make it, or something like that. All these different kinds of wood. Even I can tell it's special, and I don't know anything. And the wife can really play. We can hear her sometimes. Sounds fantastic. Like she's got fifty fingers. She's a total fucking nightmare, though. Can't get it into her head that noise is part of the deal with building work. Like we make a racket just for the fun of it. And no chance of the workers actually being allowed inside. You want a cup of tea – you bring a flask, mate. But the piano is something else. And the sound system – you wouldn't believe it. Speakers the size of wardrobes and amps as heavy as sacks of cement. He's a nice bloke, though, considering he's a banker-wanker. No side to him. You know what I mean? You could talk to him and not know he's a rich bastard. Nikos, his name is. From Cyprus. Gorgeous daughter. Hair like silk. Wicked tits and all. Sorry. But no, she's really gorgeous. Right bitch, though. Takes after her mum, I'd say. Looks at you like you've just dropped out of the trees. Spends all day at the shops, far as I can see. Scoots around in this little fucking Mazda—'

'Please,' I interrupted. If I hadn't stopped him he'd have gone on for an hour.

'What?'

'Is it impossible for you to get through a sentence without swearing? Just "little Mazda". That's all we need.'

'That's what I said.'

'No, it's not. You said: "little effing Mazda".'

'Did I?'

'Yes, you did. Please stop it.'

He apologised with an embarrassed smirk, as a son might. 'It's the way we talk, me and my mates,' he said. I told him that it wasn't the way I talked, and I was about to say that it wasn't the way Sarah had talked either, when he laughed and said: 'It's my upbringing that's to blame. Boys need their fathers.' Within a second his smile was erased, replaced with the expression of a man who thinks he's just made a bad misjudgement. 'No. Sorry. Just a joke. No. I didn't mean it. Really. It was a stupid thing to say. Sorry I said it. Really,' he gabbled. 'I'm not blaming you at all. I'm not blaming anyone.'

I assured him that I didn't regard myself as being blamed. How could I? Until a week ago I hadn't known of his existence. And this, I confessed, was something of a mystery to me. Why had Sarah never told me he'd been born? Why suddenly had he appeared?

The latter question was the one he answered, and the answer was simple: it was only last year that he'd found Sarah. By now we were on our second or third circuit of the gardens; we'd reach a tacit understanding that the privacy of this spot, in the rain, was more conducive to our conversation than any enclosed space would be. In the middle of the path he paused, arms wide, presenting himself. 'I mean, look at me,' he said. 'I ask you: do I look like I was brought up by a woman like her? No, I do not.

You don't get my type in her world, do you? Would I be talking like this if Sarah had been looking after me? No, I would not. She was a fucking mess – no offence – but I think I'd have come out a bit smoother than this if she'd been in charge. You know what I'm saying?'

The story was that, when Sam was eighteen months old, Sarah gave him up. 'She gave me away, or I was taken away. Don't know which. She said one thing one minute and another thing the next. Whatever. She couldn't cope. Didn't want to cope. I don't know,' he said, and he glared at the tarmac, seemingly upset for an instant, before raising his bitterness to smother any further signs of what he felt. 'No chance of her family taking me for a bit. Other families, the old folks would lend a hand, wouldn't they? But with her folks it was: "Here's a few grand to take care of the bastard – now fuck off." Ever see pictures of her mum when she was young?' he asked.

'No,' I answered, which was true.

'What, never?'

'No, never,' I told him.

'OK,' he said, with a sceptical shrug. 'Nice-looking woman, her mum was. Very classy. Great bones. You could see where Sarah got it from.'

Here I was being invited to remark on the beauty of Sarah, but I said nothing.

'But a vicious old bitch, wasn't she, the mum?' he went on. 'You know the story about the cat?'

I did not know the story of the cat.

'OK,' he said, delighted to be able to rectify my ignorance. 'This is when Sarah was at school. Fourteen or thereabouts. One night she stays out an hour later than she's supposed to. Not the first offence, but still – not a major crime, is it? Next day, mum decides to teach

her a lesson: so it's "Say goodbye to Lady Paws." Cat
vanishes that afternoon. Removed, just like that. Mother
never told her what she'd done with the animal. Cruel
stuff, no?'

'I knew there were problems,' I said.

'Problems, fuck yes. One way of putting it. The mother
was an evil old cow, that's another way. Never wanted
kids and should have had her ovaries bricked up to
stop her having them. And the time she put all Sarah's
stuff out in the garden? Chucking LPs out the bedroom
window. You know that one? I mean, that's no way to
treat your daughter, is it? Doesn't matter what she was
up to, you don't do that, do you? And the father, he was
a right royal pillock, wasn't he? Seemed to think that
paying the pocket money was the beginning and end of
his involvement. "I give you twenty quid a week, you
love me like I'm God all fucking mighty" – that was how
it was supposed to work, wasn't it? Banging all his secre-
taries, wasn't he? And anything else that came his way,
from what I heard. Great one for working late, if you get
me. You know about Sarah finding the knickers in his
briefcase, yeah?'

It was no longer possible to give him no response. 'I
hadn't heard that, no,' I said.

'Yeah – he's off to the office in the morning, she hands
daddy his briefcase, the thing comes open and what do
we have here? Nice pair of lacy undies. One careless
lady owner. The mother knew what was going on, yes?
That was the deal. He provided the posh frocks and the
big house and the holidays in the tropics while the kid's
farmed out to some aunt or uncle out in the fucking sticks,
and he's allowed to go sticking it into whoever will do the
business in return for a Gucci handbag or some other bit
of crap. Parents like that, no wonder Sarah was a fucking

head-case. I mean, she was a wild one, fair enough. But you've got to ask yourself: which came first? Shit parents or fucked-up girl?'

The idea, plainly, was to goad me into a defence of his alleged mother. Seeing, however, that the tactic wasn't working, he told me that Mr Williams had died a few years back; the old girl was still clinging on, but was now totally ga-ga. A lawyer had advised Sarah that her mother had become so delicate and confused that she needed to be in residential care, which was absolutely fine with Sarah, so Mrs Williams had been shipped off to some well-appointed institution in pleasant rural surroundings, where, according to Sam, she had become prey to the notion that she was in some way related to Princess Diana and had been shut away on the orders of Someone Very Powerful. 'What goes around, eh?' said Sam, with some gratification. Sarah, apparently, had been to see her once, but the old woman didn't say a word to her, except to tell her that the chief beneficiary of her will would be 'a donkey hospital, or something fucking stupid like that'. His nostrils were stiffened with anger as he said it. 'Can you believe it? Telling her that she's worth less to her than a load of knackered ponies. I should go around and give the old bat a seeing-to,' he said. 'I'm fucked up because of her daughter – well, one reason I'm fucked up – and the daughter was fucked up because of her and her useless dick of a fucking husband.' And then he said to me: 'She must have talked to you about them, yes?'

'Once or twice.'

'That all?'

'Yes. They weren't central to her life. She didn't talk about them.'

'But you must have wondered?'

'Wondered what?' I asked him sharply, because his tone now had something of the investigating officer in it.

'I mean, asked yourself: how did she get like this?'

'Like what?'

'Oh come on,' he moaned. 'You know like what. She told me. She was messed up.'

'I wouldn't say that.'

'What would you say, then?' he asked, as you'd ask someone who was denying that the earth moved round the sun.

'I wouldn't say she was messed up.'

'Are you telling me she went loopy when I arrived, and before that it was all rinky-dinky-doo? I don't think so, somehow.'

'It happens,' I said. 'Strange things can happen to a woman when she has a child. Some become depressed. It's not uncommon. Maybe—'

'Yeah, yeah, yeah,' he broke in. 'She got that all right. She told me all about it. Not a natural cuddler, and all that bollocks. But she was more than a bit mental before that. And after. Been up and down like a roller coaster since she was a kid. That's what she said. A head-case – her words, exactly.'

'She wasn't a head-case,' I stated.

The firmness of my reply made him pause. 'Well, OK,' he said. 'I'm only reporting what she told me. That's all. She said she didn't know what day of the week it was, half of the time. Her parents thought she was just being a pain in the arse. Typical moody teenager and all that shit. But she was seriously in the dark stuff and they didn't notice, or didn't want to know.'

The insinuation was obvious: that I had been as stupid or as selfish as her parents had been. 'She wasn't a head-case. If she told you that, I think she might have been exaggerating. She had a tendency to exaggerate. She liked a touch of drama.'

This prompted a glower and some furious head-shaking. 'No,' he answered. 'No. You're wrong. Touch of drama hasn't got anything to do with it. She was just telling me what had happened. "These are the facts: I wasn't right in the head." She wasn't hamming it up. She wasn't making excuses for herself, like: "It wasn't my fault. I was off my head. I'm not responsible." It was like it was someone else she was talking about. "These are the facts" – that's what she was saying. She wasn't making a drama out of it. That wasn't it. She was giving me the facts. For a long time she wasn't right in the brain. But now you're telling me she was as right as rain when you were around, so – what am I meant to think?' He jiggled his hands about, cupped, testing the relative weights of a genuine article and a fake.

I was tempted to walk away. Instead, after counting to ten, I told him that the young woman I'd known, all those years ago, was not someone I would describe as being not right in the brain. 'She had her ups and she had her downs,' I conceded, 'but not as extreme as you're making out.'

'Her ups and downs?' he repeated, as if beginning to work at the flaw in an alibi.

'Yes,' I said. 'Ups and downs, the same as a lot of people.'

'Then a lot of people are in deep trouble, that's what I'd say. I mean, she had them really bad. Really really heavy. Like it was "Hello birds, hello trees, hello pretty clouds" one day and "Fuck me, I want to die" the next.'

'When I knew Sarah she wasn't always the steadiest vessel,' I responded, 'but that's as far as I'd go.' I was dismayed by myself: I was almost bargaining with him.

'And she was doing a lot of dope, she said. Is that true, or not, would you say?'

'She wasn't the only one.'

'What? You mean you did too?' he said with a short laugh at the thought of it.

'Not a lot. Every now and then. Same as everyone she hung out with, more or less. It was just what you did. You had a drink, you had a joint.'

'Right. But we're not talking about every now and then, are we? We're talking about a lot. She said she was out of her tree for days on end. A whole week without being straight for a minute. Away with the fairies.'

The implication, clearly, was that I had in some way exploited the drug-addled young woman. 'That's not true,' I stated, with more sharpness than I'd intended. His face contorted in an expression of pained bafflement, as though he had been asked to accept two absolutely irreconcilable versions of events; he was about to speak, but I stopped him. 'Look,' I said, 'we're talking about you, not about Sarah.'

'OK,' he said, palms towards me, appeasingly. 'But it's the same thing, isn't it? I mean, that's why I'm here, because of what she was like, and I'm just trying to get a clearer picture, you know? That's all. I just want to make sense of it,' he said, but the forlorn note did not convince; he didn't strike me as a young man trying to make sense of it – the picture was already clear in his mind, it seemed to me. I pointed out that we were running out of time, so he'd better get on and tell me what he had to tell me. Well, he said, what he had to tell me was that Sarah had been a disaster as a mother. One afternoon she'd gone out to the shops and left him at home. This was not long after he'd been born, he said, so she'd have been leaking all over the place, yet somehow she forgot that he existed, and not for a couple of minutes – for two whole hours, until it suddenly occurred to her that she had a son and she'd left him asleep in her bedroom. This story prompted another: she'd fallen asleep in the park, with Sam in his buggy beside her, and didn't wake up until some shrieking woman shook her awake, to tell her that a dog had taken the baby's teddy bear, which it was ripping apart, no more than ten feet away. Another time, he said, she'd left him behind in a supermarket; and once she'd left the balcony window open and a woman had come banging on the door, because she'd seen this baby's head peering out between the bars. 'Another thirty seconds and I'd have been through,' said Sam. I was finding it hard to imagine that Sarah would have told him these stories; and if she had, and they were true, why had I never heard anything from her? If she'd been in such a state, would she never have called me? It didn't make sense, and I was going to say so, but then he was telling me about Sarah's breakdown.

One night, around five o'clock in the morning, a taxi driver found her outside a branch of Boots, hammering on the door; she seemed to think it was five o'clock in the afternoon; she was wearing a raincoat over a winter coat and not a stitch under that. Not even shoes. So Sam was placed in care; the idea was that he would be sent back to her, once she'd recovered, but the people in charge soon came to think she would never be capable of raising a child, and she couldn't muster the strength to resist them. 'Myself, I don't think she did much resisting,' said Sam. 'She told me straight out: "I should never have had a kid." That's what she told me. Like she'd forgotten I was the kid she was talking about. Know what else she told me?' His face now registered a dazed incredulity, and a grain of something comical.

'She said she nearly had me scraped out of her. Actually got as far as the clinic, but then couldn't go through with it. She told me that.'

For the next ten years he was passed from family to family. He was, he admitted, a handful. 'I had issues, as they say,' he mocked. 'It was like having a little fucking gorilla in the house,' he said. He'd ended up with Mr and Mrs Hendy, in Birmingham. (And no sooner had he said this than I could hear – so clearly that I couldn't understand why I hadn't heard it earlier – a West Midlands note in his voice. Most of the time, though, it was London – or working-class southeastern England – that I heard.) They were nice people, he said. He liked them a lot. They were very good to him – 'more patient than I'd have been with a little bugger like me'. But it was always a holding operation – they were looking after him until he was big enough to fend for himself, and fend for himself was what he wanted to do, as soon as possible. 'Families weren't for me, at that time,' he said. Neither was school: having been habitually AWOL, he left school the day he reached leaving age, with no qualifications whatsoever, unless you counted the cross-country trophies. He worked as a labourer for a while, but got into trouble with a foreman and had to move on. He fitted tyres, swept streets, dug holes in roads – and then he joined the army.

His first posting was to Northern Ireland, which was mostly dull as fuck: 'watching the rain come down in South Armagh, taking shit from the natives'. He'd joined the army to get some action, 'but the only action in Ireland was jumping out the way when some fuckwit decided he didn't fancy stopping at a roadblock. You wouldn't believe how boring it was,' he said. 'It got so I really wanted to have a go at someone,' he said, and

I could sense that we were approaching some sort of confession. 'It got to you, these arseholes giving you shit all the time, calling you a British cunt and all that, and they're standing there in a Man United shirt with Beckham's name across the back, and I'm thinking: hold up – last time I checked, David Beckham was a British cunt. Worse than that: an English cunt. I wanted to say to these fuckwits: "Look pal, it's not my fault you've got no fucking work, is it? You think I'm enjoying this?" It drove me mental, I'm telling you. I was getting dangerous,' he said, and the look in his eyes was the look of a dangerous young man. 'Every day I wanted to drop somebody. Every fucking day, I was just itching to have a pop, but there was nothing we could do. If some dickhead felt like giving you shit, you just had to take it.'

By the time the tour was over he was regretting the day he'd signed up, but then the CO walked in one morning and announced that they were going to a place where he could guarantee they'd be using their weapons. 'Those were exactly his words: "I guarantee you'll be using your weapons",' said Sam, eyes wide at the thrilling prospect. The CO was right: within days of landing in Iraq they had fired their guns in anger for the first time. 'It wasn't dull, I'll tell you that much,' he murmured. 'Fuck me, it was so not dull it'd make your head explode. From week one, it was as much action as you could handle. Drive down that road' – he stuck out an arm, envisaging the road ahead – 'and there's a one hundred per cent chance of contact. An ambush. One hundred per cent. Could be a gunman, could be RPGs, could be something nasty by the road – but it'd be something. And everywhere stank of petrol and rotting bins and shit – trenches full of it. No kidding – I've stood in piss and shit up to my armpits. You take cover, you get down, and sometimes that's the only place to go. And so fucking hot your brain turns to glue. After a month, I was having dreams of Armagh. I wanted dull again, more than anything in the world. I dreamed of standing in the pissing rain in a field of mud, counting the cows go by. I'm telling you, it was horrible. Really fucking hardcore. Horrible.'

He'd been talking quickly, non-stop, for maybe ten minutes, but now the words petered out. He halted, and wearily wiped the rainwater from his face. 'You've no idea,' he told me. It was not an accusation. 'Maybe I'll tell you about it, some other time,' he said. He checked his watch and then offered a hand; I shook it, and he kept hold of my hand for a moment, looking at me in a way that seemed to be asking what I thought about the story he'd told me. 'You don't believe me, do you?' he said.

'I do,' I told him. 'Of course I do. It must have been terrible. I can't imagine.'

'No,' he said, 'that's right. You can't imagine. But that's not what I meant. I meant you don't believe I am who I am.'

I couldn't immediately think what to say; he was right.

'You want proof,' said Sam. His eyes were dulled by disappointment at my attitude.

'Well,' I said, 'you did say you were going to bring—'

'Yes, I know what I said,' he interrupted. 'But I haven't.'

'OK,' I responded, then supplied the question he was waiting for: 'Why not?'

His reply was not immediate. For a few seconds he regarded me, sullenly, before answering: 'Because it's raining.' I couldn't tell if this was intended to be a joke of some sort. His look was asking me what I made of his answer; a smile began to form, but it was not good-humoured. He took a deep breath that rushed through his nostrils, squinted at me, and said, almost in a whisper, bringing his face close to mine: 'You think I'm lying, don't you?'

Though he claimed to be my son, at this moment I felt it was possible that he would turn very hostile, possibly violent, if I didn't measure my words. 'No,' I said, 'that's not what I think.'

He stepped back and folded his arms. 'So what do you think?' he asked. His expression now was one of disinterested curiosity.

'I think that there might have been a mistake.'

'And whose mistake would that be?'

'Sarah's.'

'Now now now,' he said, wagging a finger. 'That's bad. Can't answer back, can she? And I think if anyone's in a position to know who put the bun in a woman's oven, it's the woman herself, isn't it?'

'Yes, but—' I started to answer.

'Unless you're suggesting—?'

'I'm not suggesting anything,' I floundered.

'Oh yes you are,' he said, sternly, but then he laughed and tapped me on the shoulder with a loose fist. 'It's all right,' he said, 'I'm having a bit of fun with you. You want your bits of paper and you'll have your bits of paper. I'll show you. Don't worry.' He smiled widely – the smile of a young man who was making allowances for an old chap's crankiness. 'I have everything you need, but I didn't want to carry it around, not on a day like this. Wouldn't do to get it all soggy, would it? Tell you what – come to my place and I'll set your mind at rest. Why don't you give me your number?' he suggested. I didn't even have to shake my head. 'No. You don't want to. That's cool. Fine. Doesn't matter. You've got my number, and I know where to find you,' he said, but casually, with no implication of threat. 'OK. You give me a call when you're ready. Next week, say? Wednesday, Thursday. Now, back to work,' he said, and before he turned away he gave me a small slap on the back, for encouragement.

4

The weekend after the conversation in Russell Square Gardens, Eleanor and Gerry came to us for Sunday lunch. I was in the bedroom when they drove up. Looking out, I saw Eleanor talking to Gerry in the car: she was lightly stroking the back of his head and talking to him, while he stared ahead, nodding, as if he were about to undergo a surgical procedure and Eleanor was assuring him it was going to be nothing like as bad as he thought. He doesn't dislike us – or rather, he definitely likes Aileen. She's the next best thing to his wife, as he's been known to tell her. But Gerry's career has been blighted ever since fifteen years of systems management with a very major publishing company came to an end with the Great Warehousing Disaster, when the computers went berserk at the vast new purpose-built facility in deep Northamptonshire, and started spewing out stock figures that bore not the slightest relation to reality. Six months later the computers still weren't functioning, so Gerry – though he'd expressed his doubts about the software people long before zero hour but had been overruled by his boss – was invited to fall on his sword. Now he was back where he'd been before his adventure in publishing, in the food business, facilitating the dispatch of frozen edibles to all corners of the country.

His boss, of course, had survived the cull. It was humiliating, and resentment was smouldering in him like a fire in the base of a peat bog.

We had half an hour to wait before the roast was ready, so Eleanor requested a tour of the house: last time they'd been here we'd only just moved in and the place had been in chaos. Aileen led the way, with Gerry bringing up the rear. Eleanor loved what we'd done with the bedroom; she went to the window to take a look at the view, as you might do when you're shown into your five-star hotel room in Venice; Gerry followed suit, dutifully approving of what he could see. The bathroom so excited Eleanor that she clapped her hands at the sight of it – the shower was so amazing, she said, she was tempted to try it out right away. With a fingertip Gerry slid the shower door open and shut two or three times, hoping it would jam.

At the table, Eleanor talked for an hour with barely an interruption, about the latest round of back-stabbings in Human Resources. The introduction of certain characters necessitated a quantity of background information, which in turn tended to prompt another lengthy digression. Many people, I think, find Aileen rather abrupt. She has a way of cutting to the heart of the matter, which is a great asset in her line of work – if there's an irregularity in a client's accounting procedures, Aileen can spot it as quickly as an X-ray at airport security will spot a knife in a briefcase. In social situations she is likewise uncompromising. 'What do you mean exactly?' she'll ask. 'I don't understand the point you're making,' she might interrupt. For some she's too blunt, but I've always greatly liked her directness. Eleanor, however, has been granted a lifetime amnesty – Aileen can never bring herself to encourage her sister to hurry things along. On this occasion such encouragement was urgently needed: never concise, Eleanor tends to lose focus after a glass of wine, and now she was on her second glass. Perhaps, in my state of mind, I was less tolerant of Eleanor's ramblings than usual. Lost in the convolutions of who had said what to whom at which meeting, I excused myself and escaped to the bathroom.

I sat on the edge of the bath for a while, examining my face in the mirror, trying to read signs of dishonesty there. I looked tired, and I felt tired: had a bed been on offer, I could have slept for the rest of the afternoon. I filled the basin with cold water and lowered my face into it. That done, I looked tired and a shade greyer. Having rehearsed an attentive expression, I returned to the table.

There had been a change of subject in my absence: Eleanor had moved on to the burgeoning career of Sean, who had been informed on Friday that he was in line for a promotion in the very near future. So her son's ascent through the ranks of one of the country's biggest suppliers of office equipment has commenced satisfactorily; the family schedule anticipates his arrival at the senior executive level of a top-drawer retail organisation within a couple of decades.

Eleanor sees life as a succession of precisely defined stages: infancy – the groundwork of character-building; childhood – fun combined with consolidation of identity; adolescence – a period in which one should expect to pass through episodes of confusion before emerging into the clear light of Who You Are; adulthood – the forty-odd years (God willing) in which one accrues a family and works hard to achieve one's goals (steady ascent of the career ladder; accumulation of sufficient material goods for comfortable living) prior to the well-deserved reward of retirement. Coming to the threshold between stage two and stage three, Eleanor had been fully prepared. She had made a clear-eyed assessment of her strengths and weaknesses: she

was not as smart as her older sister, but she had a tempera-
ment that was well attuned to rules and regulations, and
she was a good listener, a patient and sympathetic listener,
a 'people person'. She consulted a careers adviser, who
suggested that she might investigate the opportunities
offered by personnel work, and Eleanor knew immediately
that this woman had hit the nail on the head. (This was,
after all, the very same adviser who had set Aileen on the
road to accountancy, which was turning out to have been a
sensible choice. Perhaps less sensible, though, was Aileen's
relationship with a woodworker whose handiwork might
have been impressive but whose financial status seemed
somewhat precarious, to put it mildly.)

By the age of eighteen Eleanor had more or less final-
ised her image of her ideal life-partner: he was to be
nice-looking but not too much so (a handsome man will
always let you down); he must want to have children (but
not too many); he would have a good job and be happy
in it (but workaholics need not apply); he would be
dark-haired (Gerry used to fit the bill); not short (Gerry
is five feet eleven); and neither a teetotaller nor a boozer.
Prepared to wait for the right man, she refused to panic
as her twenty-ninth year expired. As if by magic, Gerry
appeared in the month of her thirtieth birthday, and
marriage followed quickly. Without delay they applied
themselves to child-creation, and all went smoothly: the
son was born within the year, the daughter two years later.
Sean, after an interlude of teenage truculence, has proved
to be a young man who has his feet on the ground and
his head screwed on the right way. Cerys, however, was
something of a concern. Her parents' feelings about the
imminent show were ambivalent.

'Of course Cerys has talent,' said Eleanor. 'But so many
young women have talent,' she went on, with a wince

of pained and tender sympathy, as though it were her daughter she was addressing. 'You turn on the TV and you see lots of them: talented young actresses, very pretty most of them. You see these girls and you think: "That one's got something. That one's going to be a star." And then what happens? Nine times out of ten that's the last you'll ever see of them.'

'On the scrapheap at thirty,' Gerry confirmed, cutting his last slice of beef as if the meat had come from a beast against which he'd held some sort of grievance. 'Panto in Whitehaven, if they're lucky.'

But Aileen thought that Cerys's ambition was commendable – she would be taking a risk if she went to drama school, certainly, but what would life be without an element of risk? 'If it doesn't work, it doesn't work,' she said. 'She's young. If she doesn't take a chance now, she'll regret it later. You wouldn't want that, would you? And who knows? Perhaps she'll be the one out of ten. She might do it. Good luck to her, I say.'

Eleanor shrugged, as if to say, weakly, 'Maybe you're right.' She does not like to contradict her sister, and when it comes to Cerys and Sean a degree of tact is always required, because childless Aileen, she believes, has a special attachment to her niece and nephew, a deep affection that will never lose its tinge of sadness. During the infancies of her children, Eleanor's pride in their achievements was always somewhat tempered, out of consideration for Aileen, who for years had failed to conceive, whereas Eleanor had become pregnant within a matter of weeks of deciding that the time had come to start a family. This self-restraint became less noticeable over the years, but there is nevertheless still a certain delicacy whenever Cerys and Sean are discussed, even though Aileen has been assuring her sister since the kids were toddlers that she and I are reconciled to our situation – more than reconciled, in fact. We are happy on our own, Aileen has often told her. We have a good life; we've done a lot of things we couldn't have done if we'd had children; if we'd been that desperate for a child, we might have thought about adoption, but we hadn't been desperate; it was a misfortune that happened to some people, and it had happened to us; it wasn't a disaster. Nothing Aileen could say, however, would ever convince Eleanor that we would not have been even happier had things worked out differently, and that we know that this is the case. And so, on the subject of Cerys and her enthusiasm for the stage, Aileen was allowed to have the last word. Even Gerry smiled, as if to say that he hoped against hope that Aileen's optimism would turn out to have been justified.

The morning had been overcast but now the clouds had broken up and the garden was taking the brunt of the sunlight. Eleanor proposed to Aileen an inspection of the flowerbeds; it seemed that she wanted a word in private. I volunteered to take care of the coffee; Gerry, also picking up the hint, said he'd stay inside, as he couldn't tell a begonia from a bonsai unless there was label on it, and, besides, he wouldn't mind taking a look at the Grand Prix. He turned on the TV but didn't immediately sit down. Instead, for a minute or so he watched his wife and Aileen as they sauntered across the lawn, arm in arm, Eleanor talking, Aileen listening with what appeared to be some concern. I made a remark that was intended as a friendly gesture towards my brother-in-law: 'God knows what they find to talk about. You'd think they hadn't seen each other for months.' Gerry gave a light snort, a minimal expression of amusement, then went over to the sofa and fell into it.

Reaching for the remote control, he said: 'I can tell you what they're talking about. They're talking about me.' He found the channel he wanted and raised the volume a little before continuing. Addressing the screen, he told me that he'd let the side down a bit at the previous weekend's party, the one for which Eleanor had bought the dress. The couple whose anniversary was being celebrated were nice enough people, he said, and most of the other guests had seemed bearable, but he just hadn't been in the mood for chit-chat, so he'd taken himself off to a quiet corner, behind the marquee, where Eleanor had found him later, sitting against a tree with a champagne bottle in his hand. 'I'd been missing for an hour, apparently. She wasn't amused. But I'd had a nice time. The time simply flew by,' he said, waving the remote control woozily.

'I'm useless at big events as well,' I told him. 'I'd have joined you under the tree,' I said. The semi-joke was not acknowledged.

We watched the race for a while. He asked me how the shops were doing – he always says 'the shops', never 'the business'. The shops were doing all right, I said. He suggested that I might soon be feeling the pinch, if the recession kicks in. Then he revised his analysis, observing that 'your kind of punters are recession-proof, aren't they?' This wasn't quite true, I said: some of our customers were wealthy; most weren't. Gerry surveyed the room as I was talking, seeing yet more evidence that life hadn't dealt him a fair hand. His eye alighted on the Glo-Ball floor lamp. 'How much would that set me back, then?' he enquired. The answer was more or less what he'd expected. 'I couldn't live with something like that,' he said. 'I'm a bit of a fogey, I suppose. I like shades on my lights.'

Until this day I hadn't known that Gerry had an interest in Formula One. I'd assumed that he was watching the race as an alternative to talking to me, but it turned out that he knew his stuff. He explained why Driver A would soon be making up ground, and why Driver B would start to fall off the pace. 'That guy's going into the pits on the next lap, and when he comes out he'll be in sixth place,' he said, and the guy duly went into the pits and emerged in sixth place. For a few more minutes we watched the cars processing at high speed, and then, with no preamble, Gerry started to tell about how his mother had been taught to drive by a man who raced sports cars at the weekends. Gerry was eight or nine years old at the time, and one night this man had taken Gerry and his mother to an unfinished stretch of motorway, where a newly tuned car was waiting to be tested. Gerry had been strapped into passenger seat with belts that gripped him like the tentacles of an octopus, and they'd gone roaring up and down the tarmac. 'Middle of the night. Blackness all around. Just the headlights, trained on this strip of virgin tarmac,' said Gerry, holding his hands out, palms upright and parallel, and smiling into the space between them, as though seeing the limitless expanse of pristine road. 'Going like the clappers. Over a ton. And this bloke steering the thing into the beams, calm as you like, perfectly relaxed. The noise was incredible. I can't tell you. I had school the next day and I couldn't hear a bloody thing. Spent all day saying: "Beg pardon, sir?" One of the best hours of my life.' I'd never heard this before. 'It was fantastic,' said Gerry, looking at me for the first time since our wives had gone outside. It seemed that he was offering the story by way of apology for being so badly out of sorts.

Before I could come up with a response, he said: 'I hear you're going to be on the telly.'

'That's right,' I said.

'When?'

'Not clear yet.'

'OK,' he said, and that was the end of that.

Eleanor came back into the room with Aileen and sat down beside her husband. She tucked a hand under his arm and pulled it gently into her side. 'How much longer is this on for?' she asked.

'Ages,' said Gerry. 'I'm not really watching it.' Half an hour later they left.

I helped Aileen to clear up. She seemed preoccupied. I asked her what was on her mind. She was worried about her sister, she said, coolly, and her sister was worried about Gerry. 'He's depressed,' she said.

'He seems fed up all right,' I agreed. Continuing to load the dishwasher, Aileen made no response. 'He told me about the party,' I added.

'What party?' asked Aileen, as if keeping a pointless conversation going.

'The anniversary bash.'

'OK.'

'Overdid the hospitality, he said. Is that what Eleanor was talking to you about?'

'She mentioned it,' said Aileen.

Evidently there was no more to be said on this topic, so I changed tack. 'He was telling me about his mother's driving instructor, the racing driver. Blasting up and down the motorway at night, with little Gerry in the passenger seat. You heard that one?'

'Yes,' said Aileen, closing the dishwasher's door with emphasis. 'So have you,' she said, now facing me. 'We've both heard it before.'

'I'm sure I haven't,' I said. 'I wouldn't have forgotten it.'

'I'm positive you've heard it,' Aileen stated, giving me a look that I thought was going to be followed by a question such as: 'Now, are you going to tell me what's going on?'

Instead, what she said was: 'Perhaps you weren't listening then, either.'

The rebuke was welcome – it invited a minor disagreement, which would camouflage the unease that I was feeling. So I said: 'Well, I thought your sister went on a bit.'

'I told you,' said Aileen firmly. 'She's anxious about Gerry. When she's anxious she tends to labour the point.'

'I lost the thread once or twice.'

'That was obvious.'

'I don't think Eleanor noticed, though.'

'Oh, she did.'

'I don't think so.'

'She did.'

'She said something to you?' I asked.

'She noticed. Take my word for it,' said Aileen, moving towards the door.

I apologised for not making more of an effort. 'I'll do better next time,' I said.

'I hope so,' she replied. She left me in the kitchen and I stood there for a while, at the sink, looking out at the garden, trying to recall when we'd last had an exchange that might be described as discordant, and I couldn't remember.

5

Sam was waiting for me outside Bermondsey station. From there we walked to a side-street, where we got into a Toyota pickup that looked as though it had been pelted with rocks and driven through mud on a daily basis for the past year. Some oil had been spilled on the passenger seat, he explained, which was why it was covered with a thick layer of newspapers; I sat on a picture of a big-breasted girl wearing nothing but a football scarf. In the footwell there were three or four polystyrene beakers, a dozen cigarette butts and a couple of screwdrivers. It took only a few minutes to reach Sam's home, which turned out to be a small caravan, parked on the edge of an area waste ground, near the Old Kent Road. 'Lovely spot, don't you think?' he said as we pulled up. Low mounds of rubbish lay all around the caravan, apparently the residue of a huge tip that had recently been cleared. Tractor tracks weaved around the mounds, through pools of brown water that were iridescent with oil and petrol. A fridge lay at an angle close to the caravan, with a mattress underneath it, surrounded by wads of newsprint. The caravan itself was a tatty old thing: the windows were streaked with grime, a fringe of moss ran along the gutter, and the walls were dented and rust-pocked. A pile of breeze blocks served as front-door steps. The hinges screeched when Sam yanked the door open. 'Welcome,' he said cheerily, jumping down so that I could enter first.

The thin brown carpet was covered with dozens of bootprints and the air was rank: the smell of cigarettes was the strongest element, and then a whiff that was reminiscent of football changing rooms; cement or plaster was in the mix as well, plus white spirit and the aroma of baked beans. A small and misshapen saucepan, caked with tomato sauce, rested on the tiny cooker opposite the door. To the right was what I assumed to be a shower cubicle. To the left was a narrow bed, with sheets and pillows and quilt all stirred in together, and a second bed, which was doing service as a sofa. A table had been slotted between the beds; it had a TV on it, plus a six-pack of beer with one can missing, and a burger carton. A folding plastic chair, heaped with clothes, was tucked under the table. Carrier bags – some empty, others not – occupied much of the sofa-bed; in the centre of the vacant patch there was a videogame console, which Sam threw onto the carriers to make a space for me to sit.

He filled the kettle from a flagon of water that he took from under the sink. 'So, how you doing?' he asked. He was in a bright mood, and appeared to have made an effort to smarten himself up: his jeans were clean, the red Adidas sweatshirt was spotless.

'Fine,' I answered. I asked him how things were going in Highgate.

'It's good. It's good,' he replied, thoughtfully, spooning coffee into mugs; the tone said that some aspects of the job weren't so good, but on balance 'good' was the right word. The coffee was the cheapest brand of instant, and he made it to a strength that was undrinkable.

'How much longer will you be there?' I asked.

He gave me a look that was gauging the motive for the question. 'A week or two. Thereabouts,' he answered.

'And then?'

'And then I'll be off to who knows where. Might be here, might be there,' he sang, waving the spoon, baton-like, from one side to the other. This was why he had the caravan, he explained. He had mates all over the country, ex-squaddies who were now in the building trade, and if one of them rang him about a job and he liked the sound of it, he could just go. Last week he'd had a call about something that would be coming up soon: a huge job, ripping the guts out of a manor house in Scotland and refitting the whole place, for some film producer. 'Near Oban. You know that part of the world?' he asked. I told him I didn't. 'I might go for it. Very decent money. Nice scenery. Make a change to open the curtains in the morning and see something worth seeing,' he said, as he perched himself on the table. The caravan was so cramped, his knees were only inches from my face.

The caravan was not his only home, he told me; he owned a flat as well. When he came out of the army he'd bought a small place in Matlock. He hadn't known what he was going to do after the army, nor where he was going to live, but he knew he wasn't going to stay in Birmingham, so the first thing he did after getting back was to buy a car and drive north, and the first town he came to that he really liked was Matlock, because it was a nice-looking town that was handy for the countryside, and he'd come to feel that at heart he was more of a country boy than a city boy. For most of the year he rented out the flat, which made him a bit of a profit; only in the winter did he live there – for the rest of the time he was on the road in his caravan. He liked not knowing where he was going to be from one month to the next, though it could be a pain not having a decent bathroom. 'You could do with a good long soak from time to time, in this line of work,' he said. 'A lukewarm shower just doesn't do the business.' And then, as if suddenly reminded of the purpose of my visit, he pushed himself off the table and announced: 'I've got something to show you.'

'So I believe,' I said.

He grinned and made his eyebrows twitch. 'No, something else,' he said, and with both hands he seized the carrier bags and hurled them onto his bed. A cherry-wood bowl was uncovered; I recognised it at once. 'Ta-da,' he fanfared. 'Nice, isn't it?' he said. 'But why am I telling you that? It's yours, isn't it? You made it.' He picked it up. 'I tell you, I'd give anything to be able to make something like this,' he said, as his fingers gently caressed the curves of the bowl. He handed it to me, with great care.

I told him that it was just a question of picking the right piece of wood, and that my father had done that for me. My father was a proper woodworker, I told him, but my skills were more limited, far more limited.

Sam frowned, giving short shrift to false modesty. 'You're not telling me this was easy,' he said. I couldn't be sure if he really did think that it had been a difficult thing to make; I suspected that he did not.

'It's nothing special. Not in the slightest,' I said.

The glance he gave me said that he was trying to understand why I was taking this attitude. 'You must feel strange, looking at it,' he said. 'I should have thought of that. Sorry.' I assured him that I didn't feel strange at all, but this too he doubted. 'You must do,' he persisted. 'Fuck me, it must have been brilliant, to make things like this. I mean, I'm OK with my hands. You know, I can knock things together and they won't fall down on you. I do a good job. But this,' – he took it back from me – 'this is a work of art. I tell you, I'm impressed,' he told me. 'You still make stuff, in your spare time?'

'No,' I answered.

'Nothing?'

'No.'

'Really?' he said, astonished and doubtful.

'Really.'

'But you must miss it, no?'

'Not at all,' I told him.

'You must do.'

'I don't.'

'OK,' he said. His expression was offering commiseration, as if it were inconceivable that the bowl would not have awakened in me a sadness for a career, as a craftsman, that had failed to flourish.

The bowl was a nice object, I told him, and I was glad to find that it was still in good condition, but it didn't make me feel nostalgic. And this was true: the sight of the bowl had raised a faint reminiscence of my father, a pallid sense of bereavement, but no regret for the period of my life that it represented. It was disconcerting that the bowl had come to be in his possession. Otherwise, what was uppermost in my mind was a question: why does he want me to feel what he thinks – or is pretending to think – I'm feeling? His intention, unmistakably, was to discomfit me.

Noticing that I had become uncomfortable, he diverted the subject down a different route, albeit a parallel one. It was a disgrace, he said, that this country, the cradle of the industrial revolution ('the fucking industrial revolution'), had become a bit-player in the world of manufacturing. His father ('my dad – the other one – the one who brought me up – Mr Hendy') was an engineer who had worked for MG 'when MG was a proper company, making proper cars'. He'd learned his trade in Abingdon and he'd worked there until the Abingdon plant was shut down, when he'd moved to the Midlands to work at Longbridge. 'At Longbridge they weren't really making MGs – they were just slapping the badge onto cars that weren't fit to wear it, but he was still making things, even if they weren't as good as before, and that's better than nothing, right?' said Sam. 'And then it all went down the fucking tubes, didn't it? Out on his ear, he was. So now what does he do? He fixes cars. He doesn't make them, he fixes them. All day long, fixing Japanese cars, French cars, Italian cars, German cars, Spanish cars, cars from Korea, even cars from the bloody Philippines. It's not right, is it? How the fuck did it happen?' he demanded. 'You tell me – how did it happen? The Philippines, for fuck's sake. We used to be the best, now we're shit. How did that happen? Tell me,' he urged, but there was no pause in which to answer. His father – 'Mr Hendy, I mean' – still drove an ancient Riley, as some sort of protest. 'Flying the flag, even if it's the slowest fucking thing on the roads of Britain.'

Britain nowadays, Sam proclaimed, was a country of 'management consultants, bankers, shit-brained celebs and hairdressers. We make weapons and money, and that's about it.' Did I know, he asked, why the economy looks good, even though we don't make anything any more? 'I'll tell you. It's because the moneymen in London, our banker-wankers and all their mates, make more profit out of the money they invest abroad than the foreigners make out of the UK. That's your reason. We make our money out of what the foreigners are making. That's a fact. Fucking madness, isn't it? I was reading about it the other day,' he said, looking around as if searching for the source of this information, but there was not a book or magazine anywhere in the caravan – just a copy of the *Sun*, sticking out of one of the carrier bags. He enjoyed his work, Sam

told me, with the vehemence of someone making a statement of a fundamental principle of his way of life. At
the end of every day there was something to show for
his efforts. He'd done something substantial; he'd added
something. Most people in this country never have that
feeling. 'It's all about satisfaction with what you've made,
isn't it?' he said. 'When you made that bowl, making it
was enough. It was nice to get some cash for it, yes, but
the money wasn't what it was about, was it? I mean, the
money let you go on working, but the money wasn't the
purpose, was it? I'm right, yes?'

He had become so heated in his enthusiasm, it
wouldn't have been wise to qualify what he was saying.
My workshop, I agreed, had not been a money-spinning
enterprise.

'Exactly,' he said. 'That's not why you did it. But for
most people in this country it's the money that justifies
the job, right? You do the job to get the pay, and you want
the pay so you can buy things, lots of things, because in
the end that's what makes you think your life is worthwhile, that it means something. If you have lots of stuff,
you have a life. I'm right, aren't I? That's how people think.
Most people,' he said. It was as though he believed he was
talking to a righteous pauper. 'And the problem with that
way of thinking,' he went on, 'is that you never arrive at a
place where you're happy to stop. You always want more.
There's always the faster car, the bigger house, the better
holiday. There's never an end to it. Heaven is always just
over the horizon, right? The way we live, there's no such
thing as enough, is there?' he said, then he looked around
the caravan again. He laughed, but it wasn't clear what
had amused him – the lunacy of the way we all lived,
or the fact that he was someone who certainly didn't yet
have enough.

I said I was assuming that Sarah had given him the bowl. He confirmed that she had, and added that she hadn't had much else to pass on. She'd given him some money as well – not much, but enough to knock off a few weeks' worth of mortgage payments. 'Things had changed since you knew her,' he said, at which point he went over to the sink, opened the cabinet above it, and took down a padded envelope. He rummaged in it for a few seconds, lifted out a photograph, and passed it to me. 'Three years ago,' he said. This woman's face was not recognisable as Sarah's – it was very much thinner than the face I had known, with deep lines to the side of the mouth. The hair was a dull grey-brown crop, whereas Sarah's had been a tangle of thick auburn curls. The lips were too thin; the jawline was wrong. Yet the eyes, as I studied them, began to become similar to the eyes I remembered: intelligent, faintly suspicious, suggestive of an erratic vivacity.

'She'd had some bad habits,' Sam explained. 'Habits not compatible with a healthy lifestyle, if you know what I mean. Her parents gave her a wad of cash to stay out of their lives, and that's where most of it went.' This was said not with any hint of grievance, nor for that matter with much discernible compassion. He spoke, rather, as though he were merely reporting the misdemeanours of an incorrigible old friend. 'She'd been in a really bad way for years, she told me,' he went on, 'then she got into a serious relationship with some bloke and she'd straightened herself out for him. He didn't work out, in the end, but she stayed off the shit. Takes a toll, though, doesn't it? You want to see where she was living? I'll show you,' he said, rooting around in the envelope. He produced another photo, which at first sight showed only trees; on closer inspection, though, a row of windows could be made out, through the lower leaves. When Sam had found her she was living here, in an old train carriage. 'See,' he said, pointing to the windows, 'there's two of them. She lived in this one,' he said, tapping the photograph, 'and guess who lived in the other one? Go on, have a guess.' I couldn't guess. 'I'll tell you. Cats. Loads of fucking cats. Paying guests, some of them. But breeding the buggers was her big thing: breeding these exclusive Siberian cats, five hundred pounds a head. No kidding – five hundred quid just for something to stroke. Beautiful animals, but for fuck's sake, let's get things in proportion, shall we? Then again – good business. Not good business like your places are good business, but decent. Bloody amazing, how many people are ready to pay stupid money for a fucking cat. Mad, isn't it? You a cat man?' he asked, cocking his head to one side to appraise me. 'You don't strike me as a cat man. Dogs more your kind of thing, I'd say. Am I right? You're not going to tell me you have a five hundred quid cat, are you? No, it can't be. Tell me you don't.'

'I don't have a cat, no,' I said.

'Dog?'

'Nor a dog.'

'Bloody nuisances, I say. Worse than having a baby around the house. If I had to choose, I'd go for a dog. Not much of a one for cats. Dull fuckers, if you ask me. Only interested in Number One. But Sarah, she was mental about them. She have a cat when you were an item?'

I had an urge to answer that we were never an item, but said instead: 'She didn't.'

'Well, she got the cat-bug big time somewhere along the line. Six of them she had living with her, in her carriage. All of them super-special. Each one unique, according to her. Real personalities, like people. Far as I could see, they were bloody identical, apart from the fur. Even then, you had to look hard. They used to bring her presents: a rat or a mouse or rabbit with its head pulled off. She'd get out of bed in the morning and there'd be blood all over the floor. Rabbit guts in her slippers. Nice, eh? Women like them a lot more than men do, I find. Apart from queers, of course. What about your wife? What does she think?'

I balked at the mention of my wife, but Sam either didn't notice a reaction or pretended not to notice. 'We don't have pets,' I replied.

'Sarah was crazy about them,' he continued. 'One time, she told me, she'd had a dozen of the fuckers living with her. She was meant to be selling them but couldn't bear to let them go. There was a top cat – had some stupid fucking name, something Russian. They all had these poncey names. Anyway, this Russian cat had made himself indispensable, she said. Can you believe it? "Made himself indispensable." What, like he can fix the drains and pour the milk on your fucking muesli, can he? I mean, I liked her. We had a rocky start, but I liked her in the end, a lot. But it's got to be said: she was flaky as fuck. Magic crystals and horoscopes and all that shit. A lot of purple in the wardrobe, but no hairbrush. You know what I mean? I have to say, I can't quite put you and her together, know what I mean? You don't seem a match. Don't take this the wrong way. But you strike me as a guy with a clear head, and she was a girl with some loose parts up top, no? I mean, it's hard to imagine: you and her. She must have driven you nuts. And vice versa, I suppose. No offence.'

I told him that it had happened a long time ago; he nodded, but obviously regarded this point as an irrelevance. 'I had to laugh,' he resumed. 'It made me feel kind of weird, you know. There she was, fussing over these fucking animals, going on about them as if they were her kids, and there I am – the kid she let go. I think it's what you'd call ironic, no? Preferred cats to men, she told me once. She didn't mean me – she was talking about men she'd been with. Deadbeats, the lot of them. The thing about cats, she said, was that they don't judge you. Total bollocks, I know, but that's what she said. I mean, the fuckers do judge you, don't they? "You got a tin of food for me? A bit of fresh fish? No? Well, you can piss off then." That's judging you. But Sarah reckoned they didn't, and that was where they scored over the deadbeat boyfriends. Like I said, the wiring up top wasn't in one hundred per cent working order.' He smiled at me, but the eyes were waiting to see if the full significance of Sarah's alleged remark had eluded me. I gave him, in reply, the blankest face I could muster.

Then he slapped his thighs and cried: 'Anyway, time is short: agenda item number one.' From the envelope he took a piece of paper that was handed over without comment, and I found myself holding a birth certificate for Samuel John Williams: born in Canterbury on September 5th, 1981; mother – Sarah Clementine Williams (Occupation: Musician); father – Dominic Pattison (Occupation: Carpenter). The date made his story possible – but barely, I thought. But whereas Sam's name and Sarah's name were written in ink from a fountain pen, mine was in ball-point ink, and the script was obviously different. The thing was a forgery, a crass forgery, and it was all I could do to prevent myself from laughing at it. Did he really think I would be so unobservant as not to notice that he'd tampered with it? 'This doesn't prove anything,' I told him, neutrally. I pointed out that the space for the father's name had originally been left blank, and that someone had filled it in later.

'That's right,' he said, as though I'd confirmed a point that he himself had been making. 'She filled it in. For me.

Look.' And now he took from the envelope a small sheet of paper, on which was written a poem. I didn't read any of it closely except the last line, which was her name and the words: 'for Sam'. His smile offered sympathy; he understood that I must now be feeling rather foolish. 'See? Her writing here, her writing there,' he said, retrieving the page and the certificate. 'She filled it in, so I could have it complete.'

The poem looked as though it was in her handwriting – the long tail on the letter *y* was familiar, as were the general size and shape of the words. And my name on the certificate was formed like the words of the poem – that much was undeniable. But it was almost inconceivable that Sarah would have rendered the certificate invalid by writing on it. Sam had forged her handwriting: this was the obvious conclusion, the only conclusion.

Perched on the table, Sam was watching me with his knees drawn up to his chin, like a child enthralled by a show. I couldn't look at him. The behaviour of a man stupid enough to think he could get away with so transparent a trick could not be predicted. Eventually I spoke: I said that I was surprised by the word 'Musician'. Sarah could play the guitar a little; she wrote songs in her spare time; but when I knew Sarah she'd been working in a stables, for pocket money. As far as I knew, she'd never performed for an audience. He shrugged, to signify that this was neither here nor there. 'But Sam,' I said, trying to sound like a man softening the blow of disappointing news, 'this doesn't prove anything.'

He sighed and rolled his eyes, and at this point I saw clearly a resemblance between him and Sarah, in the fold of the eyelids and the slight protrusion of the bone below the eyebrows. 'Something else for you,' he said, fishing a photograph from the envelope. He slotted it gently but firmly between my fingers, like an uncle giving a banknote to a favourite nephew who was reluctant to accept the gift. 'You took it, I believe,' he said. The picture showed Sarah leaning on an old wooden gate, with tall bushes, brilliantly sunlit, behind her; she was wearing a big red shirt over white jeans. The colours in the photo had gone milky with age, but I could recall the original crimson of that shirt; I had no memory of taking the picture, however, and no idea as to where it had been taken.

'Those were the days, eh?' said Sam. 'The clothes, I mean. And that's not the worst,' he said, delving into the envelope again.

I raised a hand to stop him, and accidentally came into contact with his fingers. He regarded my hand, then glanced at me, loading the moment with a meaning it did not rightly have. 'Some other time,' I told him.

'Sure,' he said. 'That's fine. A lot to think about. I understand.'

I handed the picture back to him, but he told me I could keep this one. 'It's a copy, for you,' he said.

Still holding the mug of coffee, I peered at my reflection in the tepid black liquid, unable to meet his gaze.

'Here,' he said, easing the mug from my grip, 'give me that.' His voice was low and solicitous, like an undertaker's.

I asked him if he had any idea why Sarah had never said anything to me about her being pregnant. He had an answer at once: 'You were a bad mistake. You and me – we were her two biggest mistakes,' he said. 'And maybe it was a way of getting her own back,' he suggested. 'If she'd been short of money, it might have been different, but she wasn't, at the time, so she could do what she liked. She wanted shot of you.'

'Own back for what?' I was on the point of asking him, but I kept the thought to myself.

Sam yawned and stretched, as if ready for bed, and said: 'We'd better get going – don't want to make Aileen suspicious. I'll drop you back at the Tube.'

The use of my wife's name was another shock. 'How did you know her name?' I asked him sharply.

'Get a grip, old chap,' he answered, grinning. 'I've read about you. Done a bit of research as well. The internet. Handy thing, I tell you. Amazing, the things you can find out.'

I rose from the sofa-bed. I felt as groggy as a man who'd been interviewed for hours.

'It's going to be difficult to tell her,' he said. 'Take your time. There's no rush. I'm a patient bloke. When you've had to spend days watching the Irish grass grow, you learn to be patient. Give me a call when you're ready. In your own time.' We were at the door when he said: 'You want me to show you where she is?' I couldn't think what he meant. 'Sarah,' he said. 'Where she's buried. Take us about an hour to get there. Hour and a bit. Think you can you swing it? Come up with a story for the wife?'

I said I'd call him.

6

The following week, Otis Mizrahi came to film the interview. Short and chubby, he had a face that made me think of a slightly less bug-eyed version of the young Peter Lorre, and remarkably long-fingered hands, with which he drew elegant shapes in the air as he talked. Much care and money had gone into his self-presentation: his hair – perfectly black – had been cut into a complicated facsimile of unkemptness; the suit – black, with wacky lapels – was from Yohji Yamamoto and had cost him a good four-figure sum, as Aileen learned within minutes; the radiantly white shirt was likewise from Yohji; the spectacles were Danish, titanium-framed. His voice was pleasant on the ear; he was impressively articulate, and his loquacity – in combination with the creaseless brow and the brightly confident gaze – was suggestive of an expensive education.

His questions were well-considered and precise, and if the nodding and chin-stroking and intensely receptive eye contact with which he received my replies – as if he were hearing the pronouncements of Le Corbusier rather than merely the remarks of a man who sold furniture for a living – struck me as being a little too much, there was no doubt that his enthusiasm was genuine. He was knowledgeable.

Off-camera we talked for another hour or so, and he showed me, online, the work of a team of young Swedish designers of whom I'd never heard. I showed him the dining chair that my father had made, and he recognised it as a replica of a George Nakashima piece. He was intelligent and ambitious – he had other TV projects in the pipeline, and a book too, and was preparing a catalogue for a museum in Finland. I liked him, as did Aileen.

While the cameraman was loading his equipment into the car, she and Otis were chatting in the hall. Standing outside the front door, I overheard them: they were talking about how the business had developed. Aileen told him that we'd had some lean years; that at one point it had looked as if we might go bankrupt. 'It was pretty awful,' she said cheerfully. 'There were days when I thought we wouldn't come through it.' At which Otis remarked: 'What doesn't kill me makes me strong.' Aileen laughed at this, and together they came out. The interview had been great, Otis assured me, and he'd loved the house. He gave Aileen a kiss on the cheek.

'Lovely boy,' she commented as the car turned onto the road, and I agreed. He was easy to talk to, she said, and he wasn't one of those people who, on learning that she's an accountant, assume that she's a drone whose interests in life are limited to money and tax law. She'd been concerned that, being a TV person, he'd turn out to be glib and slick, but he wasn't glib at all.

I agreed again: Otis was a serious-minded and very personable chap, I said, and nicely turned out, as well.

'Very nicely,' Aileen concurred.

'"What doesn't kill me," eh?' I quoted.

'It's a good line,' said Aileen.

I followed her into the kitchen. For a few minutes I helped her to clear up, then asked: 'When you said you thought we wouldn't come through it, what did you mean?'

'Didn't I say "might not"?' she answered, loading the dishwasher. 'That's what I meant to say.'

'Sorry, yes. You did.'

Aileen carried on with what she was doing.

'You were talking about us as a business, yes?' I suggested.

'Yes,' she said.

'But not only as a business?'

'Not only, no,' she answered, still with her back to me.

'Really?'

'Well, yes,' she said, glancing at me over her shoulder as she crouched at the machine. 'We had a very bad patch. You know that. We came close to splitting up.'

'We did?'

'We did,' she said. 'Another month or two and I'd have been packing my bags.' She smiled at me as she said this, and it was said lightly, as if she were talking about a holiday that, in the end, she hadn't taken.

I knew she wasn't joking: this wasn't Aileen's kind of joke. 'Did you say that at the time?'

'Perhaps not in as many words.'

'I don't remember you saying anything.'

'Maybe I didn't,' she said. 'But it was obvious. There was no need to say anything. Hardly matters now, does it?'

Aileen would have left it at that, but I wanted to hear more. I had been impossible to live with, she duly told me: irascible, unreasonable, unaffectionate. I couldn't take issue with this, but I was a little surprised to be told that I'd been almost as unpleasant, occasionally, in the year or two before we'd left Canterbury. There had been days, she said, when she'd wondered if we had a future. 'And you felt the same. I know you did,' she said. If I had felt the same, I no longer had any recollection of having felt that way. Neither did I recall the weeks during which I'd stayed in the workshop till late and would barely speak to her when I came back to the flat.

'Really? Weeks?' I said.

'Weeks, yes,' she repeated, giving me a quick amused frown, as though I'd forgotten what day of the week it was. 'You were miserable in Canterbury,' she said. I thought that 'discontented' would have been a more accurate word.

There had been a lot of friction between me and my father, she reminded me. One evening she and I had been due to go to my parents for a meal and I'd cancelled at the last moment because I just couldn't face him. This too I had forgotten. Some tension, certainly, had come into my relationship with my father since I had decided to work on my own. He would have been happier had I stayed with him; he didn't greatly care for the pieces I was producing; at times, being fully aware that my skills were not and would never be the equal of his, that my work was assembled rather than crafted, I didn't much care for what I was making, either; I had far fewer customers than he did; in short, I was failing. These factors all complicated the situation with my father, but I had no memory of being unable to face him.

On the one hand I didn't recognise myself in Aileen's words; on the other hand I was sure that her version of that period of our lives was more faithful to the facts than was mine. It was troubling to be corrected in this way, and it was even more troubling to learn – or to be reminded – that Aileen had almost left me. The exposure of my complacency was unsettling, and I knew that I was ridiculous as well: it was ridiculous to feel – as I did feel –

in some way slighted by a rejection that hadn't actually happened, and it was doubly ridiculous to react in such a way when I was the one who had been duplicitous, in addition to being so difficult to live with. And of course what was going through my mind while Aileen answered my questions was that the affair with Sarah would almost certainly have had something to do with my having been irascible, unreasonable and unaffectionate, though it wasn't clear to me what was cause and what was effect. Nothing was clear to me. Indeed it crossed my mind – when Aileen looked me in the eye and said, 'You weren't yourself' – that she had suspected what was going on and was now about to tell me that she'd suspected, but this panic lasted only a second or two. If she had suspected anything, I told myself, she would have confronted me at once, when it was happening. Aileen was always direct, and never dissembled. I repeated this to myself many times, throughout the rest of the day.

I was appalled by my duplicity, yet when Aileen went out the next morning I was up in the loft within minutes to retrieve the picture of Sarah, which I had hidden with pointless thoroughness, in a box of old paperwork at the bottom of a trunk. Since hiding it I'd been congratulating myself for managing to leave it alone; now there was an excitement, a brief and guilty excitement, in finally ceasing to resist. I sat on the trunk, under the bare light-bulb, and looked at the photograph as you might look at a memento and await the arrival of a memory – the image and sounds of a beach from a stone you'd gathered there, for example; the atmosphere of a town from a postcard; the events of a particular day from a ticket for a concert. I looked at Sarah, at the gate, at the high bushes behind her, willing a meaning to emerge from this square of washed-out colours. The shadows in the foreground were crisp and the foliage of the upper branches was bright in the higher reaches; her clothes suggested a day that was warm; on the margin of the picture, a rhododendron was in full blossom. The belt that Sarah was wearing – I remembered that: she had bought it in Cordoba, and the leather still bore a smell, ten years later, that hinted at the reek of the tannery. After a while I had the notion that, had the camera been aimed a little higher, the spire of a church might have come into view; I seemed to recall a church that was reached by a path that ran under bushes, and that the path was closed by a gate, but I didn't know if that path was the path in the photograph, nor where that church was located, for that matter. It was not in Canterbury, I knew that for sure, which meant that we must have driven to wherever it was, and it must have been on a weekend when Aileen was away somewhere, because I wouldn't have closed the shop in order to have time with Sarah – or had business been so dire that a couple of hours here or there didn't seem to make any difference? Or had I been so infatuated with her that I hadn't cared about the possibility of missing a customer? I must have been infatuated, because otherwise why would I have become involved with her? Unless, that is, things with Aileen had been bad enough to make the temptation of Sarah irresistible. That was a possibility, although I tended to regard the dissatisfactions of that episode of my life as dissatisfactions with myself and with my livelihood rather than with Aileen. Yes, there had been disagreements, but the affair with Sarah had not, I believed, been indicative of any crisis in my relationship with Aileen. It was indicative, rather, of my selfishness and weakness. I hadn't given so much as a passing thought to the possibility of my being unfaithful before Sarah had appeared – or that's how I remembered it.

I stared at the face in the photograph, as if to ask it why I should have been so entranced by her. If you were to happen upon this picture in a sheaf of old photos in a jumble sale, it's unlikely that you would give it a second look. Bringing the photo as close to my face as I could without making it blur, I focused on the eyes, and soon I saw again the boldness of them, the gaze that was more challenging than flirtatious, and sardonic too, as if hinting that you may not be adequate to that challenge. Looking at her as she leaned on the gate, I remembered the quality of her stillness, which had something of the latent energy of a dancer or gymnast. And the precision and sudden-ness with which she would gesture, as though seizing an invisible object in mid-air – I remembered that too, and the way she raked her hair back with her fingers. She was exciting. Aileen, on the other hand, was good company, a good person, warm, kind, generous – but 'exciting' has never been an adjective that would spring to mind were I to be asked to describe her.

She would say the same about me, I'm sure. We weren't lovers who had found each other in a flash of recognition: rather, it had been a sort of gentle, protracted confluence, as acquaintance deepened into easy friendship, which in turn, over the course of several years, had deepened further. 'You were made for each other,' my mother would often say; 'She's sound, very sound,' said my father, for whom there could be no higher praise. Her soundness, her genuineness, her decency, impressed people immedi-ately.

There's an incident that I recall in unusual detail, perhaps because it had taken on the character of an anecdote as it was happening. We were in a pub one evening, not long after we'd moved into Chatham Street, and a red-faced man was sitting at the bar, sinking pint

after pint. Every few minutes he gave us several seconds
of his close attention. Eventually he stood up and came
over to our table. He was in his mid-fifties and around
six feet two, well in excess of twenty stone, with no
more than five visible teeth and hands that resembled
rubber gloves that had been filled with thick grease.
'You take good care of this girl,' he told me, putting a
hand on Aileen's shoulder. 'You take good care of her,
or I'll do it for you,' he said. His face was directed at me
but his eyes were swivelling like a blind man's; he was
alarming, but Aileen smiled and assured him that I did
take care of her. 'You better do,' he said to me. And then,
to Aileen: 'If I was younger, he'd have to watch out, and
that's no lie.' Aileen managed to appear charmed by this
gallantry; as a result it took a good ten minutes to get rid
of him. Placing a big soft hand on Aileen's bare forearm,
he offered, in a whisper, to buy her a drink. She patted
the hand and answered: 'Thank you, but I think we've
all had enough.' The reaction was unnerving: he closed
his eyes; he pursed his lips like a kid who's told a fib
and has been caught out; the hands closed on his knees
and gave them each a few small thumps. Trouble seemed
to be inevitable. The eyes opened; he squinted at Aileen,
lowering his head down an inch or two, as if looking
through a keyhole; the mouth widened in an expression
of what seemed to be pain, which suddenly became a
grin. 'You're right,' he said. 'Enough's enough. Enough is
enough. You're right.' Now, having more or less ignored
me since inviting himself to sit down, he looked at me.
'She's a good 'un,' he said. 'No side to her. I like that. I
do.' He lurched upright from his chair, then brought his
mouth to within an inch of my ear. 'You watch your step,
pal, OK?' he whispered, with a glance that was momentarily sober and distinctly unfriendly. Before leaving us,

he lifted Aileen's hand from the tabletop and planted a kiss on it; it was, she said later, like having a gigantic snail stuck onto her hand.

It's not impossible that this character had observed something in me that I'd never perceived in myself. When he said 'you take care of her', I wonder if he had sensed that I had to be warned. I thought of myself as a decent man, yet it could not have been more than a year later when I became involved with Sarah. But it had never occurred to me that he was doing anything other than complimenting Aileen. It was nice to hear her being praised, even though the praise was coming from an oaf who was reelingly drunk.

He was right about Aileen, it goes without saying. Aileen said what she thought, and this has always been, for me, one of her most appealing qualities. 'I'll come to your place on Thursday and I'll stay' – that's how we came to spend the night together for the first time. (That must have been exciting, to have it stated so plainly that we were about to become lovers; it must have been.) She foresees consequences and ramifications with great clarity; she can quickly assess and summarise the positives and negatives of any given situation. She is remarkably efficient and remarkably competent, and is reluctant to attempt anything for which she doesn't possess what she takes to be the requisite knowledge and abilities. Trial and error is not her way. Aileen has always made life run as smoothly as possible. And perhaps that's part of the explanation for what I did: I was excited by the possibility of an interval of disorder, a diversion from the responsibilities of my life, with a young woman who patently did not live to a plan, was not transparent, was not – by definition – someone whose principles were of the same order as Aileen's. But why, I asked myself, had I betrayed Aileen at that particular time, with that particular woman? Had a frustration of which I now retained no memory reached a critical pitch in the weeks before I met Sarah? Or was it because the foothills of middle age were then beginning to come into view that I'd succumbed to the flattering interest of a good-looking twenty-four-year-old?

Sarah had been good-looking – much more so, I knew, than appeared from this image of her. Again I studied the face in the photo. Looking at the mouth, I recalled that her lips, when she wasn't speaking, seemed often to tremble slightly, and that this had been enticing. Her eyes sometimes would widen momentarily, by a fraction of a millimetre, as if at an amusing, or alarming, thought. There was something, too, about the movement of her waist when she walked, the suppleness of her body, that was alluring. I closed my eyes, and I saw her momentarily, in motion, as if she'd stepped up to a pane of frosted glass and then withdrawn. I saw that movement of her waist, and the curves of her back. Her skin was remarkable, I remembered: running a finger across her back was like stroking the surface of a liquid. And at the thought of her skin – even though I was merely recalling the fact of its texture, rather than reviving the sensation of it – I felt a weak stirring of desire, which was not something I'd experienced much in recent years. Then it struck me that the body of Sarah might have been the single most important element of the explanation for what had happened. Was that all it had been: the attraction of one body to another, reciprocated, albeit less strongly? And the rest of it – all the emotional tumult of the affair – had been mere smoke, the mind's self-justification for what the body had done. Was that the truth of the matter? It was a banal idea, but credible.

Then again, credible is all that it was. I spent more than an hour with that photograph. At the end of the hour I had recovered a few pieces of memory but I knew nothing more than I had known an hour earlier. I gazed at my hands: they had touched the body of the woman in this photograph. That much was incontrovertible, I told myself. And in the next moment even this fact lost its truth: wasn't it the case that every single cell in these hands had been replaced many times over the years? Sarah's body was now bones in the ground; mine was no longer the one she had known. Was the man who took this picture, I argued, as dead as its subject? 'Yes, he is,' I answered. 'No,' I countered, but largely from a sense of obligation.

I went downstairs, as furtive as an adulterer coming home from a rendezvous, and searched – as some sort of antidote – for pictures of myself and Aileen from the year of the photograph of Sarah. Our lives are somewhat under-documented in comparison with the lives of Eleanor and Gerry. They have hundreds of photos, miles of videotapes, scores of DVDs. It comes of having kids, they tell us – you don't want to lose a minute of their growing up. Aileen and I, by contrast, have a couple of photo albums and a miscellany of plastic wallets, which were crammed in a drawer in the bedroom. Most of the pictures are from our first two or three years together; after that, it's mostly holiday pictures. I found some shots of us on holiday in Brittany, which perhaps belonged to the year in question. There was Aileen at Carnac, standing by a dolmen; she was frowning slightly (she's never liked having a camera pointed at her), but the frown seemed to be a superficial detail – a sense of wellbeing was what the picture most strongly conveyed. In the same batch there was a snap of me, sitting on my workbench, wearing a vile mustard-coloured top, holding a plane as though it were an object of immense value – every inch the pious young artisan. If this character were to walk into the room, I said to myself, I'd head for the door.

7

On a Saturday morning Aileen went up to London for the day and I told her a lie: I said I'd arranged to visit the studio of a pair of designers whose work I'd admired at one of last year's degree shows. In fact, I'd arranged to meet Sam in the car park of the Bluewater shopping centre.

The Toyota had been hosed down and its interior improved since my last ride. The floor had been cleared of cups and fag-ends, the dashboard had been given a wipe, and the passenger seat was covered with a freshly laundered white towel, which had the name of a hospital stitched in blue along its borders. Sam waited until I was buckled in before starting the engine, then pulled smoothly away. For the first few minutes he barely spoke. His driving, while we were in traffic, was positively sedate: I could have had a cup of coffee in my hand and would not have spilled a drop. As soon as we were out in the country, however, he became a man in a hurry: leaning back, with one hand on the wheel and the other dangling out of the window, he took us beyond the speed limit within a minute of turning into the first clear road. At a warning sign for a dangerous junction he didn't slow down at all. 'Didn't you see that?' I asked him.

'See what?'

'The sign,' I said, as we sped across the junction.

There was no chance of getting killed when he was driving, he told me. 'King of the Road, I was. That's what they called me. I could slot a Land Rover down an alley at sixty, with an inch to spare left and right, and there wouldn't be a scratch on the bugger. I've been in ambushes and fire-fights. Had bullets pinging off the doors. RPGs zinging in. Never lost a man. You're with me – nothing's going to happen to you. I'm good, and God takes care of me,' he proclaimed, smacking a fist into his chest with force.

At one point, having become distracted by the sight of an ascending hot-air balloon, it suddenly struck me that the fence-posts were reeling past very rapidly indeed. I checked the speedometer and saw that we were doing more than seventy. Not only that: Sam wasn't even looking at the road – he too was watching the balloon. 'If a tractor comes out of one of these fields, we're dead,' I said.

'I'll see him,' he answered, but he eased off the throttle. After that, he more or less kept our speed within the bounds of legality. For a few more minutes there was no conversation, and then we were held up behind a lorry. 'You wouldn't want me to overtake, would you?' he asked, having craned his neck out the window three or four times. I confirmed that I wouldn't. He told me again that nothing could happen to me while I was being driven by him.

'There's always a first time,' I said.

He drummed his fingers on the steering wheel as we crawled in the wake of the lorry. 'Here's a story for you,' he announced after a minute, then he told me about an incident from his time in Iraq. They had left the base to take some equipment across town and bring an officer back, and had been told that the chances of contact were high. They reached the building where the equipment was to be dropped off; the journey had been uneventful so far. At one point along the road back they had to pass a cluster of market stalls. It was a very hot afternoon, and Sam was feeling a bit groggy, which is perhaps why he was too slow to notice that there were no kids around. This was a sign that something was about to kick off, but it was only after it had kicked off that Sam realised that the kids were missing. 'It was like a millisecond later,' he said. 'I saw the fucker in a hole in the wall, and I saw the RPG coming in, and then – before it had arrived – it struck me: there weren't any kids.' The grenade skimmed the bonnet of the Land Rover: with one hand Sam showed me the angle of the bonnet, and with the other he mimed the flight of the grenade; the lorry had turned off and he was now accelerating, steering with his knees. 'Thing was,' he continued, 'there were gunmen in the neigh-bourhood as well, and they started up at the same time, so we had rounds coming in right and left. One of them went straight through us. In one window, out the other. If I hadn't had my head back it would've taken my face off. That was lucky enough, right? But even better, the RPG guy was a real heavy-duty idiot. The silly bastard decides to have another pop. Steps out into the open, ready to fire. Fuck knows what he was thinking, but it was last thing he ever thought. He suffered a very rapid downturn in his quality of life, I can tell you.' Sam giggled, shaking his head at the recollection, but his smile swiftly faded into a sombre stare that seemed, worryingly, to be fixed for a moment not on the road ahead but on a mirage of the ambush. With another shake of the head he was back in the present.

'Something like that, it gives you a buzz like nothing else,' he resumed. 'When you know you were just one twitch away from being extinct, it's better than sex, better than drink, better than drugs. You feel like fucking Superman. That's what I felt like. It was great. Mr Invincible. But second time it happens, it makes you think. Made me think, anyway. The second time really got to me. You want to hear about it?' I said I was happy to hear it if he would just pay closer attention to where we were going and slow down a bit. 'Sure thing,' he said, giving the brakes a token dab, then he told me about an evening when he'd been up on the roof with a couple of mates and a new lad, a huge Fijian called Pita. (He spelled it out for me: 'P-I-T-A. Not Peter.') They were sitting against the parapet, playing cards, under netting. He'd had a beer, it was late, it had been a long hot day, so again he wasn't at his sharpest. There was a sound he recognised but didn't process instantly, then the netting came down and a lump of metal was skittering around on the roof. His mates were diving for the steps; Pita, however, strode over to the angle of the wall in which the mortar had nestled, picked the thing up, and hurled it out into the darkness. There was no explosion. 'Now that got me thinking,' said Sam. 'Three strikes and out. You've had two – the next one's going to do you. It's crap, I know, but that's how I thought. And the other thing I thought was: when I get out of here, I'm not going to waste a fucking minute. That's what I thought: I'm going to live life to the max,' he said, grinning salaciously, eyes wide, at the wonderful prospect. The grin faded quickly; the eyes stared vacantly. 'I was going to be Jack the fucking lad,' he sighed, shaking his head.

'That's not how it worked out,' he went on. He'd had plenty of opportunities to run amok, because his first job, after coming out of the army, was working the door at a club run by a 'Turkish sleazebag' called Mehmet. 'I say he was sleazebag, because that's what he was,' Sam explained. 'But the guy I worked with, Col, he wasn't any better. He was into anything that had a skirt and pulse. The things some women will do to get to the VIP bar – it's incredible. He had women in the back office, women in the bog, women in the alley out the back. One of them gave him a blow-job behind the bins, while the boyfriend was looking for a place to park. Amazing, eh?'

'Heartwarming,' I said.

'But I couldn't do it,' he went on. 'I couldn't be like Col.'

My wordless response could have been taken to signify that I was glad to hear that this was the case.

'I just couldn't click, most of the time. I had a few women, don't get me wrong. But it kept going wrong. I'd be talking to some girl, and suddenly it was like I didn't have a clue what I'd just said to her. Or she'd be talking and my brain couldn't comprehend what she was saying. It was noises, not words. The brain wasn't processing it. Which wasn't much of a mystery.'

'Meaning?'

'Meaning I was off my face, nine days out of ten. That's how I got the maximum. A bottle of Scotch a day, easy. Plus a few beers. I did a lot of coke, plus dope. Then I saw the error of my ways,' he said, almost primly, with no apparent irony. 'It just hit me one day: *this isn't right.* It was the proverbial bulb going off. I'm lying in bed in the morning, with some girl whose name I don't even know. There's a bottle under the bed. I'm taking a swig, then: ping! *This isn't right*, this voice says in my head. *You haven't been straight for a month. There's a girl in your bed but you don't know anything about her. You don't know her name. You don't even know how she got to be here.* He did a sort of squirming movement in his seat and ran a finger around the neck of his sweatshirt, as though the thought of what he'd done was making him uncomfortable. 'That's what it was like,' he went on. 'Like a conversion, except God wasn't anything to do with it. I had this voice saying to me: *this is totally wrong. This isn't you.* But the thing is, I didn't know what was me any more. Does this sound like a load of wank to you?' he asked, in the tone of a keen student asking his teacher if he was on the right track.

I told him that what he was saying seemed absolutely reasonable, a remark that he took with the smile of someone receiving an unexpected and valued compliment.

'OK. OK,' he went on. 'Good. Right. Good. So I knew this wasn't me, yes? And I'm wondering what that means I am. A year ago, I knew what I was. It was obvious: I was a squaddie. Being a squaddie suited me. It was a good fit, till it all started to go a bit messy, and then I knew it wasn't like a one hundred per cent fit. The fighting, the buzz and all that: some of the blokes can't get enough of it. By the end, I'd had my fill. Don't misunderstand me: I'd learned a lot and I'd seen a lot. I was better for having done it. But I didn't want to see any more, thanks all the same. Enough was enough. And now, what was I? I was a bouncer and a piss-artist and a coke-head, and that really wasn't a good fit. So I stopped being a piss-artist and a coke-head, and I stopped being a bouncer, and I did some stupid non-jobs that weren't me at all. Then I got into building, and that was good. I liked it. I could do it. But still something wasn't right, you know what I mean? Is this making sense?'

This time the encouragement did not seem necessary; he wasn't going to stop talking.

'It was like: this is the right thing to do, this is what I should be doing, it fits me, but there's something not right with the me that it's fitting. Are you following? It was a good fit, but it was like something fitting a dummy. I mean, not really a dummy. Of course not, not literally. I wasn't brain-dead. But there was something missing. Like this hollow feeling, you know?'

He pressed a hand to his heart at this point, and gave me a searching look, the look of a man tormented; everything – the gesture, the look, the phrase 'hollow feeling' – struck me as having a rehearsed quality to it, and I knew what was coming next.

'And then I thought – maybe it's not knowing my real parents. My real parents, I mean,' he went on. 'Obvious now, I know. But honest, it hadn't occurred to me. I'd been well looked after, when I was a kid. Mr and Mrs Hendy, they'd done a good job with me. They gave me everything I needed. They were nice people, lovely people, but we were never really mum and dad and son. They were the people who looked after me. And I was fine with that. I didn't need to belong to a family, you know what I'm saying? I was OK as I was. Home was good, but I was my own man, and I proved it in the army. I didn't need anyone, not me. The women, they came and went. Could have done better with some of them. Would have been nice to have had a steady one, but it was no big deal. I didn't need to be with someone. And then I realised: maybe I'm wrong. Maybe I do need something. Not that I needed to be loved by my mum, OK? It wasn't like: "Please won't somebody love me?" It wasn't about self-esteem. That's your standard excuse nowadays, isn't it? "Not my fault – I have low self-esteem. I blame my parents." That wasn't it. My self-esteem is fine, thank you. What I mean is just that I didn't know my parents, and maybe that was having an effect, like some sort of weakness in your bones that you don't know about for years and then one day you find you're walking weird. Something like that. So I thought I'd have a go at finding my mother. Boys need their mums above all, eh? I thought: what's the worst that could happen? She could tell me to fuck off. I could think she was horrible. I was ready for that. So I went looking for her, and I tracked her down, in her little woody hideaway. Took a while to find her, but I got there. You don't have to be Sherlock Holmes, just determined. I'm not the sharpest tool in the box, I know that, but I don't give up. I never give up. I'm like a fucking terrier, me.' He pulled a face, as though checking his terrier-like qualities in a mirror. For a few moments he appeared to forget that I was with him.

'And then?' I prompted him.

'Then what?' he said, scanning the skies to left and right, as if on the lookout for something.

'You found her, and then—?'

'It was cool,' he said.

'Really?' I said, with what I hoped wasn't too strong an ingredient of scepticism.

'Sure. It was cool,' he said again. Then, after a pause, he cackled to himself and said: 'Not absolutely cool right away. Of course not. I mean, you couldn't expect her to be overjoyed when the little bastard comes looming out of the mists, could you? It wasn't exactly going to be "Glory Hallelujah, my boy is back – thank you, Jesus," was it?'

'Might have been,' I said.

'Well, I don't think so, in the circumstances,' he said, shrugging. 'She was mixed up about it. She felt bad about what had happened, but she wasn't going to pretend she'd been pining for me all these years. She was honest about it. I liked that. She shouldn't have had the kid, and the kid was better off with someone else. She hadn't been eating herself up about it. But there I was and she was glad to see me. It was cool. I felt a lot better. I did. I felt better right away,' he said. He seemed to have talked himself out, and not to require any response from me. A melancholy cast came over his face. For a minute or two we drove without talking, then he said, softly, as if waking me up: 'This is it.'

The church was a plain old building with a stocky bell-tower and walls of pale sandstone. From the road a path of stone slabs rose over the flank of the low hillock on which the church stood, curving in an arc towards the dark wooden door. A dilapidated wooden gate opened onto the path, and the wall into which the gate was set was crusted with bright lichen. Ivy almost covered two of the church's side windows. A gnarled old yew filled a corner of the graveyard, which was an expanse of undulating grass, on which the gravestones leaned at all angles, like sails at sea in a gale. It looked like a film set, I thought, and then Sam stooped to set down the flowers he'd brought, and I was standing at the grave of Quentin Williams and his daughter.

When Sam had told me that Sarah was dead, I had believed him. There was no reason, that I could think of, for him to be lying. There were moments, later, when I wondered if anything that Sam said could be believed absolutely, but when he offered to take me to see where she was buried, I knew that any last vestige of doubt had gone. So I'd known for some time that Sarah was dead – but until now I'd known it as a proposition, which was a different kind of knowing from what I experienced as I stood before the upright slab of limestone, reading its inscription. At the top was the name of her father:

QUENTIN WILLIAMS
BORN FEBRUARY 2ND, 1926
DIED OCTOBER 2ND, 2002

Below came a gap, where his wife's name would one day go. The inscription resumed at the base of the stone:

SARAH CLEMENTINE WILLIAMS
BELOVED DAUGHTER OF QUENTIN & ISABELLE
BORN JUNE 12TH, 1956
DIED AUGUST 13TH, 2008

What did I feel as I stood there? I can't honestly say that it could be described as grief. What I felt, I think, was something like what you'd feel if the ground suddenly fell away in front of you and you found yourself standing on the brink of a vast pit. There was a sensation – a sensation strong enough to make me light-headed – of an immense emptiness right in front of me, and also a flush of fear. This does not reflect well on me, but it is what I felt – afraid, for myself. *She was younger than you and now she's dead; soon it will be you.* That was the idea that quickly became strongest: *soon it will be you.* Regret, too, was part of what I was feeling – and not regret solely because of the situation that had now descended on me. I regretted that we had become involved with each other, that I had deceived Aileen. I suppose that, as I stood tracing the letters on her stone over and over again, I was apologising to both of them, pointlessly. Grief, however, would not be the right word for what was going on in my head.

A squat stone vase stood in the grass at the foot of the gravestone. A wilted bouquet had been in the vase when we arrived; Sam had removed the dead flowers and carried them to a bin by the churchyard wall, then he'd taken the steel insert out of the vase, replenished it at a nearby stand-pipe, and now was trimming his flowers with a penknife. He snipped each stem at precisely the same angle, and when the flowers had been arranged he carried the pile of trimmings to the bin on an upturned palm. Every action was performed with a strange gentleness and precision – like some sort of ritual, it struck me. Back at the grave, he knelt on the grass and bowed his head; his hands were joined loosely in his lap. It appeared he was praying, and when at last he spoke again, his voice came out in a murmur that sounded reverential, but for only for a fraction of a second, because what he was saying was: '"Beloved daughter" my arse. Makes you want to go round and tip the old coot's wheelchair over, doesn't it?'

I said I'd find it hard to imagine a nicer place to be buried. The setting was beautiful, and the gravestone was beautiful as well. Nowadays, I remarked, you don't often come across a stone that had been properly carved. I pointed out where the lettering showed that it had been incised by hand.

Sam considered the lettering, as though taking mitigating circumstances into account. 'Nice if you're a Bible basher,' he said. 'Which she wasn't. And her old man was about as much of a Christian as Attila the Hun. Same goes for the old woman. Not a Christian bone in her entire fucking body. Arseholes, the pair of them.'

I conceded that he might well have a point regarding the parents' Christian principles, or lack of them, but we should look at the grave simply as a grave. It was in a nice spot. It was tasteful. There weren't any angels on it, or quotes from the Bible. It didn't even have a cross on it.

'Yeah, but it's got "Beloved daughter" on it, which is a lie, and it's got her father in it,' he answered. 'And any day now the old bitch is going to be joining them. That's not what Sarah wanted. She didn't want to be tucked up with those two until the end of the fucking universe. She hated the bastards, didn't she?' I was going to suggest that perhaps she hadn't hated them, but I thought better of it when he started muttering to himself: 'It's not right. It's not right. It's not right.' At the last repetition he shook his head so violently I thought for a moment that he was trying to fend off a wasp. He started sweeping invisible dirt off the top of the gravestone.

'But it's not such a surprise, is it, not really? It's what people do,' I said, and I would have said more, had Sam not cut across me.

'I tell you what,' he said, scanning the graveyard as though he saw a hostile crowd there and was prepared to take them on, 'I fucking hate religion. All of it. I do. I fucking hate it.' He told me that when he first arrived in Belfast he thought it was a place just like home: 'a bit of a dump, in other words. But it wasn't anything like home. It was a madhouse. I'll tell you how mad it is,' he said, standing up. He planted his feet far apart and shook his shoulders, as if steadying himself prior to a martial arts routine, then he told me about the afternoon, in his first week in Belfast, when his patrol had gone up to the top of a hill overlooking the city. 'This is right on the edge of town, OK? The hill's here, the houses start here,' he said, chopping at the joints of his outstretched fingers. 'And if you put your hand out and stick up a thumb,' – he did that, lining up his thumb with my face – 'you're covering two enemy camps. Shankill here, Falls there. Side by side. Neighbours who fucking hate the sight of each other. And why? Because of this bollocks,' he said, indicating the church and its environs with a sweep of his arm. 'People carrying on like the seventeenth century happened last week, and it's all because of religion.'

He seemed to have finished what he had to say, so I remarked, quietly, that the situation in Northern Ireland was perhaps not quite as simple as that.

Sam reacted as if he'd been crushingly patronised. 'I know it's not as simple as that,' he snapped. 'I'm not a total fucking moron. I can read, you know. I did talk to people. I wasn't just stomping around telling the Micks to go fuck their mothers. I know it's not as simple as that. It's the economics; it's the politics. I know. But this shit is what's at the heart of it. This is where it all comes from, in the end. Catholic or Prod – it comes down to that. And I'm just saying I can't be doing with it. Not the Catholic shit, not the Protestant shit, not the Muslim shit. Iraq, right? Same fucking crap. What are you: Sunni or the other fucking crew? And if you don't get the answer right, we'll pull the eyes out of your head and piss in the sockets and then we'll burn your fucking house down and throw you in it. And if you're a woman, tough fucking luck either way, because the word of God round these parts is that you lot will do what you're fucking told. Speak when you're spoken to, cover your face, and walk ten yards behind your lord and fucking master. I hate it, all of it. It's total fucking bollocks.' He'd half turned away from me, and was rocking from one foot to the other, gazing at the ground and rubbing his neck as he did so. He had the look of a man who had a friend beside him, telling him to calm down. 'Chuck the fucking Pope in the slammer, that's what I'd do,' he growled. 'And make him share a cell with a couple of ayatollahs and a gang of fucking rabbis.' He kept rubbing at his neck; after several deep breaths he smiled at the turf and said: 'Maybe the Buddhists are on to something. I don't know.' When he looked at me he was blinking exaggeratedly, as if coming out of a fit.

Having scrubbed his face for a few seconds, he nodded towards a grave to his left. 'One of the clan, what'll you bet me?' he said. I read the inscription: it was another Williams – John Jeremy Williams, born on an illegible day in July 1884, died April 22nd, 1916. 'Who the fuck was he, eh?' said Sam. 'Who the fuck were any of them?' he said, scanning the cemetery, smiling in commiseration with the dead. 'Once your grandchildren have gone, that's it,' he said – 'that's when you're finally, utterly, totally dead. Once the last person who knows what your voice was like, who heard you talk and saw your face – once they've gone, you're finished.' Pointing to the stone of John Jeremy Williams, he launched a monologue about the men who had fought in World War I, about how none of them will be left in a few months from now, and then nobody will know what that war was really like. 'As soon as those old men have gone, that human link,' he said, 'that's when it all becomes history.' He gave me a long and solemn look, by which I was to know that this was a subject to which he was accustomed to giving deep thought. 'And eighty years from now, ninety, nobody's going to know what Iraq was like. There'll be hours and hours of films, and loads of books and all that – but what it really was, that'll die with us. What's in here,' he said, giving his head a knock with his fist, 'that's what true. And you can't get it all out. It's not possible,' he said. 'What you know, what's in here—' he began, jabbing a thumb against his brow, but he abandoned the sentence with a rueful half-smile. Then he asked me: 'You ever seen a corpse?'

'Yes,' I replied. 'When you get to my age, it's inevitable.'

He carried on as if he'd heard 'No.' He told me he'd seen a lot – 'and I mean a lot,' he emphasised. He asked me if I knew what a corpse was, and told me immediately what it was. 'A broken machine,' he said, severely, in a tone of rebuttal. 'You understand? A broken machine. It's not something that's no longer whole. It's not the mortal remains, and soul of the dear departed has flown away. Nothing's flown away. That's all there is, and it's broken. Same as a TV. Same as a computer. When a computer breaks, you don't think it's lost its soul. All the parts of the machine are there, but they just don't work. And that's what it is with a dead person. It's a broken machine. Do you get what I'm saying?'

I replied that I did indeed get it, but his eyes were searching mine, failing to find evidence that I had truly understood.

'Can I have a few minutes on my own?' he asked abruptly, putting a hand on the gravestone as though for support.

The church door wasn't locked, so I went inside. Filtered by the ivy, the light in the nave was an easeful pale green; it was so quiet, all I could hear was the scratching of leaves at the glass, and the gushing of my pulse in my ears. The latter was louder – I'd been alarmed by Sam's outburst, and could still feel a fluttering in my chest. I was intrigued by him, and somewhat frightened too. And although I wasn't convinced that he was who he said he was, I became aware, as I sat in the cool high-ceilinged church, with its comforting green light and its smells of rising damp and whitewash and furniture polish, that I was coming closer to an acceptance of the idea. The impossibility of it had become diluted, as it were. I wondered what I would do, should we arrive at the day on which the last piece of doubt was dissolved. I had no idea what I would do. I imagined myself telling Aileen, but could get no further than the arguments that would follow. Seeking distraction, I studied the flower-heads that had been carved at the end of the pew. They were not in any way remarkable, but I managed to pretend to myself that they were fascinating. As I was working my way from pew to pew the church bell began to ring; the sound was an unmusical clanging, like a strip of scrap iron being hammered. I heard Sam laughing raucously outside, and went out to see what was so funny, which was clearly what he wanted – the laugh had the tone of a call.

'Says it all, doesn't it?' he shouted as I emerged from the church. He was sitting on the wall, near the gate, and pointing up into the tower, where the bell was hanging, motionless, as the clanging went on. 'It's a recording, isn't it? They can't be arsed to ring the bell, so they've got a tape instead. And a fucking crappy recording at that. I mean, if you're going to fob us off with a CD, at least give us the bells of Westminster Abbey or something half fucking decent. Not a monkey in a breaker's yard.' He pushed himself off the wall and came over to me. 'You OK?' he asked, as though I'd been distressed and had gone into the church to get a grip on myself.

'Fine,' I told him.

He asked if I wanted any more time here and then, being told that I was happy to set off, he suggested a walk. There was a nice path, he said, that went from near the church down to a small reservoir, through a bit of woodland. It would take us forty minutes there and back, that's all. He was asking a favour of me, I thought, and so I agreed. It was indeed a pleasant stroll, even though the path deteriorated into thick mud in a couple of places. Sam led the way, holding back any branches that might have obstructed me. We didn't talk much. Two or three times he asked me to identify a particular tree; growing up in the

Midlands, he said, he had learned to identify any make of
car from a range of two hundred yards, but he still didn't
know his trees as well as he should. At one point, as Sam
was leading us on a detour around a tract of swamp, he
started and turned sharply to his left. 'We're not alone,' he
whispered, aiming a finger through the foliage. I'd heard
nothing and for several seconds could see nothing in the
thicket into which he was pointing, but then I made out
a man in a Barbour jacket, and, a few moments later, a
golden retriever. Sam winked at me and said: 'Good,
eh? Ears like a bat, eyes like an eagle. I'm the man.' He
was making a joke of it, but it was nonetheless meant to
impress me, and it was quite impressive, I have to admit,
even if it was something of a performance, a display of
soldierly prowess – and I could tell that he saw that he'd
achieved something of the desired effect. A short distance
further on, as the reservoir came into sight, he plucked a
hornbeam leaf and asked me what it was – having demonstrated his special competence, it seemed, he now felt it
necessary to invite me to show mine. The reservoir wasn't
interesting – just an irregular oval of water, as motionless
as lacquer except in the middle, where the breeze raked a
bit of movement into it. Last time he was here, said Sam,
he'd seen a kingfisher on the opposite bank.

We waited for five minutes, but no kingfisher appeared.
We did see something remarkable soon after, though. On
the way back we took a different path, a path that went
right through the heart of the wood, whereas the one we'd
followed to the water had taken us close to the boundary.
When we were more or less in the middle, Sam began
murmuring, in a rising voice: 'Fuck – fuck – fuck – fuck.'
And then, smiling with delight, he directed my attention
to what he'd seen: an expanse of bluebells, twenty yards
away, like a small bank of radiant blue fog, or – as Sam

put it – a patch of blue summer sky lying on the ground. 'That's just amazing,' he kept saying, as we stood on the edge of the clearing that the bluebells filled. He stood with his hands on his hips, nodding and grinning, as though someone had put the flowers there to astound us and had succeeded spectacularly. 'Incredible. Absolutely fucking incredible,' he said, and it appeared to me that his joy was genuine, rather than something that depended on his having me for an audience.

On the drive home I found myself talking to him in a way I hadn't done before – by which I mean that I did more than merely react to whatever Sam said. In other words, we had a conversation. I told him about the vicar who'd asked us – my father and me – to make a cross for him. The cross was to be huge – about twenty feet high – and would stand outside the vicar's church, which was out in the middle of nowhere, but within sight of the train line to London. The idea was that the weary commuters, catching sight of the magnificent cross, would be prompted to consider the vacuity of their lives and turn back to God. Father Gorman was the vicar's name, and we hadn't warmed to him: a smug little zealot, my father thought he was. The mighty wooden cross, my father said, was the sanctified equivalent of the Bentley parked in the drive. It wasn't a commission that we wanted to take, but we might have taken it had the vicar not jibbed at the cost and tried to persuade us to donate our labour in the name of the Lord. In relating this episode to Sam, I failed to make it clear that the cash had been the sticking point. Instead, I implied that we'd turned down the vicar on principle. And the reason I misrepresented the situation to Sam, I think, was that I knew that Sam would be more receptive to this slightly skewed version than to a truer one. This seems obvious now, and seemed obvious later that day, but at the time it didn't occur to me that I was courting his approval.

One reason I was slow to comprehend my own motive is that within a minute or two of having told Sam about Father Gorman's commission, I'd clashed with him. And shortly after that, things took an even sharper turn for the worse.

The situation changed when, apropos of absolutely nothing I'd been saying, Sam asked me: 'What did you think of her? Sarah. I mean, I know you fancied her. Obviously you fancied her. But as a person – what did you think?'

I was taken aback, not just by the suddenness with which he'd changed the subject, but by his manner. It was as though we were a couple of lads who'd been out on the town and now he was asking me what I'd thought of a girl we'd been chatting to. I told him that I didn't want to talk about it.

'You what?' he screeched, as if I'd said something incredible. 'You're my dad and I'm asking you what you thought of my mum, and you're telling me you don't want to talk about it? After what we've just been doing?'

My answer to this was that I had known Sarah, briefly, a long time ago, and no purpose would be served by going over what had happened between us.

'Well,' said Sam, 'what happened between you and Sarah was me, wasn't it? So I think I have a right to know.'

'I don't think you do,' I said. 'And please slow down,' I added, because we were now travelling as fast as we had been on the way down. Sam decelerated by perhaps two miles per hour. 'A little more,' I said. This provoked a stamp on the brakes, and a brief episode of ostentatiously cautious driving. In the middle distance, ahead of us on the road, there was a livestock lorry. We were soon right behind it; when we came to a long corner at which it might have been possible to overtake, Sam made no attempt to pass. He stared dully at the rear of the lorry, in obedience to my tedious instructions. A protracted silence was broken by the ringing of my phone. I saw from the screen that it was Aileen, so of course I couldn't answer it, because she'd have heard the noise of the Toyota and I'd have had to invent an explanation for where I was. I held the phone until it switched to the answering service, then repocketed it; Sam smirked.

We drove on, not talking, stuck in the wake of the lorry. Then I looked in the wing mirror and saw a car, a silver open-top BMW, so close that most of its radiator grille was hidden. I'd been glancing in the mirror every minute or so, I suppose, and the road behind us had been empty last time I looked, so the car must have been doing quite a speed before it caught up with us. Its headlights flashed, and Sam put a hand out of the window and stuck up a finger. The car fell a little further back, flashed, and came up even closer than before. 'Wanker,' Sam grumbled. He prodded at the brakes, which prompted a long blast on the horn from the driver of the BMW. In the mirror I saw a hand making a motion as if slapping something aside. The BMW moved into the right-hand side of the road, preparing to overtake; Sam eased the Toyota a yard to the right, and peered round the lorry. 'No fucking way, sunshine,' he hissed, getting back in lane a few seconds before a van flew past in the opposite direction. Again the BMW sidled out; again Sam did the same. Headlights flashed; Sam touched the brakes; the BMW's horn blared; I could see the driver's face contorting with fury.

We were on a long blind corner, on the flank of a hill, when the BMW came alongside. With one hand the driver was pressing the horn; with the other he was gesturing that we should get out of his way. Sam put his head out and shouted: 'Cunt!' At this the BMW driver seized the steering wheel in both hands, accelerated past, then turned sharply into the gap between us and the lorry, a gap that was barely larger than his car. We came into contact with the rear of the BMW, not as forcefully as had seemed inevitable, but with enough strength to shatter some glass. The BMW slewed to a stop at a right-angle to the road, and the driver got out.

He was a man in his late thirties, somewhat shorter than Sam but thick-set and broad-shouldered – he looked like someone who spent hours of each week in the gym. He had spiky hair that was unnaturally blond, and wore an expensive-looking black jacket over a brilliant white shirt, the top two or three buttons of which were undone. He was wearing sunglasses, which were removed as he bent down to survey the damage. The inspection completed, he stood up and scratched at his chin, frowning as if he'd been the victim of a serious act of vandalism. The frown was directed at Sam, who was now breezily inspecting the Toyota, which had thick steel bars across its front and was more or less in the same state as it had been before the collision. Waiting for Sam's attention to come his way, the man adjusted his expression to one of lavish incredulity at Sam's casual reaction to the mess he'd made. Meanwhile, the lorry had come to a halt a couple of hundred yards away, and the driver was walking towards us. Ignoring the driver of the BMW, Sam strolled down the lane to meet the lorry driver, crunching through the pieces of glass and plastic that littered the tarmac. They exchanged a few words; Sam made some reassuring gestures; the driver handed Sam a piece of paper before returning to his lorry and driving away.

Having concluded his dealings with the lorry driver, Sam was walking back down the lane towards the Toyota, without so much as a glance for the BMW or its owner. Realising that Sam intended simply to leave, the BMW man darted forward and put himself between Sam and his vehicle, at a distance of maybe ten yards from where I was. I couldn't hear what was being said, but it was clear that the man was insisting that Sam take a closer look at the damage that had been caused to his car. Sam shrugged, followed him, gave the dented stern of the BMW a cursory examination, shrugged again, and turned away. Before he'd taken more than a couple of steps, he'd been grabbed by the arm. Sam's gaze travelled slowly from the man's hand to his face, then he smiled and said something that resulted in the prompt removal of the hand. The man moved closer to his car, and urged Sam to look at the mess that had been made of the area around the rear light. Sam's response was to raise a foot and tap at the cracked glass with the toe of a boot. Winding down my window, I heard: 'What you going to do about it?'

This made Sam laugh; turning away, he muttered: 'Go fuck yourself.'

The BMW driver's face was now so strained with anger, it looked as if invisible hands were throttling him. He sprang forward, seized Sam by the shoulder, yanked him round and threw a punch – which missed by several inches, because Sam pulled his head back while the fist was in flight. After doing a sort of dance which I think was intended to make him look like a trained boxer, the man threw a second punch, which Sam similarly dodged. A third punch followed immediately; Sam dealt with it by seizing the wrist in mid-air and pulling the arm down slowly, like a stiff lever. As he did this he said something I couldn't hear clearly, and produced a look that was so

grim it would have made any rational person immediately
reconsider his tactics. However, the moment his arm was
released the man launched another punch, and this one,
though Sam ducked away from it, caught him on the bicep.
Rubbing the arm where he'd been hit, Sam looked up at
the sky as though giving thought to what he should now
do, then warned the man that if he didn't go back to his
car right now and get the fuck out of here, he'd be leaving
the area in an ambulance. I heard this warning distinctly;
it was uttered in a perfectly even voice, as though Sam
were discussing a consequence as unavoidable as night
following day.

The man called Sam a cunt, but seemed to have understood that he'd pushed his luck as far as was wise. 'OK,'
said Sam, with a dismissive wave of the hand, and
he started to walk towards his side of the Toyota. He'd
covered five yards when the man decided to follow. Sam
wheeled about and shouted, as if dealing with a dog that
was making a nuisance of itself: 'You. Fuck. Off.' He
turned his back, whereupon the idiot hopped forward and
shoved Sam between the shoulder blades.

Sensing that the situation was in danger of deteriorating
rapidly, I opened my door, but before I could get out, let
alone tell anyone to calm down, the man shouted at me:
'You keep out of it.' Sam motioned that I should stay
inside, and in the split second in which I was closing my
door and not looking at the two of them, Sam struck out. I
saw the man bend double with his hands to his face, and
when he straightened up there was a streak of blood down
the front of his shirt. He uncovered his face and stared at
the blood in his palms, and as he was doing this he took
another punch to the side of the head, which put him on
the ground, on his back. As though waiting for a drunken
friend to get to his feet, Sam propped himself against the

Toyota, arms crossed, gazing at the fields beside the road. Slowly the man raised himself onto his knees. Sam had a fist cocked. The man raised his hands, cringing, which persuaded Sam to lower the fist. Upright now, the man pinched his front teeth and grimaced. Blood dribbled from his mouth. For a few seconds they stood facing each other. 'Done?' said Sam. The man tugged at the sleeves of his jacket, dusted them down, and kicked Sam in the crotch. The kick must have been painful, but Sam barely reacted. Instead he squinted, as if peering through fog at something apparently odd, before hitting the man with a punch to the jaw that was so strong it made him stagger sideways in four or five little steps, as if the ground had tilted thirty degrees; a fast punch to the nose sent him backwards. Sam shadowed him, leaning forward and mouthing a few quiet words, as if to enquire if everything was all right.

By now the man's face was daubed with blood from nose to his chin, and he was having to hold onto his car to stay upright. Sam seemed to take pity on him. Holding him by the shoulders, he shifted him so that he was sitting on the top edge of the nearside rear door, with his feet braced on the road. The man was too dazed to resist being manoeuvred in this way. Sam searched the pockets of the man's jacket and took out a mobile phone, which he lobbed onto a front seat. He pointed to where the phone had landed, and gave him a pat on the back. Looking down, the man nodded as he massaged his jaw; then Sam pushed him firmly on the chest, toppling him backwards into the car. A foot remained resting, motion-less, on the door. Sam knocked the foot off and sauntered towards the back of the pickup. When he reappeared he had a wrench in his hand and was striding towards the BMW.

Terrified by what I thought he was going to do, I flung open the door and yelled 'Stop!', but he took no notice of me. He looked into the car, holding the wrench by his side, then he went to the front and, with one sharp and precise blow, as if striking a gong lightly, he shattered the windscreen. That done, he returned to the Toyota, glancing to left and right as he strolled, wholly at ease on this fine afternoon, in this fine little corner of England. Having tossed the wrench into the back, he knelt by the verge to wipe the blood from his hands; unhurriedly, as though washing himself in the morning, he swept his hands back and forth through the grass. While doing this he noticed that a car was now coming towards us. As casually as a person going to greet the postman, Sam stood up and walked a few yards down the road, taking up position in front and to the side of the BMW. The car stopped and the driver wound down his window; Sam stooped to talk to him, placing a hand on the roof and standing in such a way as to limit the view of the scene. Assured that everything was under control, the driver drove away, with a small wave for Sam and another for me.

Sam waited until he was out of sight, then went to the back of the Toyota again and reappeared with a large white water canister, which he emptied over the rear seat of the BMW. For a moment a hand appeared, trying to grab onto the door. Sam walked off, returned the canister to its place, and swung himself into the driver's seat. As we pulled away, the man was struggling to sit up; blood was coming out of a gash across his nose. 'What a fucking plonker,' Sam muttered, and that was all he said until we were back in town. I said nothing; I wanted to get away from him as soon as possible, and a variety of consequences were running through my mind. His face was clenched, but once or twice I thought I detected a sign of self-annoyance in his eyes. He dropped me back at Bluewater. 'See you,' he said as I got out, and within seconds he was gone.

Aileen wasn't yet home when I arrived. This episode would have repercussions, I was certain, so I had to have some sort of story ready. I told Aileen that I'd been a witness to a road rage incident, and the police might be in touch. I played it down, and skimped on the details. It wasn't possible to tell the truth at the moment. I was praying that I would never have to.

8

The police were soon in touch. Fortunately I was the one who took the call, and to avoid complications I arranged to be interviewed at the station rather than at home.

Two officers led me to the interview room. My anxiety, I thought, must have been conspicuous, especially after their opening enquiry: they asked if I could confirm that the incident had happened as Mr Williams and I were returning from the cemetery where his mother was buried. The next question, I was sure, would be something along the lines of: 'Mr Williams says you're his father – is this correct?' In turmoil, despite the officers' sympathetic manner, I answered that this was indeed the case. Then I volunteered that Mr Williams' mother was a friend of mine from many years ago. This must have accorded with what Sam had told them, because the discussion now moved on to the fight itself.

The crash, I told them, had been the other driver's fault entirely; Mr Williams could not have done anything to prevent it. I described in detail how the collision had occurred; I drew a diagram. And how about the alterca-tion that had followed? Without compromising myself I could tell them that Mr Williams had not started the brawl. The other man – his name was Terry Fenway, they told me – had seemed hell-bent on having a fight, whereas Mr Williams had made several attempts to deter him. I told them that Mr Fenway had struck Mr Williams first, and Mr Williams had not retaliated. One of the officers made a note of this, before remarking that there was a notable difference between the injuries sustained by Mr Fenway and the injuries sustained by Mr Williams. Mr Williams, in fact, would appear to have emerged unscathed; Mr Fenway, by contrast, had sustained a broken nose and extensive bruising. Did I have any comment to make on this discrepancy? Mr Fenway, I said, had been extremely aggressive from the outset, but most of his punches had missed; Mr Williams, on the other hand, had not missed. I was asked about the blow that had cracked Mr Fenway's nose; I hadn't had a clear view, I answered – and managed to persuade myself that this was broadly true.

Mr Williams had admitted that he'd smashed the windscreen of the BMW, they told me. His action, they proposed, was an act of criminal damage. I said that I had tried to dissuade him, but Mr Fenway's actions had so enraged Mr Williams that he was in no frame of mind to listen to me. Would I say, they asked, that Mr Williams' assault on Mr Fenway was as excessive as his vandalism of Mr Fenway's car? This was the trickiest part of the interview. Of course I thought that Sam had lost control, but if I were to say as much, and thus incriminate him, who was to know what he might do? It was highly likely, I thought, that at the very least he would retaliate by telling his story to Aileen, and I couldn't run the risk of that, so I repeated that Mr Fenway had attacked Mr Williams, who had restrained himself for longer than most people would have found possible. For how long, they asked me, did Mr Williams continue hitting Mr Fenway once he'd decided he had no option but to use physical force? Only a few seconds, I replied – which made one of the policemen raise an eyebrow, though I'd given them an honest answer. And that, more or less, was the end of the conversation. When I left the police station I was convinced that worse was soon to come.

I now had a spasm of anxiety every time the phone rang. It was only a matter of time, I was sure, before the police or Sam called me. But the half-hour at the station turned out to be the end of my involvement in whatever investigation there was. Neither did any insurer contact me. It wasn't long, however, before Sam reappeared.

Early on a Saturday afternoon, a fortnight after the crash, I took a call from Geoff Collingwood, the manager on the North Street branch. There had been an incident. A man had come into the showroom an hour ago, 'a scruffy individual', said Geoff. When Geoff had asked if he could be of assistance, the man had said he was just looking; he made some remark about the price of everything, but he wasn't abusive, not at first. Geoff left him alone. Two women – a mother and daughter – were also looking around. The man said something to the daughter to which she took exception; he then seemed to try to make out that it had been intended as a joke. The mother, sensing that there'd been an unpleasant exchange with the man, asked questions of her daughter, after which she informed Geoff that one of his customers had been making objectionable comments. She pointed out the offender. Geoff told him that a complaint had been made. The man seemed to find this both surprising and interesting; he requested further information. 'You know perfectly well what we're talking about,' said the older woman. 'I'm afraid I don't,' said the man, the soul of innocent politeness. The mother said that she had no intention of repeating verbatim what he'd said to her, but was astonished that he should pretend to have no idea what this was about. 'Not the slightest,' Sam sighed. It had come to something, he said, as he prepared to leave, that a man could not compliment a woman on her appearance without being accused of making a nuisance of himself. He smiled sadly, as if grievously disappointed that he could have been so slandered, and took his leave. At the door he stopped and beckoned Geoff to come over. Looking steadily at the women, as if intending that they should suspect that they were the subject of whatever he was saying, he said: 'Do me a favour. Tell Mr Pattison I dropped by, will you? Tell him today, there's a good chap.' Having given him an intimidating little tap on the shoulder with a rolled-up newspaper, he swaggered off.

I rang Sam right away and asked him what he'd been playing at. The question received no answer. 'Oh, hello,' he said, with weighty sarcasm, as if I were a supposed friend who'd been unaccountably out of touch for rather a long time. Again I asked him what he'd been doing in North Street. 'Same as everyone else – planning a lifestyle upgrade.' Immediately he added: 'Only kidding. Nice stuff you got there. Really nice stuff. Silly prices, to be frank with you, but nice stuff. Nice people too. Staff, I mean. Nice staff. Some of the customers I'm not so sure about. Up themselves. You know what I mean? Like: "Look at us. We spend as much on a fucking chair as you'd spend on a car." But nice staff.'

I tried again: 'What happened this morning?'

There'd been a misunderstanding with a couple of stuck-up women, he said, and before I could ask him to clarify he said that we should meet.

'What are you doing here?' I asked.

'Doing where?'

'Here. In Guildford. Aren't you working in London?'

'Well, obviously not,' he answered.

'You're working here? In this area?'

'What's the big deal? You telling me I need a passport for Surrey or something? I just thought I'd take a look around. Anyway, I've got something for you. A surprise,' he said.

I told him that I was still recovering from his previous surprises and would rather know right now what was in store. 'You'll see,' he said.

'Where are you living now?' I asked him.

The caravan was berthed in a field near Elstead. He'd done a deal with the farmer who owned the land, he explained: in return for repointing the side of the farmer's house, he'd been allowed to tuck himself under the trees for a month or two. I proposed that we should meet there, and he gave me directions.

We met the following morning. He was sitting on the bonnet of the Toyota, holding a cylindrical package that was wrapped in brown paper. 'You don't want to go inside,' he said, jabbing a thumb back at the caravan. 'It's in a bit of a state. Needs a good clean. Lovely spot, though, isn't it? Better than the last shithole,' he said, presenting the panorama of the fields.

I agreed that it was.

'Doing my best to lower the tone of the neighbourhood,' he joked. 'Peter Sellers used to live around here. Did you know that?'

I didn't know that.

'With that Swedish bird. Actress. Blonde. Tits. What's her name?'

'Britt Ekland?'

'Yeah. Her. Tasty number, she was. Here you go.' He

held the package out to me, saying nothing, as if this meeting had been arranged by me, so that I could take delivery of the item. I asked him what it was, though I could tell it was a bottle. 'Open it,' he said. I peeled back a ribbon of paper, and saw the name Laphroaig on the top of the tube inside. 'Very nice stuff, I believe,' he said. 'You like whisky, I hope?'

I don't much like whisky, but I thanked him, before asking why he was giving it to me.

He said it was by way of an apology. 'I put you in a situation,' he said, 'and I wanted to say sorry.'

The apology was offered as if in compliance to an order, like a young hooligan forced by his parents to apologise to a neighbour for breaking a window. 'How did you know my address?' I asked. His look of perplexity made me hope for a few seconds that all he'd given the police was my name, and that they'd done the rest. 'The police,' I prompted him.

'They called you in?'

'They did.'

'OK,' he said. Then, after a sustained pause, he asked: 'So what did you tell them?'

I hesitated, but not for as long I should have, before replying: 'I told them you were a maniac.'

For the past minute or so he'd been staring at the ground. Now, startled, he looked me in the face, with such alarm in his eyes – and something else as well: grief at my betrayal of him – that I immediately regretted my semi-joke. 'Of course I didn't,' I said. 'I told them the crash was the other driver's fault. You didn't cause it.'

'What about the fight?'

'He wouldn't back off.'

'That's what you told them?'

'Yes.'

'Really?'

'Yes,' I repeated.

'You didn't tell them I'd gone over the top?'

'I didn't. But they might have drawn their own conclusions.'

Sam released a long breath. 'Thanks for that. I appreciate it,' he said.

'But you did overdo it,' I told him.

Gazing into the sky, he grimaced as though recalling what had happened and being slightly puzzled by it. 'I did,' he stated. He lit a cigarette and let his head fall slowly back onto the windscreen. 'I could have killed him,' he said.

'I thought you were going to.'

'So did I,' said Sam. Smoking his cigarette, with his head lolling on the glass, he now – no more than a minute after seeming to believe that I had told the police that he was a madman – had the look of a man on holiday.

Suppressing my irritation, I asked if there had been any further developments. 'Heard nothing,' he said. Having finished his cigarette, he stubbed it out thoroughly on the door of the Toyota.

'Now, how about an answer to my question?' I suggested.

'What question's that?' Sam replied.

'Did you give the police my address?'

'Well, yeah. Obviously,' he answered. I began to wish that I'd continued to pretend that I'd not covered for him. 'Otherwise it was my word against his. Smoothie in shiny BMW versus yob in van. BMW smoothie all knocked up; low-life unmarked. We all know which way that one would have gone, don't we? I get some trainee on legal aid, if I'm lucky. He gets some cunt who plays golf with the judge every Sunday morning. Go Directly to Jail; Do Not Pass Go; Do Not Collect £200.'

'What I'm interested in,' I said, 'is how you came by my address. And phone number.'

'What's the big deal with that?'

'I'm just curious.'

'It's easy. I'm not as thick as I look, you know,' he said, taking another cigarette.

'I don't think you're thick,' I said. 'You're obviously not thick.'

'Thanking you kindly,' he responded, with a small mock-deferential nod. 'But what are you saying? The cops say to me: "Who was the gentleman who was with you?" And I'm supposed to say: "Fuck me if I know"? Is that it? Is that what I was meant to do? Keep you out of it?'

'No. Of course not.'

Having swung round so his legs dangled down the side of the truck, he jabbed his elbows onto his knees and set his head in hands, as if locking it into place. He spat out a pellet of smoke and said: 'So what exactly are you saying?'

I tried to formulate a reply, but before I could come up with anything Sam leaned forward, aiming the tip of his cigarette at me. 'I'll tell you what the interesting question is,' he said. 'The interesting question isn't how I know where you live. Any fuckwit could find that out. Takes a few minutes. If you want to know how I did it, I'll tell you, but it's not interesting. The interesting question is why you're so wound up by the idea that I know. That's what's interesting.'

'I'm not wound up,' I answered.

'Oh yes you are,' he said, with a smirk that had some malice in it and also some sense of injury. He let some smoke dribble from his mouth and drew it up into his nostrils, taking a steadying shot of nicotine. 'And another interesting thing,' he went on, 'is that you've been steering clear of me.'

'That's not—'

'Two weeks and not a dicky bird. Only one way of reading that situation, it seems to me. In my book, that's the cold shoulder.'

'I've been very busy.'

'Whereas I haven't, of course? I've been lying around on my sunbed and sipping Bacardi all fucking day long.'

'No, but—'

'We're all busy, mate. Point is, it takes ten seconds to make a call. Don't matter how busy you are. President of the United fucking States of America finds time to ring his family from the office. Not telling me you're busier than the President of the United States, are you? I mean, I know business is good, but that's ridiculous. You've been avoiding me. That's the truth. That's what's been going on,' he said, placing a full stop on the air between our faces with his cigarette.

Unable to think of a plausible way of disagreeing, because of course it was true, I contradicted him with a mumble.

'You're my father,' he protested. 'You shouldn't be avoiding me. I know we had a bit of a setback with that dickhead, but I didn't expect you'd just vanish like that. I don't think that's right. It's not right, is it? I mean, you should have called. For all you knew, I was in the slammer, for fuck's sake.' He was no longer aggressive – his manner was plaintive, and aggrieved. Yet there was still something that jarred. When he said 'You're my father', it didn't sound like a son talking. Rather, it was as if 'father' were some kind of job title and nothing more, like: 'You're the driver.' What's more, crucially, by now I'd observed him closely for several hours altogether, and had yet to discern even the slightest resemblance between us.

Suddenly he bared his teeth and began scratching at the tops of his thighs, as though there were ants crawling over his skin. That done, he turned to me and gave me a pursed-lips smile. 'But I know what it is,' he said. 'I know why you've been keeping your distance. I do. You're scared of me. That's what it is, isn't it? You really do think I'm a head-case.' Sustained eye contact now followed; his look was not challenging – it said instead that he was patiently awaiting an honest answer, and would wait for as long as was necessary.

Lying outright was impossible: I told him that I couldn't deny that the accident and the fight had unnerved me.

This elicited a smile, the smile of a confessor who was glad – for my sake, of course – that I had at last unburdened myself. 'That's OK,' he said. 'I understand. I'm scared of me as well.'

Pleased with this turn of phrase, he paused so that I could register my reaction to it. If my face showed anything, however, I think it would have been something like dismay. It was plain that Sam intended to treat me to a confession of his own, and I was sure I wasn't going to enjoy hearing it.

'I go off sometimes,' he said, smacking his hands together, cymbal-style. 'I snap. I lose it. Totally. And there's fuck all I can do about it.' He gave me a few details about his employment history that had been omitted from the first telling. His career as a doorman had come to an end after an altercation from which a trio of lairy lads had emerged in a very much worse state than Sam. A spell as a warehouseman was terminated after a disagreement with a workmate, who had escaped serious injury only because Sam managed to divert his rage onto his surroundings, causing so much damage to the stock that the compensation he was obliged to pay his employers more than cancelled out the pay he was owed. Various pubs had taken him on for a while, but sooner or later some rat-arsed twat had pushed him too far and he'd gone nuclear. A doctor gave him tranquillisers; they made him feel like his head was stuffed with socks. He was gradually getting better, he reckoned. Smashing up the BMW was the worst he'd been for months, but he knew that it would happen again some time, no matter what he did. 'It's a flood in the brain,' he said. 'Like a dam's burst and there are all these fucking chemicals pouring out.' He grasped his skull in both hands and pressed so hard his arms shook. If this was a pretence of anguish, he was an astonishingly good actor, and the distress in his eyes, when he brought his hands down and stared across the grass, seemed equally authentic.

'I never used to be this bad,' he muttered. 'I was a handful when I was a nipper. Don't get me wrong. I could be a right little cunt. Beg pardon. But I wasn't a mental case. I liked a scrap, but I didn't go berserk like I do now. Easy to work it out, though, isn't it? I reckon half the squaddies are cracked by the time they come back home from that place. Some of them fill it with drink, some of them fill it with drugs, some of them go off the deep end. With me, I get the flash-flood and an hour later I'm back on dry land. Other blokes, they'll drive into trees or they'll try to kill the wife. They go wandering off to the other end of the fucking country and they haven't got a clue how they got there. Like they're sleepwalking. For weeks. Some of them can't sleep. An hour's kip at a time. I sleep OK. But I get the horrors. Two, three times a week, I'm seeing things in my sleep like they're really happening. I wake up, but I'm not awake. Not properly, not right away. For a second or two I really think it's happening, and I'm clouting the wall because what I'm seeing is some horrible little fucker with a gun in his hand. Or I'm running for cover. In a caravan. You can't run anywhere in a caravan. I've smacked my head so many times, you wouldn't believe it.' He laughed briefly but wholeheartedly, as if recalling a bit of slapstick he'd seen on TV. 'I tell you, it's fucked up a few relationships before we've got past square one. Women I thought I'd clicked with. Early days, very early days, but we were going somewhere, maybe. Then one night they're having their sweet little dreams and suddenly they've got Mr Psychokiller screaming about blood on the ceiling. That sort of thing can really make a girl rethink her priorities. You get sympathy, from some of them, but even when they're talking you down and telling you it's OK, you know it's fucked. Who wants to be shagging a mental-man, eh?' He shook his head and sustained for as long as he could a smile of resignation, but soon his face went slack and his eyes became hazy. 'Fuck it,' he sighed, lighting yet another cigarette. He blew a long jet of smoke skyward.

Nothing but inanities came to mind: 'It must be difficult,' I said.

He did not respond. It wasn't that he seemed lost in thought – rather, he appeared to be wholly absorbed in the smoking of his cigarette. Watching the smoke dissolve above his face, he might have been following the flight of a rare insect.

'Have you talked to anyone about it?' I asked. 'A doctor, a therapist.'

'A doctor gave me the tranquillisers,' he replied, as if the whole medical profession were thereby demonstrated to be useless.

I suggested that it might be worthwhile going to see someone else. This was followed by a louder expulsion of smoke. There was no point, evidently, in continuing with this line of conversation, so I waited for him to say something. After a full minute's silence he said, quietly: 'The things I've seen. You can't imagine.'

'I'm sure you're right,' I said.

Again he leaned back against the windscreen, then he turned to face me, smiled, and proceeded to tell me – like a man in a deckchair on the beach, chatting idly to the person in the deckchair next to him – that when a tank round explodes in sand it vitrifies the sand, so anyone who's standing in the way gets ripped apart by a blizzard of glass as well as the steel shrapnel. 'A mouse dropped in a blender. That's what it's like,' he said, nodding his approval of the accuracy of his description. One afternoon, he went on, they'd followed a smell down an alleyway and come across a man whose head had been removed with hammers. 'And it takes a lot of hammering to destroy a head. I mean really destroy it. Make jam of it. There was a bit of jaw intact, but apart from that – a mush of bone and skin and brain, with an eyeball in it. Just one. Like a marble in a pile of red cabbage.' I said that I'd got the picture, but Sam wasn't to be stopped. It was amazing, he told me, the different ways a human being can disintegrate. 'You'd think it was like a big toy coming apart, wouldn't you? All the attachments come away. Arms come off, legs come off, head comes off. Pop pop pop.' I agreed that this is what the layperson would imagine. 'But no. That's not how it is,' said Sam, giving me the smile of a man who knows a scandalous secret. Then he told about the day they'd arrived at a spot where a car-bomb had gone off. The dead had been taken away and the ambulances had carried the injured off to hospital, so the scene was now composed of wreckage and rubble and a lot of wailing people. Sam

and his patrol were walking across a road when someone
noticed what appeared to be a piece of cloth stuck to
a wall, high up, between two windows. 'Know what it
was? Guess,' said Sam. I declined to guess. 'A face. It was
a face. A whole face, ripped off and stuck on the wall.
Like a rubber mask with a fringe of hair. A bit of beard,
a bit of ear—'

'I can see it,' I interrupted him.

He regarded me for a few seconds, as though trying
to find in what I'd said something that could give him a
reason not to give in to his impulse to lose his temper.
He blinked slowly. 'Ah, but you can't,' he said. 'That's
the point. I can see it. You can't see it. That's the whole
fucking point,' he said, placing heavy stress on the last
three words. 'How can you possibly see it? I tell you
about it, but that's not seeing it. Going to see it on the
telly, are you? Of course you're not. They're not going to
show you what's going on. They've got a message to get
over, and people blown to shit aren't part of the message.
Fucked-up squaddies aren't part of the message. People
here, they haven't got any fucking idea,' he snarled.
This, I made the mistake of suggesting, wasn't entirely
true. He thumped the bonnet with the base of a fist –
so hard, it left a dent. 'Not a fucking clue,' he repeated,
'and that's the way they like it. Got to keep the blinkers
on,' he said, glaring at me with such animosity I couldn't
withstand it.

In turning away from him, I gave Sam further proof
that the great British public hadn't the stomach for his
message. Within seconds he'd embarked on a furious
monologue, an incoherent rant of which the essence was
that he wanted to put his foot through the screen every
time a politician appeared on TV, that Iraq was totally
fucked up, and that Britain had been totally fucked

up since Thatcher had got her hands on the country. Everything is disposable nowadays – this was Sam's refrain. 'Your DVD player breaks down – chuck it away. Washing machine breaks down – chuck it away. Fridge broken – chuck it. Workers giving you trouble – bin them, then get yourself another gang of throwaways. Dumb fucking squaddies come back with legs missing – chuck them away.' The papers shouldn't have Page Three girls, they should have Cripple of the Day. Anyone heard using the words 'flexible workforce' should be forced to sweep the streets for a month, barefoot. Look at the crap on TV – 'you want ratings, just point the cameras at a bunch of shit-thick proles and let the middle-class cunts have a good laugh.' People no longer care about anything, he kept saying, and the implication was unmistakable: I was one of the uncaring. 'But fuck it, eh? Fuck it. Yeah, fuck it,' he finished, as though I'd remarked that there was no point in wishing that things were different and he was aping my cynicism. He was on his feet now, rubbing his hands quickly up and down his face. 'Look,' he said, 'I'm doing a job back in London. A week. Ten days, tops. Let's get together when I'm back, OK?' This was said in the tone of someone making some sort of concession for the sake of preserving good relations. Then, after another bout of face-rubbing, he added: 'And there's something you need to do while I'm gone.'

'What's that?' I said.

'You know what,' he said, with a chastising finger-wag. 'If you don't, I'll have to.'

I was so annoyed by the gesture that I didn't give him an answer.

He smiled to himself and put a cigarette in his mouth. 'Sorry, but I have to go,' he said, as if I'd been asking him to stay. He slid off the truck, then asked me to wait a moment. He went into the caravan, and emerged after a minute with a pair of photographs. 'I had copies made for you,' he said, placing them onto the roof of my car, one at a time, like a gambler playing a winning hand. Without another word he climbed into the Toyota and drove away.

Sitting in the car, I looked at an image of myself, as I had been more than a quarter of a century earlier. On a footpath that crossed a field of grass stood a young man who looked as if he'd last had a haircut three months previously, and had done the job himself, with knives; he wore a black zip-up jacket and jeans. I had no idea as to where the picture had been taken, and neither could I recall the jacket. Across the grass in the foreground lay a shadow that must have been Sarah's, and in the photograph of Sarah – standing atop a tree stump, with perhaps the same field stretching out behind her – most of her body was overlapped by a shadow that must have been mine. She wore a cerise T-shirt; I recognised that. The clouds, the crispness of the shadows, the tones of the colours – every clue suggested that the two pictures had been taken at the same time, but I couldn't locate them.

Two days later I received a letter at home – or rather, a note. The note was wrapped around another pair of photographs. The first showed an expanse of sandy ground in front of a wall that was the same colour; in the foreground there was a large puddle of brown and oily water; in the middle of the puddle stood a boot, with a rod of bone sticking out of it. The second photo showed four soldiers looking askance at a figure that was sitting against a wall, a figure charred so badly the head looked like a huge block of coal, except that there were ice-white teeth in it, parted in a howl; the soldiers were looking at the corpse as if it were just a man begging for the price of a cup of coffee, and one of the soldiers was Sam. On the note, five words were written in dark pencil – I AM NOT A LIER.

9

I ran the war pictures through the shredder and put the shreds into an envelope, which I dropped into a rubbish bin in London the next morning. Had it been simply a case of myself against Sam, I might have gone to the police at this point, but this wasn't a feasible course of action, the circumstances being as they were. Throughout the day I had visions of returning home to find Aileen waiting for me, with another letter, opened, in her hand. I imagined him phoning the house and Aileen answering. By lunchtime I had become so uneasy that I rang her on a pretext, just to make sure that nothing had happened; at three o'clock I called again, and then I rang Sam, to stall him while I tried to think what I might do. I went out into the street to speak to him, so I could use the traffic noise as an excuse for keeping the conversation short. Immediately, before I could say anything more than his name, he apologised for the photographs. 'A bit strong,' he said, wryly dismissive, as if he thought I might follow his lead and make light of it. I told him, with the greatest possible coldness, that I was acknowledging receipt and would call him again in a couple of days to discuss the situation. The tone might be taken, I hoped, to imply that a strong response, perhaps involving legal sanctions, was imminent. He was talking when I hung up on him. For a few seconds this felt like a victory.

Once the first shock of Sam's photographs had been absorbed, I had simply wanted to be rid of him. If someone had said to me that in return for a hefty payment they could remove him from my life, that they wouldn't harm him but could guarantee that he'd never trouble me again, I would have written a cheque on the spot. But perhaps, in that very terse conversation on the phone, there was something in the last words I heard him speak, a momentary suggestion of desperation, that elicited a spark of sympathy; or perhaps, after cutting him off in mid-sentence, I became conscious of having handled the exchange with less than perfect dignity, and a tinge of sympathy proceeded from that self-rebuke. Whatever the explanation may have been, by the time I returned to my office I was in a slightly less unforgiving frame of mind. I told myself that his photographs, and the way he'd forced them onto my attention, confirmed that I was dealing with a young man who was deeply disturbed, and that the only way of resolving this crisis was to find a way of persuading him to submit to some sort of counselling. Inevitably, as the dialogue with his counsellor brought him closer to a more stable condition, he would abandon the fantasy of being my son, and all would be well, or well enough. On my journey back home that evening, I was rehearsing the words with which I would persuade him to talk to a professional; I would undertake to make enquiries on his behalf; if it turned out that private consultations were the best course, I would offer to help with the payment. Even if he refused, I reasoned, he would see that I was trying to help him, and accordingly would give me more time, at least.

In the morning I phoned him again, but had to leave a message on his voicemail: I said I'd call him that night. Aileen was away for a couple of days, visiting her father to get him settled into new accommodation. This in itself was some relief – for forty-eight hours there would be no risk that Sam might put me into an inescapable corner. Relatively unworried, fairly confident that I would be able to persuade him to accept my proposal, I worked in the London office until lunchtime. In the afternoon I had a meeting in Greenwich, which finished a little sooner than anticipated, so I went for a walk in Greenwich Park.

It was a glorious day, with a shimmer of heat on the grass, and the towers over at Canary Wharf gleaming, and the walls of the Queen's House as bright as new paper. People were picnicking under the trees; every slope had a dozen sunbathers – there was an air of ease and wellbeing about the place, and I caught something of that air. Everything would soon be resolved, it seemed to me, as I strolled around the park, and when I was in the car, moving swiftly through light traffic towards the motorway, I had a sense that my life was being restored to the right path, that I was making progress back to clarity. This being the case, I don't understand why I did what I then did.

Approaching the slip-road for the motorway, I saw the sign pointing straight ahead for Canterbury; I had driven past this sign many times, and the name usually had no greater impact on me than any other I passed. So it seemed on this occasion: speeding by, I registered the word 'Canterbury' as I registered the words 'Dartford Crossing'. I stopped at the lights, where the various slip-roads merged. The lights changed; I drove to the next set of lights, where again I had to stop. Here I saw another sign for Canterbury, of which I took note, along with various other items of equivalent information. The lights turned green, and I switched lanes – not, I think, from any sudden desire to revisit the city in which I had been born and had lived for more than thirty years, but rather as if I'd merely decided to call heads instead of tails. I re-joined the road that I had left two minutes earlier, and drove forty-five miles to Canterbury. I had been back three or four times in the year after my mother died, and only once since then, more than five years ago.

I pulled up outside the house that had been my family's. Nothing in particular came back to me as I looked at the building, nothing in any detail. What I experienced was instead a vague, fond, warm regretfulness, a banal and generic kind of feeling, a run-of-the-mill happy-sadness such as one might be expected to have in such a situation. More than any memory, what engaged my attention was a plastic cat that peered skyward in the centre of the front garden; after a minute or two I realised that it was staring at another plastic cat, which had been placed in the lower boughs of the apple tree. Having observed the second animal, I drove on to Chatham Road, to the house in which Aileen and I had lived. Here too I failed to muster a response of any intensity. The place had been smartened up, I noted, and was no longer divided into flats; the whole street was smarter now, with some high-quality exterior paintwork on show and a number of expensive cars parked along its length. I gazed at the window of what had been our kitchen. This was a significant location, I had to tell myself. We had lived here, happily for the most part, and I owed it to Aileen that I should now feel something stronger than a sense of deep familiarity. So I stayed in Chatham Road for a while longer, honouring the time we had spent here, recalling things that had happened here and managing to experience something – an almost expired echo – of the contentment of those years. From Chatham Road I went to where my workshop had been, and found the premises occupied by a shoe-repairer who, it appeared, had recently gone out of business: a few pairs of shoes were heaped on the counter, beside a stitching machine, but the windows were grimy inside and out, and letters were spread over the floor. A voice in my head murmured: y*ou once worked here. This place was yours.* It might as well have been telling me that the shop was associated with someone of whom I'd never heard.

But a gorgeous evening was beginning: warm, with a few thickening strokes of cloud and just enough of a breeze to put some movement into the trees. I left the car in a backstreet and walked to the cathedral. Approaching it, I was conscious that I had walked along this street with Aileen dozens of times, but the scene through which I was moving gave rise to no specific memory: the buildings seemed, instead, to confirm simply that we had been among them, together, many times. The days of our past in this city were like the swirl of a great flock of birds, in which no single bird could be seen clearly amid the thousands.

And yet, an hour or so later, when I was gazing at the river in Westgate Gardens, the memory of a single day in Canterbury did detach itself from the mass, and I could picture Sarah as she appeared, unexpectedly, on the path to my right, by the flowerbeds. I was pleased to see her, but uneasy too: however hard I tried to act as though we were only acquaintances, I would certainly betray myself in ways of which I would be unaware, and we might be seen by someone who knew me as Aileen's partner. Sensing my discomfort, Sarah hooked my arm and made me walk with her for a minute. 'Would lovers make such a show of it? Of course not. Double-bluff. Relax,' she said, laughing. It was a windy day, and when she released my arm she walked on with her eyes closed, guiding herself by sound. Hearing, she said, was the truer sense, being passive: sight makes you think you own the world. 'Try it,' she said, but I wouldn't. She turned to walk away backwards and called out, when she was almost at the bridge, ten yards in front of me: 'Come on. Try it.'

I stayed in the park for a while longer, chiefly, I think, to try to hold this image of Sarah in my mind. And as I strolled around the park it became clear to me, as though it were an errand that could no longer be postponed, that I would be leaving the park to go to the one site that remained to be visited: where Sarah had lived.

It was on the opposite side of the city, so I decided to get there by car. The drive took longer than anticipated: the traffic was heavy by now, so heavy that once or twice I was on the brink of turning back. Then I lost my bearings at a road junction that I didn't recognise, and having found the right street, I drove past Sarah's flat without realising what I'd done – she had lived nearer the end of the road than I remembered. Eventually I was standing at the foot of the steps that rose to her door, up the side of the building. I looked at the door, and within a few seconds it became the door on a different day: I was standing, in the past, where I was standing now, looking up the steps. The day was cold and the stamps were black with moisture, and slippery. The door had been closed on me. I looked at the closed door, and experienced a glimpse of Sarah. For a moment I could see her, standing in her flat, arms crossed, chin tilted up, telling me to leave. I could hear the contempt in her voice, see the contempt in her eyes. She'd spent the night with someone – Thomas, I think his name was. On the table stood a cigarette lighter that was his. No sooner had I arrived than she'd told me. I was less surprised than I made out to be. I was affronted more than surprised. 'And what, exactly, are your grounds for complaint?' she had said. She was right, of course. And although wounded, I was grateful that she'd done it, that the ending which I'd been too ineffectual to bring about had now been delivered. Yet her admission – it wasn't so much an admission as a statement of fact – had also caused a convulsion of jealousy that made me furious: the angriest, perhaps, that I had ever been. But barely a trace of those emotions could now be revived. I could recall that she'd closed the door as soon as I had stepped out, and had shut it with such force that the flap of the letterbox had clattered. Now I felt a small wince at the thought of that instant, and an insipid pang at the recollection of that cigarette lighter on the table. Otherwise, the recollection of this final confrontation had no effect on me, almost as if the scene had happened in a film I'd seen many years ago.

I returned to the car but found that I couldn't drive off: a mood of deflation had overwhelmed me. The idiocy of what I'd done with Sarah was incomprehensible, and neither could I understand what I'd just been doing. Years ago I had been a fool, and now I was almost old, and there was my non-son to deal with too. But the light in the street was beautiful and a ring-necked dove was springing about in a tree on the opposite side of the road. The evening was delicious. I got out of the car and walked back into the centre of the city, where I found a café that seemed pleasant. I ordered a coffee, then decided to eat there. At one point an intriguing-looking character took a seat at a nearby table. He was wearing a paisley waistcoat over a shirt that had once been white but was now the colour of week-old lilies, plus a bow-tie patterned with lime-green flowers on a brown background. The trousers were capacious brown corduroys, which rode up to reveal lime-green socks. A fastidiously trimmed little moustache and tiny goatee, and a thick topping of dark and slicked-back hair, completed a look that had something of the music-hall entertainer about it. He was in his late thirties, I'd have said, but his skin had an exhausted pallor and dryness, especially around the eyes, and his hands were deeply wrinkled, as if overwashed. Two pots of tea had been set on his table, and against them he'd propped a book that had a picture of Pope Benedict on the cover. With an expression of earnest bafflement he scanned the pages, moving his lips as he read, and before turning each page he would make notes on a piece of card, scribbling aggressively, as if putting together an argument. This is a very strange person, I thought. It was only some minutes later that it occurred to me that he would have had the same thought, if he'd seen me an hour earlier, standing at the bottom of the steps, and someone had told him the facts of the situation.

As I was walking back to where I'd parked, I rang Sam. It was my intention to be as sympathetic as I could, to gently bring him round to the idea that he should seek help, but this strategy was defunct within a matter of seconds. His immediate response, on hearing my voice: 'So, have you told her?'

'No,' I said, 'I haven't told her. Not yet.'

'Oh,' he said, and the way he said it was peculiar – it was as if he'd expected a different answer and was now nonplussed. There was a silence, then – as I was about to make my proposal, in words that I'd rehearsed a dozen times in the café – he went on: 'I thought you might have had a bit of a tiff.' Missing his meaning, I asked him why he would have thought that. 'Gone back to her mum and all that,' he said. He waited for me to understand.

'How do you know?' I demanded.

'Know what?' he replied, insultingly disingenuous.

'That she's not here.'

'Lucky guess,' he said. Again he paused; he started to chuckle. 'Oh come on, come on, come on,' he coaxed, like a teacher running out of patience with his slowest pupil. 'Get a grip. The pictures.'

'What about the pictures?'

'No stamp on the envelope, was there? Therefore . . . ?'

He wanted me to lose my temper, and I might have done, had a woman not been walking a dog ten yards behind me. 'I know there was no stamp on the envelope,' I hissed, clamping the phone to my jaw. 'I know the postman didn't bring the bloody thing.'

'Nice choice of words—'

'But it doesn't follow that you're spying on me. It doesn't—'

'I was in the neighbourhood. I passed by a couple times. No sign of her car. So I thought—'

'Harassment. That's what this is.'

'No,' he said, calmly, as if I'd misidentified a species of tree. 'That's not what it is.'

'Harassment is exactly what it is. And harassment is an offence. It's a criminal offence. If you—'

'No, no, no, no,' he murmured. 'It's not harassment. It's a cry for help. That's the phrase you want. That's what I'm doing. I'm making a cry for help,' he said, with a parodic tenderness for himself. It was all I could do to stop myself hurling the phone across the road; I held it away from my face, as his voice chirped: 'Hello? Hello? Hello?'

I told him that I could take the photographs to the police.

'Not sure that would get you very far,' he said.

I was saying something else about the photographs when he interrupted. 'Look,' he said, his tone peremptory. 'As soon as she's back, you tell her. OK?' I started to make an objection; again he interrupted. 'As soon as she's back, you tell her,' he repeated, like a machine. 'You tell and then you call me.'

Aileen came home; I didn't tell her about Sam.

10

Two days later I took the train to Leeds, where we'd opened our third branch the previous year. I was walking down Queen Victoria Street, on my way to the showroom, when I received a call that gave me such a jolt that I can remember the circumstances of it in precise detail: in front of me a middle-aged woman in a navy blue trench coat was having words with a teenaged girl who had just dropped a Starbucks cup on the pavement. The argument was becoming heated as I looked at my phone and saw that it was Aileen who was calling. A Mr Hendy had turned up at the house five minutes ago, she told me. I was steadying myself for the moment of crisis when Aileen went on: 'He says you asked him to look at the roof. Is that right?' I apologised; it had slipped my mind, I told her; I asked if I could speak to him.

A few seconds later I was talking to Sam the jolly workman. 'Good morning, Mr Pattison. How are you?' he said. The cheerfulness had a triumphant edge.

I wanted to ask him what the hell he thought he was doing. Instead I said that I was fine, and reminded him that I'd been going to phone him.

'No problem. Absolutely no problem,' he said, in an effusion of helpfulness. 'Just driving past. Thought I'd take a look at what we were talking about.'

'And what were we talking about?' I asked him.

'From down here, I'd say the chimney stack was a bigger priority than the tiles. I mean, you're right – some of the tiles are dodgy. But your pointing is in a worse state, I'd say. And you said something about a wall in the garden?'

I was certain I'd never said anything to Sam about the house; he'd taken a look over the side gate, which is how he knew about the wall; perhaps he'd even climbed over and walked around our garden. The turbulence of these thoughts prevented me from replying, but Sam continued, as if in response to something I had said: 'Yes, sure. OK. Yes, that's fine. I'll pop up on the roof for a minute. I've got the ladders with me.'

I started to say something but Sam cut across me, speaking to Aileen. 'That's all right with you, Mrs Pattison? Wouldn't be disturbing you? Be done in ten minutes.' I heard Aileen say that he could go ahead. Judging by the sound of her voice, they were standing in the kitchen, and the thought of Sam inside the house made me feel nauseous. 'Right then, Mr Pattison, I'll talk to you soon. Have a nice day,' he said, reverting to the strenuous cheeriness with which he'd begun. I told him that I'd give him a call. 'No need, sir,' he replied. 'I'm in the area. I'll do you a quote and drop it through the letterbox at the end of the week. No trouble. Really, it's not. See what you think. No obligation. Up to you. Take care now. Have a nice day.' He handed the phone back to Aileen and I told her I'd speak to her in the evening. I'd be staying in Leeds overnight.

I waited a couple of hours before ringing Sam – a period of time in which I was in a state of constant and extreme anxiety, at the thought that he might, at this very moment, be telling Aileen his story. His phone was on, but he didn't answer. I left a message, saying I'd call back in half an hour. Again he didn't answer, but this time I hung up. Every fifteen minutes I redialled. On the eighth or ninth attempt I spoke to him.

'Nice of you to call,' he said.

'What's going on?' I asked him.

'Exactly what I was wondering,' he said. 'You were going to call as soon as Aileen came home.'

'That's right. I was going to phone you.'

'Don't believe you,' he said, dully, as though I had let him down so many times in the past that this answer had become a routine.

'I said I would phone you and I would have phoned you. If I say I'll do something, I'll do it,' I said, and immediately regretted the pomposity.

'Sure,' said Sam.

There was a silence of a few seconds. 'I'm not happy about you barging in on Aileen. Very unhappy, in fact,' I went on.

'I didn't barge in. I knocked and spoke politely. She asked me in. That's not barging.'

'You shouldn't have done it. This is a difficult situation. We need to go slowly.'

'I don't need to do anything,' he corrected me.

'If what you want is for you and I to have some sort of relationship,' I answered, 'then you can't carry on like this. That is what you want, I assume?'

'And what about you? Is that what you want?'

'My main concern, at the moment, is Aileen.'

'And yourself,' he added.

'My main concern is Aileen,' I reiterated.

'She's very nice,' said Sam, as though her niceness had been unexpected.

'Yes,' I said. 'I know.' I had been making enquiries about DNA testing; this was the only way to clarify the situation, but I was afraid of proposing the idea now that

Sam had inveigled his way into the house. There was no knowing how he might react.

Another short silence was ended by Sam. 'Don't worry,' he said. 'I'm not going to tell her anything. That's what you should be doing. And you and I should also be getting our story straight.' The story, he told me, was that he'd been working on a roof a few doors down from North Street; we'd got talking, and I'd mentioned that I had a few bits and pieces that needed doing, and I'd asked him to drop by. 'Got that?' he asked.

'Just out of interest,' I said. 'How did you know about the garden wall?

'How do you think? Nice place you got there, I have to say. Very nice. Not what I expected, mind you.'

'And what had you expected?'

'Well, it's quaint, isn't it? Chocolate-boxy. I'd imagined something less cute. No offence. But I thought you were a bloke for the modern stuff. Wife's choice was it?'

'Joint choice.'

'Must have cost a packet. Been there long?'

I suspected that he already knew how long we'd been living there. 'So why exactly did you drop by?' I asked.

'You said you'd call. You didn't. I thought something might have happened to you,' he answered.

'I appreciate your concern,' I told him.

'You're welcome,' he replied.

I told him I'd be grateful if he didn't come to the house at the end of the week. 'I'll call you,' I said. 'I promise.'

'Thing is,' said Sam, 'I already promised your wife. She's expecting me. Friday, eight o'clock. It's arranged. I wouldn't want her to think I'm not reliable.'

'It's got nothing to do with being reliable.'

'I'm in your neck of the woods anyway. Two-minute detour. Easy-peasy.'

'I'd rather you didn't,' I said, in a tone that was more of a plea than I'd intended.

Now he abruptly changed tactics. 'Look, Dad,' he said, 'it's tough for you, I know. A big adjustment to make. It's not easy for me, either. Not exactly been open arms from you, has it? Opposite, in fact. But that's fair enough. I understand. It's hard for both of us. I think we have to give it some time. A lot of time. To get to know each other, you know?'

'Precisely,' I said, 'which is why—'

'OK,' he jumped in, 'so I'll be there. Eight o'clock. On the dot. See you then.'

I tried to say something more, but he'd cut me off. There was little point in ringing him back – he was determined to come to the house, and there was nothing I could do to dissuade him. There was, however, one good thing about this conversation: he was no longer at our house, and Aileen hadn't phoned me; therefore he hadn't said anything about our alleged relationship. On the other hand, it was always possible that he'd let slip a remark that would have revealed to Aileen that the connection between us wasn't quite as casual as he'd made out.

So I wasn't entirely relaxed when I called her, and it was clear right away that she'd found this episode perplexing. Why hadn't I said anything about talking to a builder? I said I thought I'd mentioned it. 'No, you didn't,' she said, and she knew she was right. And if I'd thought we needed to get someone in to fix the roof or the wall in the garden, why hadn't I discussed it with her? We had discussed it, I said. When we bought the house we knew that a few things would require attention soon. 'True,' said Aileen, 'but that's not the same thing as discussing it. We didn't agree to go ahead and do something this week.' This was true, I had to admit. I'd thought we were in agreement that something had to be done sooner rather than later, but I agreed that we hadn't actually decided together to take action now. It was peculiar enough, she persisted, that I'd not so much as mentioned to her that I'd asked someone to come round and give us an estimate, but it was even odder that I'd asked this man in particular, because as far as she could make out he was a jobbing builder rather than a roofing specialist. 'Well,' I replied, 'I was impressed by the work he'd done, and it's not as if we're contemplating having the whole house rebuilt. It's just a patch here and there. But if you have bad feeling about him' – Aileen thinks of herself as someone who can sniff out the untrustworthy, and has often been proved right – 'we can simply not take him on. If you like, I'll tell him we'd be happier with a specialist. Do you want me to do that?'

But Aileen did not have a bad feeling about Sam. She was surprised by the way I'd gone about it, and had initially been on her guard when this slightly fierce-looking young man had appeared on the doorstep with no warning, but her subsequent impressions had been favourable. Unlike the plumber who'd recently made a complete hash of fixing the boiler, he'd been very courteous – he'd even offered to remove his boots at the front door. And he'd seemed very professional. The mortar in the chimney had crumbled so badly that he could push a screwdriver between the bricks, he said, and he'd taken a picture of it with his phone, so she could see that he wasn't exaggerating. Parts of the roof were more delicate than we'd thought (again, he took pictures of cracked and slipped tiles); he recommended that we take action before the winter. There was no danger that the garden wall would collapse imminently (he'd led Aileen to believe that I was worried it might), but we should think about straightening it out within the next year or so. All of these repairs he could do himself, he'd said, but he understood that we might want to approach other builders for an estimate before proceeding. Those were more or less the words he'd used: 'I understand you may want to approach other builders before proceeding.' Articulate and pleasant and thorough and not at all pushy – he'd made a good start with Aileen. 'But I just wish you'd told me,' she said.

'I'm getting forgetful,' I apologised. The excuse was plausible and was accepted; my errors of absent-mindedness – mislaying of keys or a book or a letter – were becoming quite frequent.

11

At eight o'clock on the Friday morning Sam arrived, precisely on the hour. He'd made something of an effort to smarten himself up: the sweatshirt seemed new and the jeans looked as if they'd been washed very recently, leaving only a few pale splashes of paint. Whenever I'd seen him previously he'd had a day or two's growth of stubble, but this morning he was clean-shaven. The hair had been washed too – there were no dots of plaster in it – and a pungent whiff of antiperspirant came off him. He shook our hands with a hand that had seen the nailbrush and clippers that very morning.

From a new manila folder he took an estimate for the various jobs he'd discussed with Aileen and handed it to her. His attention was directed chiefly at her from the outset, as if he believed that it was Aileen he needed to impress in order to secure the work. We placed the piece of paper on the kitchen table and read the estimate together. Headed with the rubber-stamped words 'Sam Hendy – Builder & Decorator', it was written in block capitals on an A4 sheet of good-quality paper, had a misspelt word on nearly every line, and valued his labour at considerably below the market rate. 'This is very reasonable,' said Aileen, at which Sam, encouraged, opened the folder again and slid onto the table a yellow plastic envelope, which contained testimonials from satisfied clients, plus photos of garden paths, expanses of roof, various lengths of handsome brickwork, and a fish-pond. The testimonials, all hand-written and grammatically correct and free of spelling errors, seemed to be genuine.

'May I?' asked Sam, crouching at Aileen's side to extract from the assortment a picture showing a roof that was very much like ours. With the tip of a broken pencil he traced for us the boundary between the original tiles and the ones he'd inserted in their midst. Removing her glasses, Aileen leaned forward to peer point-blank at the photo, and as she did so Sam smiled at me across her back, in a way that momentarily disarmed me, because it was the diffident smile of a son who was looking for his father's approval. I drew the picture closer to me and nodded my appreciation of his work – and if it did indeed show what it was said to show, the repair had been so skilfully done as to be seamless. 'You'll want to get some other estimates,' said Sam, gathering up his paperwork, 'but if you decide you'd like me to go ahead, I could start very soon. Middle of next week. Tuesday, maybe. And if you'd like me to do just one job and the rest some other time, that's OK too. Or maybe get someone else to do the rest, if you're not entirely happy with what I do. Whatever. It's up to you. But if you want me to go ahead next week, it'd be handy if you could let me know a.s.a.p., because as things stand I'm free, but in this line of business you have to say yes to whatever comes your way. Someone might ring tonight with something for next week and if it was a definite job I'd have to say I could do it. But as I say, at this moment in time I'm yours.'

All of this was addressed to Aileen, to an accompaniment of apologetic shrugs and quasi-boyish smiles. Aileen assured him that we would not keep him waiting, and then, as we got up from the table, she gave me a look that said, 'Why not?' The look was noticed by Sam, who nonetheless made sure not to appear confident of success. 'Speak to you soon, I hope,' he said at the door, shaking hands with both of us once more. His parting shot was a compliment on the house. It was, he told Aileen, exactly the sort of place he'd buy if his lottery ticket came up. There was nothing I could do. Aileen phoned him that evening, to say we'd like him to start work the following week, and to do everything that was on his list.

Next Tuesday, at eight o'clock on the dot, Sam arrived for work. An hour later the scaffolders arrived. By ten o'clock the flank of the house was covered in scaffolding and Sam was up top, scraping away at the chimney, singing along to his radio. His timekeeping was exemplary: every day he'd turn up on the stroke of eight and leave on the stroke of five. Aileen, who was working at home for most of the time, couldn't recall ever having come across a more conscientious workman. He allowed himself only half an hour's break in the middle of the day, to eat his sandwiches; at the end of the day he'd spend twenty minutes clearing up – sweeping the path, cleaning his tools, stacking them neatly in the outhouse. He was as hard-working and fastidious as an apprentice working under the eye of a demanding boss.

The first day that Sam was at the house, I was too anxious to think straight. In a meeting with the representative of an Italian lighting firm I had a moment when I realised that I couldn't have repeated anything he'd told me in the preceding five minutes. Coming back on the train, I managed to read about two pages of the newspaper then forget whatever I'd read the moment I turned the page. At any moment, I was thinking, the phone would ring and Aileen would be telling me that we had to talk. Or perhaps, watching Sam at work, she'd been struck by something that had made her wonder – a similarity between myself and him that seemed incontrovertible to her but had eluded me entirely. It was unlikely, but not impossible. I imagined her remarking on the resemblance as a strange coincidence, and then seeing in my face something – the tiniest twitch of an eyelid – from which arose the notion, incredible though it seemed, that this was not a coincidence at all.

Disaster was inevitable, I told myself. Rather than take a taxi from the station I walked home, feeling like a fugitive who had no option but to turn himself in. From the front door I saw Aileen in the kitchen, at the chopping board, and when she turned and gave me a smile that showed that nothing had changed in the course of the day, it was all I could do to stop myself from laughing. She'd spoken no more than a dozen words to Sam. Mid-morning she'd made him a cup of coffee, which he'd taken up onto the roof straight away, as if he hadn't a minute to lose; in the afternoon they'd had a brief conversation – he'd wanted to know how we'd feel if he were to work on Saturday. He'd understand, naturally, if we preferred to have the house to ourselves at the weekend, but if we didn't mind he'd prefer to crack on with it. And there was a couple of other things: the soffits had some rot in them, and in places the pointing on the side wall was in worse shape than he'd thought. He'd asked Aileen to stand at the foot of the scaffolding to watch as he raked the point of a screwdriver through the mortar, raising quantities of dust. If we wanted him to fix it this week, he could; it would take him two days, no more, and he'd mix the mortar to match perfectly with what was there; the soffits would take another day or so. It made sense, said Aileen, to get him to do it all at once, didn't it? Of course I agreed.

Sam was up on the roof when I left the next morning. He called out to me and came down, descending through the scaffolding with alarming speed and jumping from the bottom level instead of using the ladder. He began to report on what he'd found the previous day; I told him that Aileen and I had discussed it and we'd like him to do whatever was necessary. 'I'll do you another estimate,' he said. There was no need, I told him, and this statement of trust was accepted with a curt nod, that's all. There was no meaningful eye contact during the two or three minutes that we were talking, no under-meaning to anything he said. Once the business stuff had been concluded we exchanged a few words about the weather, how nice the garden was looking, this and that. It was as though I was having a chat, in passing, with a friendly workman whom I'd never met prior to that morning. Aileen, had she seen us talking, would not have suspected a thing – but I didn't have the impression that Sam was conducting himself in this way because of the risk of our being observed. It seemed instead that he had decided, having tricked his way into close proximity to me, that he was simply going to be himself, to allow me to see who he was – to see that he was, at heart, someone quite unlike the hooligan I'd seen a few weeks earlier.

Or this is what I found myself hoping, and for about as long as it took me to drive to the end of the road I managed to push to the back of my mind the knowledge that nothing had been resolved, and the near certainty that, whatever resolution was to come about, it could only be calamitous. Nonetheless, I was fairly confident that there was no immediate danger, and that was enough to keep the feeling of dread at a less acute level than it had been the day before. It was like having an indefinite stay of execution.

Day two of life with Sam in attendance was uneventful – again, Aileen's interaction with him was limited to handing over a few cups of coffee. On day three there was even less contact, because Aileen had a meeting up in London, so she was out of the house for most of the day. She gave him a key and put the cafetière and coffee jar on the work surface for him, but when she came home nothing in the kitchen had been touched, as far as she could tell. The weather during these first three days was consistently fine. On the Friday, however, the morning began with drizzle. Sam set to work, with a baseball cap, and the hood of his sweatshirt pulled over it, as protection against the rain. By mid-morning the drizzle had become heavy. Aileen stepped outside to check on him: there he was, sitting on his plank below the eaves, doing something to the soffits, with his arms and head sticking out of a black plastic bin liner that he'd converted into a rain-jacket. She asked him if he was OK up there. 'Hunky-dory, Mrs Pattison,' he called back, giving her a thumbs-up. An hour so later there was a downpour so sharp and sudden it made Aileen look up, thinking that something had flown into the window. The windows of the Toyota, she saw, were steamed up, so she assumed that Sam was sheltering in it. Grabbing an umbrella, she went out. The temperature had fallen by several degrees and the rain was bouncing off the path. Sam wound down his window and assured her that he was fine where he was. 'Early lunch, Mrs P,' he said, waving a sandwich. The persuasion of the kindly and shivering Aileen could not be resisted, however. Holding the umbrella over her head, he escorted her to the kitchen door.

She made him a mug of coffee. It turned out that he liked a lot less milk in his coffee than she'd been giving him, but he'd not said anything. A shy boy, she thought he was, after this conversation in the kitchen. The assurance with which he'd presented himself when he'd appeared on the doorstep, and when he'd brought the estimate, was but a superficial layer. That's what she told me that evening, when we talked about him. He would meet her eye only for a split second at a time, she said, and it was a while before he'd give her replies that were longer than a single sentence. Eventually she'd managed to eke out of him that his father had been very keen on DIY, and that Sam had picked up a lot of his skills from him. 'He could do anything,' Sam had said, with a tone from which Aileen had deduced that Mr Hendy was dead, but she didn't like to ask if this was the case. I was about to say, 'It isn't', but I bit back the words in the nick of time; as Aileen relayed Sam's words to me, I had to concentrate on listening as though this was the first time I'd heard them. He'd told Aileen that he'd grown up in the Midlands, but not that the Hendys weren't his birth parents. She'd quickly desisted with the personal questions, because it was obvious that he was uncomfortable talking about himself – so uncomfortable, in fact, that she'd begun to form the impression that this was a young man with an unhappy past. They'd spent about half an hour in each other's company. Sam had told her about the Highgate banker with the cost-no-object music room, and was markedly more at ease with a topic that was not focused on himself. Then the rain had abated and Sam announced that he should be getting back to work.

At this point something remarkable had happened. Sam was carrying his mug to the dishwasher (tidiness and helpfulness – more feathers in his cap) when Aileen, having put the milk back in the fridge, accidentally closed the fridge door more forcefully than she'd intended. It's a very large fridge, so the door can make quite a boom when it slams, as it did on this occasion, and the sound so startled Sam that the hand in which he was holding the mug jerked upwards, spilling the dregs on his jeans. He grimaced, as though he had committed some terrible gaffe in front of people he had wanted to impress. Glancing at Aileen, he saw that she'd seen what had happened, and this prompted another grimace, less extravagant than the first. It was the expression of a man who knows he has to make a difficult decision immediately.

'I'm sorry,' he said, 'but I get jumpy sometimes. That sounded like something else.' She asked him what it was, and he replied that it was like the noise a grenade launcher makes. 'I was in Iraq,' he said, as you might explain something trivial, like having a suntan. 'You should see me if a car backfires. Dive into dustbins, I do,' he said, making light of it, but Aileen could tell he was shaken and that it was best to let him go without saying anything more.

'Strange, don't you think?' Aileen asked me. 'Half an hour he was sitting there, and he never so much as mentioned the fact that he'd been in the army. From the way he'd talked, she'd thought he'd been a builder for years and years.

Keen to change the subject, I said I didn't think it was so strange that Sam hadn't said anything about his having been a soldier; perhaps he wanted to forget all about it, I suggested.

12

In other circumstances I might have developed some sort of liking for Sam. In fact, for a few days I did find myself liking him from time to time – when I wasn't wondering what was really going on with him, that is, and wishing he weren't there.

On the first Saturday morning he had been at work for an hour or so when I went out to buy the newspaper. As I was closing the gate he whistled to me and came down from the roof, again at reckless speed. He asked me how I felt about going up onto the roof, because he'd like me to take a look at what he was doing and what he'd already done. 'And I could do with having a word with you as well. In private,' he added. This didn't strike me as ominous; it seemed rather that he was embarrassed about whatever it was he needed to discuss. So as soon as I'd returned from the shop I climbed up the ladders to join him.

Sam was sitting on the ridge, eating from a tin of rice pudding with a plastic spoon. 'Mid-morning snack,' he said, before slithering down the roof on his backside. There was a ladder he could have used; hooked onto the ridge, it lay to the side of an area that had been stripped of its tiles. The discarded tiles were stacked where I was standing, on the narrow platform at the top of the scaffolding; the platform shifted an inch when Sam landed on it. 'Making progress,' said Sam, indicating the area of exposed battens. He was wearing a T-shirt, so for the first time I could see clearly the tattoo on his forearm: the words were 'Villa Forever'. The burn scar on the other arm held my attention for a fraction of a second longer. He noticed this, and I thought for a moment he was going to make a remark about it, but instead he put down the tin of rice and lifted an old tile from the heap. With no effort he snapped off a piece of it. 'Most of them are this bad,' he said, and he broke another to show that this was true. 'Surveyor should have picked this up,' he remarked, giving me a look that said I'd been duped. The replacements were going to be a bit brighter than these, he said; it wasn't possible to match them exactly, not unless he used tiles that were as wrecked as these. He was going to muck up the new ones before putting them down, so it wouldn't look too much like there was a bloody great sticking plaster on the roof. 'More like a toupee, if you like,' he said.

He directed my attention to the repairs he'd made to the chimney stack. 'This is new, and this, and that, and that,' he said, indicating his handiwork with a trowel. If he hadn't pointed out which parts were his I'd have had great difficulty distinguishing them: the colour of the new mortar was identical to the colour of the old, and the texture was the same. What Sam had done was different only in that it was so meticulous – each vein of mortar had been finished off at a perfectly even angle, a few degrees off the vertical, as precisely as a picture frame. He'd tidied up the flashings as well, he told me, leaning on the roof so that he could show me exactly where the invisible restoration had been carried out. 'There's one other thing,' he announced, and he strode across the platform with so heavy a tread that it quivered like a rowing boat on water. He noticed that I was nervous, I think, but he said nothing except 'Look here,' as he crouched to show me where the seams in the guttering were coming apart.

We discussed the pros and cons of cast iron, aluminium and plastic; without much consideration of the matter, I commissioned him to undertake the priciest of the various alternatives. 'That's what I'd do,' he said. 'No point in cutting corners if you don't need to.' It appeared that our conversation had now ended. I reminded him that he'd asked to have a word with me. 'Oh, yeah,' he said, smacking his forehead with the heel of his hand. 'The thing is, I'm a bit out of pocket at the moment. Cash-flow problems. I've had to pay that wanker for a new windscreen. He's agreed he won't press charges if I cough up. Can you believe it? So I was wondering if you could advance me a few quid. Say a couple of hundred?' I told him that this would be fine; he said he needed cash, and he needed it today, if possible. That could be arranged, I told him – I'd be going into town in the afternoon and would call at a cashpoint. I was happy to get more, if that would help. He blinked at me as if I'd offered him a lavish bonus. 'That'd be great, yeah,' he said. 'I appreciate it.' Then, as if on an impulse, he seized my hand and shook it.

The sudden gesture was disconcerting enough, but it was accompanied by an expression of such fervent gratitude that I was forced to look away. 'I'll leave you to it,' I said.

'You're happy with what I've done?' he asked, though there could not have been any doubt that I was.

'Yes,' I said. 'Thank you.'

'That's good,' he said, as though my approval meant that our relationship was making progress. He nodded, raised his eyebrows, blew out a breath: a worry had been cast away, he was letting me know. It was an exaggerated performance, as was the way he now grabbed the scaffolding handrail and inhaled greedily, like someone who had been driving all day and, having at last arrived at his seaside destination, was getting his fill of the cleansing sea air. 'Fantastic day, isn't it?' he said. The intention was to detain me for a while longer. It wasn't a fantastic day: the air was mild and very still; fat white clouds occupied most of the horizon to the south; overhead the sky was more or less blue – a washed-out blue. It was a pleasant day, that's all.

'It's very nice,' I replied.

'Gearing up for the summer over there,' he said, pointing towards the Jermans' house, where a thick hosepipe wound across the grass and drooped into the water of the kidney-shaped pool. To the right of the pool, Claire Jerman was steering a large mower around the cherry trees. The Jermans have the biggest house in the vicinity, so I was expecting from Sam an observation on the lives of the idle rich, but instead he let out an abrupt and very loud laugh, and started telling me about a friend of his from his army days who'd met this girl at a club and they'd gone back to her place, which turned out to be right at the top of a high-rise block – 'which wasn't a problem right away, because it was dark and they had other things on their minds, but in the morning she opened the curtains and he really freaked out, because he had this thing about heights and there he was with all these pigeons flying about below him and only a pane of glass between him and the big plunge. Put a bit of a dampener on the relationship. His place was a pit, but if they went back to hers he had to stay away from the windows. Should have seen him in a helicopter,' said Sam, delighted at the recollection of it.

'Sweat pouring off him. Pints of it, and this is Armagh I'm talking about, not the desert. The watchtowers – he could just about handle them. Higher than that: not a happy boy. Great shot, though. Could shoot the knackers off a hedgehog from two hundred yards,' he said, aiming an imaginary rifle in the general direction of Claire Jerman. 'How about you?' he asked. 'I get the feeling you're not too comfortable up here. Being up high, I mean.'

'No,' I said, 'I'm fine.'

'You sure?' he asked me, doubtfully.

'I'm fine,' I repeated. 'But I should be getting back to ground level.'

Sam smiled, as if at the laudable stubbornness of a doughty old man. 'I love heights,' he went on. 'Always have. Gives me such a buzz,' he said, smacking a palm against the scaffolding bar, making the platform quiver. When he was a boy his parents – 'Mr and Mrs Hendy', he clarified needlessly – used to take him to Kinver Edge on Sundays, and at Kinver there was a special tree that he always had to find. He would clamber right to the top of it while Mrs Hendy watched him, gnawing her fingernails to the quick because she was thinking of the afternoon he'd been climbing a tree in the park with a friend and the friend had fallen out and broken a leg so badly that he could hardly kick a ball straight after the plaster had come off. More than anything else, Sam had wanted to be a pilot. For a while he'd even thought of trying for the RAF, before his teachers told him not to waste his time. 'Need more up top than I had to offer,' he explained. He couldn't stand it when kids in his class would come back after the summer having flown to Spain for their holidays, while he'd had to make do with a week in the Black Mountains, 'which aren't really mountains, either'. One year they went to Snowdonia, he told me, the words coming out of him with barely a gap between them. Snowdon was a real mountain, and he'd imagined himself standing on the summit 'like Edmund fucking Hillary' but it had rained nearly all week and when it wasn't raining it was either dark or 'the cloud was so thick you might as well have been standing in a fucking bus stop in Coventry'. (It had struck me that he'd not been swearing as much as usual – hardly at all, in fact – and that this must have required some effort on his part. Now that he was getting up a head of steam, the swearing had resumed.) 'Used to really piss me off, it did,' he went on. 'All these kids getting on planes like it was no different from catching a bus. I suppose we could have afforded a crappy package deal to Torremolinos, but that wasn't my folks' idea of fun and I can't say I blame them. Fresh air and loads of greenery, that's what they liked. And it was OK. Don't get me wrong. I had some good holidays. Some fucking grim ones, but some good ones too.'

There followed immediately a recollection of a good one – the best holiday of his life, no less. They had spent a fortnight on the west coast of Ireland ('my mum, Mrs Hendy, has some cousins there'), in the course of which they had visited the Cliffs of Moher. 'Fuck me, the Cliffs of Moher,' Sam declared, with a sort of elated yelp, raising his hands to gesture at the cliffs' immensity. It was, he said, 'totally amazing. You're lying on the grass, on the edge, with your face hanging over this drop, and there's hundreds of birds – gulls and guillemots and whatever – wheeling around in the air. And these fucking birds are like moths, they're so far below you, and the sea is hundreds of feet below where the birds are. You can see all the foam on the sea. You can see the water smacking up against the cliffs. Tons of spray. But you're so far up, you can't hear it. It's weird. It's like you're watching a film of the sea and someone's turned the sound off. You been there?' he asked me. I shook my head. 'You should. You really should,' he said, exhilarated, as if he'd come from the cliffs this very morning and was urging me to set off right away. 'Such a blast. Like it was all I could do to stop myself from jumping off. You know what I mean? You've got all these hundreds of feet of air below you,' he said, leaning out to gaze down into the empty air below us, 'and there's part of you that just wants to fall through it, to have that buzz for a few seconds. You must have had that feeling sometimes. No? Once or twice?' Told that I'd never had that feeling, Sam was momentarily deflated, not – it seemed to me – by my implication that the impulse to fling himself off a cliff was perhaps not entirely healthy, but simply at learning this was not an area of experience we could discuss on an equal footing.

He recovered with a question that was the sort of thing a boy might say to someone he's desperate to befriend, and for that reason it was touching, in a way. 'You ever been in a helicopter?' he asked me. I told him I had not. 'It's fantastic,' he said. 'You should do it. Like floating in a bubble. Well, not floating. It's noisy as fuck, so it's not floating. But you know what I mean. There's just this skin of glass around you and you're at just the right height. High enough to see for miles, low enough to see what's going on at street level. The best thing about Ireland was the chopper rides. You're coming in so close, the TV aerials are bending over, and then you bank and shoot right up. One moment you can count the cups on the kitchen table, five seconds later you can see all the way to Belfast. Fucking brilliant,' he said, watching his hand as it swerved and dipped between us, and then he glanced at me and brought his hand down, with a sideways flicker of his eyes, which might have been an expression of irritation at what he took to be my unresponsiveness.

I told him that I wasn't sure I had the nerve for a flight in a helicopter. 'If the engine on a jet fails,' I said, 'there's another in reserve. And the thing can glide. But if the engine fails on a helicopter—'

'You're fucked.'

'Exactly. You have a problem.'

'Which is a major part of the excitement.'

'If you say so.'

'You don't know what you're missing,' he said, in a slightly coaxing tone.

'Safety first, that's me,' I said, and as the words were leaving my mouth I sensed that Sam wouldn't let the irony pass unremarked.

But in fact he merely shrugged, signifying that there was nothing more to say on the matter. 'It was good to have a talk,' he said, though it hadn't been much of a conversation – I'd uttered one word for every two hundred of Sam's. 'We should do it again. What are you doing at lunchtime?' he asked.

Wrongfooted, I started to bluster: 'Well, I think Aileen has—'

'I was joking,' he interrupted, shaking his head and giving me a pat on the arm – a soft and patronising pat, as if to say: 'Don't worry, old chap.'

For a while I sat in the kitchen, reading the paper with Aileen. The background noise of Sam hammering on the roof made it impossible to concentrate – it was like hearing a saboteur at work. Aileen was going to take some stuff down to the recycling centre. I went to fetch a few bits of junk that we'd thrown into the shed; crossing the garden, I glanced up at the roof and saw Sam watching me – he gave me a wave that was almost a salute. A few minutes later, I opened the gate while Aileen was getting into her car; again Sam was watching, and again he gave me the salute-wave. I'd intended to go into town in the afternoon but I went now instead, largely to get away from him. Walking back, I had the image in my mind – for the twentieth time that day – of Sam explaining the situation to a distraught Aileen.

That wasn't what I found when I got home. What I found was Sam on the roof, straddling the ridge, screening his eyes from the sun and gazing fixedly in the general direction of the Jermans' place. It took me a few moments to realise that he was peering through a pair of binoculars. Clearly focusing on something in particular, he was immobile for perhaps as long as a minute, and then, as if he'd known all along exactly where I was standing, he turned to me and beckoned. 'Come up here,' he shouted, waving the binoculars. 'Hurry up. It's worth it.' He was very happy about something.

I don't know what I imagined he was looking at: Claire Jerman had crashed the mower, maybe, or David Jerman was doing his t'ai-chi routines in the middle of the lawn, or Sophie was sunbathing topless. 'You need to see this,' he said, when I'd reached the top of the scaffolding. He gestured me towards the ladder that he'd hooked to the ridge of the roof. 'Come on,' he urged. I crawled up the ladder, belly to the rungs, until my chin was resting on the ridge tiles. Sam leaned towards me, pressed a hand to my back to clamp me to the ladder, and held the binoculars to my eyes. I took hold of them, gripping the ridge with my other hand. 'Find the pool,' he directed me, 'then go left. Slowly. To the edge of the trees. See?' In the shadow of the trees a badger was foraging; three cubs were wrestling nearby, on the grass. 'Now that's something you don't see very often,' said Sam. I'm not sure which surprised me more: the spectacle of the tumbling cubs or Sam's pleasure in the sight. 'You ever seen that before?' he asked me. 'Badger cubs, in daylight? Lovely, no?' he said, as if remarking on a good-looking girl. Yesterday, he told me, he'd seen a pair of jays right by the pool. All through the afternoon they'd been in the garden, off and on. 'There is no more beautiful bird in the world,' he said. The statement was so incongruous, I remember it exactly: 'There is no more beautiful bird in the world.' He spoke the words as though they were a quotation from a famous ornithologist. 'Except the lyre bird, of course,' he added. 'Nothing touches the lyre bird. Or you could argue about hummingbirds, I suppose. But for me the jay is right up there. If I see them again, I'll give you a shout,' he offered. I thanked him and began to descend the ladder. Sliding down the roof, he escorted me back down to the platform.

He put the binoculars into the khaki canvas bag in which he carried his box of sandwiches and coffee flask. 'Wasn't that something, eh?' he said, grinning like a lad who's just seen his team win a big game. 'Just fantastic. Amazing.' There was an ingenuousness about this enthusiasm, a quality that made me think that I was seeing an aspect of his character that was essential to who he was, rather than something that was being presented for a purpose – whatever that purpose might have been. 'Glad I called you up? I mean, that's the sort of thing you only see in documentaries, isn't it?'

'It is,' I said, and then I laughed. It was a brief, one-breath laugh, but it somewhat took me by surprise. I couldn't recall having laughed at anything recently. I gave him his cash in an envelope; he thanked me, with a smile that wasn't quite that of a hired worker, and lobbed it into his bag. As I was turning away he asked me how we'd feel if he were to come to work the following day, on the Sunday. The weather forecast said there was a chance of rain on Sunday evening, so he'd like to get the roof finished off before then. 'But if that's at all a problem, don't worry. I can get a tarp over it. Not as good as getting the tiles down, but it'll keep the worst of it out.' I said I didn't think it would be a problem.

Aileen had no objection, but she felt sorry for him. A young man like Sam should be with his girlfriend on a Sunday, not working. From the way he'd said to her, when she'd asked him if he was absolutely sure he didn't want to take the day off, 'I've nothing better to do, Mrs Pattison,' she'd had the impression that there was no girlfriend, which was odd, she thought, because he was a nice-looking boy. She'd felt sorry for him ever since she'd learned that he lived in a caravan.

From what I could tell, I said, he seemed to like the arrangement.

Aileen doubted it. That might be what he said, she conceded, but she thought there was something sad about it. There was something sad about Sam himself, she thought – something vulnerable in his eagerness to please. 'He needs someone to look after him,' she said.

He struck me as a chap who was more than capable of looking after himself, I told her.

'In some ways, yes,' said Aileen. But there were moments, she said, when she felt quite protective of him. At lunchtime, she then told me, Sam had come indoors for a cup of coffee and noticed, on the side of the fridge, a flyer for Cerys's show. She told him that our niece was in it, and he said that he liked musicals, as long as they were old-fashioned Broadway ones. There was such a sense of loneliness in the way he made the remark and the way he looked at the flyer, said Aileen, that she found herself asking him if he'd like to come with us.

I raised the newspaper to cover my face. 'That was nice of you,' I said, feeling as if I had a ball of bread wedged in my gullet. 'And what did he say?'

'He appreciated the offer, but didn't think he could make it on the night we're going.'

'Oh well,' I said.

'He said he might pop along, if it turned out he was free. I'm sure he's free, but I know he won't come. He's worried about intruding – that's what it is. So I didn't press the point. Do you think I should have tried to persuade him?'

'Best to let it lie. You did the right thing,' I said. This was my last word on the subject.

At nine o'clock the next morning the Toyota appeared. It was warmer than the previous day had been; and it didn't rain, contrary to the forecast that Sam had supposedly seen. Aileen and I had lunch in the garden, as we often do in summer. It would have been one of our typical Sundays – slow and easeful and satisfying – had Sam not been there. But Sam was there – and worse, Aileen insisted that he join us. He accepted the invitation with gratitude. The food itself – pasta salad, followed by homemade chocolate cake – was received with copious compliments. 'This, Mrs Pattison,' declared Sam, circling a fork above his plate, 'is absolutely wonderful.'

He smiled at me, and the smile said that he knew that I now knew about the flyer, and that there was nothing I could do prevent him outmanoeuvring me again. I could hardly bring myself to look at him, let alone talk to him, but Aileen of course kept things going with ease, which only increased the torment of the situation: she was such a kindly person, so engaging, so warm, and I might lose her if Sam decided to talk. The prospect of that loss changed what I saw. I looked at Aileen in her chair, and I looked at the garden around her, and it was no longer a place in which she and I necessarily belonged – we were merely two bodies occupying a small part of this space at this particular moment, and I might be removed from it with just one sentence from Sam.

'Dominic tells me you're a birdwatcher,' Aileen remarked, having accepted Sam's praise with due modesty.

'It's a bit of an obsession, Mrs Pattison, to be honest,' he replied, with a bashfulness that struck me as being at least seventy-five per cent bogus. On days off – 'So you do take days off?' Aileen interjected, relieved to hear it – he might drive right across the country sometimes, if there'd been a report of a rarity. Suffolk was his favourite spot – especially a place called Minsmere. Last year he'd had an amazing experience at Minsmere: he'd seen a bird called a Baikal Teal. Just one of them, paddling through the reeds. The Baikal Teal, he informed us, is a migratory species (for a minute his style of speech was that of an instructor with an adult education class), which breeds in the forests of eastern Siberia and spends the winter in Japan, Korea and China. The world's total population of Baikal Teals, some 300,000 birds, lives in a single flock, Sam explained – 'So God knows what that one was doing in Suffolk.' This was notable too – 'God knows', he said, whereas with me it would have been 'Fuck knows'. In Aileen's presence he didn't swear once – not on this occasion, anyway.

'A duck,' he said. 'I saw one little duck and that was a highlight of the whole year. How sad is that?' he said. A self-deprecating grimace, deployed for Aileen, produced the desired result.

'Not at all,' she answered, and asked him to continue.

He'd sat around half the day, eyes trained on the reeds, waiting for a glimpse of that bird. Patience was something he'd learned in Ireland, in the army, he told Aileen, who was duly intrigued. 'People think it's all Action Man stuff,' he said. 'I thought it was going to be Action Man stuff. But it wasn't. It was boring, a lot of the time. Dead boring. Stag is the most boring occupation you could imagine,' he said. The dash of jargon – dropped into the conversation carelessly, or so it appeared – prompted a request for clarification. Stag, he explained, was guard duty, lookout duty, hour after hour of standing in a little room on the top of a tower, watching the sky change from grey to greyer. Yet he'd learned things doing stag, he said. For one thing, he'd learned that he was capable of doing it, which he wouldn't previously have thought was possible, because he'd been a boy who always had to be on the go, doing stuff. But he'd found that he liked having time to think, and even when it became so boring that he couldn't really think, sometimes being bored to the bone was a good thing, he discovered. 'Rather like meditating, I suppose. Emptying your mind. It can be good for you. You know what I mean, Mrs Pattison? Or does that sound daft?' It did not sound daft in the slightest, Aileen assured him. And the other thing he'd learned, Sam continued, was that wildlife was fascinating. He'd found himself in the same company as a lad from Dorset, a real country boy, Jake by name, who knew everything there was to know about the birds of the British Isles. 'Bit of a nutter, if I'm honest with you. Black belts in everything. But he did love his birds. For some reason we clicked, and he taught me a lot. Got so I could spot a bird from way off and put a name to it right away. No confusing martins and swallows with this boy. A good teacher, he was,' said Sam, giving the last sentence a touch of wistfulness.

'Are you still in touch with him?' Aileen asked.

Jake, we were told, was currently a guest of Her Majesty, as a consequence of having over-battered an Irish barman in a pub in Plymouth. 'Well, two Irish barmen, actually,' he said. 'Like I said, he was a bit of a psycho, and he had a thing about the Irish. His attitude to the natives didn't exactly chime with my way of seeing things.' Sam eluci- dated the differences between their ways of seeing things: whereas he'd had a lot of sympathy for the nationalist community (this sounded like a phrase parroted from the news), perhaps because there was a bit of Irish in the family ('as I was telling Mr Pattison'), as far as Jake was concerned the Catholics were either scumbags who left bombs in pubs and blew children to bits, or idiots who thought that these low-lifes were heroes. 'And don't get me wrong, Mrs Pattison,' said Sam, leaning forward and lowering the voice, as though to impart information in confidence. 'There were some evil characters hanging around. When we arrived we were shown this book – The Catalogue. Pictures of killers and their associates. Known killers – this wasn't just rumours. And you'd pass these specimens on the streets, knowing what they'd done. It was hard, and to Jake's way of thinking it was all wrong. Instead of talking to these creeps we should have given the SAS enough time to finish the job. Let them off the leash, kill all the bad guys, job done. As far as I was concerned, if we'd done that we'd have been fighting till the sun went cold. But I didn't go out of my way to broad- cast my views on the topic. I did once tell him I thought things weren't black and white, and he looked like he was about to smash my face in for me. He was rather a dangerous boy, it has to be said.' He stopped for a moment and glanced to the side, frowning – it appeared – at the memory of mad Jake.

Twice Sam had used the word 'rather'. The word had jarred the first time, because it sounded inauthentic coming from him; the second time, it occurred to me that it was a word that I often (too often) use myself. Instantly I was convinced that Sam was copying me, consciously. And now, as Aileen looked at distracted Sam, it seemed to me possible that, having heard the echo of me in what Sam had been saying, she was beginning to detect another resemblance. She was turning to me, questioningly – but her face, I saw, was simply requesting me to speak. I was aware that I hadn't said anything for a while. 'So,' I said to him, 'this Jake – is he the one who couldn't stand being in a helicopter?'

There was a vagueness to Sam's expression, as if he were emerging from sleep. It took him a couple of seconds to reply. 'No, it wasn't,' he said. 'That was someone else. Barry. Barry Mettyear.'

Sam was telling Aileen about Barry Mettyear – how he'd forced himself to go up the Eiffel Tower to try to get over his problem, but had keeled over in the lift before he was halfway up – when the phone rang. It was Eleanor; this, as I told Sam, could take a while.

What I wanted him to say, and expected him to say, was that he should be returning to work, and it did at first seem – as he placed his knife and fork carefully on the plate, folded the napkin neatly, sipped the last of his water – that he was going to leave the table. But then he settled back in his seat and said to me: 'You know, I really do like your wife. She's great.' The remark was made in a way that seemed to signify that he was glad to have found her so likeable, because he was going to be around her for a long time. 'The thing that gets me,' he said, 'is that she's an accountant. I mean, I'd never have guessed. Not in a million years.'

'And why is that?' I asked.

He assumed a lavish expression of incredulity. 'Come on. She's cool. Accountants aren't cool.'

Many different adjectives might come to mind upon making Aileen's acquaintance: steady, calm, capable, congenial. I doubt if anyone – including Sam – has ever thought her cool. 'Not all accountants are dull little bean-counters,' I said.

'No,' he conceded, 'but still, you wouldn't think she was in that line of work.'

'And what line of work would you think she was in?'

Sam scratched at the nape of his neck and scowled as he considered the question. 'Don't know,' he answered. 'A cook? That would fit. A top-notch cook.'

'Something more womanly – is that what you mean?'

'Lot of male cooks nowadays,' he countered. 'Turn on the telly, there's a geezer with a frying pan.'

Aileen, I informed him, was the one who'd made our business work. I might have had the idea, but without her financial know-how we'd never have got where we were today.

'And where would that be?' asked Sam. I told him that I didn't understand the question. 'Only joking,' he soothed. 'I can see where you are,' he said, surveying the garden. 'You've done well. I'm impressed. Very impressed. This is a nice place. And you've got a smart operation going. Nice shops. I take my hat off to you,' he said. 'And Mrs Pattison, of course.' Standing up, he placed a hand on each shoulder in turn and swivelled his arms, like a swimmer warming up. 'Making a go of it, being your own boss – I admire that. Really, I do,' he said, looking everywhere except at me.

'Aileen deserves much of the credit,' I said.

'If you say so,' he said, with a face that said – but only if you didn't look too closely – that he commended my modesty. He was moving away from the table, rotating his arms and turning his head this way and that. 'Who picks the staff? In the shop. Is that you?' he asked. 'North Street, I'm talking about.' I told him that the manager did the hiring. He nodded deeply, as though something had now been explained. I refused to ask the question he wanted me to ask, so he volunteered that the new girl was very nice. 'Polish girl. You seen her?'

'Agnieszka. Yes, I have.'

'She's something, isn't she?' he said. This might have been intended as nothing more than a comment on her appearance (which was pleasant enough, but not – I'd have said – remarkable), but might have been taken to imply that he had an interest in her. The latter, it seemed to me, was intended.

'She seems a nice young woman,' I said.

'She is. She is indeed,' said Sam, gravely, as though we were discussing someone who merited our profoundest respect. Then he added, as his parting shot: 'Good workers, the Poles. Never let you down.'

By the time Aileen had finished talking to Eleanor, Sam had been back on the roof for a quarter of an hour. He seemed such a nice boy, she commented. It was remarkable how suddenly he'd come out of himself. 'He really likes you, I think,' she said.

13

The family convened for Cerys's show, for which the venue was a school hall in north London. The hall had an under-air of sweat and there was as little legroom between the rows of hard plastic seats as you get on a budget airline. And I had Sean sitting next to me. Arriving at the last minute, he at once informed me, with a cheerful grin and a brisk rub of the hands, that he'd had a bugger of a day. Having imparted this information, he scanned the audience. 'Well, Broadway it isn't. But nearly a full house. That's good,' he commented, nodding, as if bestowing his approval on the achievement a team of amateurs whose performance had gratifyingly exceeded his modest expec-tations. I too inspected the audience, in search of Sam. A glimpse of the back of a young man's head – short-haired, dark – made me catch my breath; the young man turned; I half-covered my eyes; and I saw through my fingers a face that looked no more like Sam's than Sam's resem-bled mine. Meanwhile, Sean was giving closer scrutiny to the row in front of us; a woman with bird's-nest hair and huge faux-Celtic earrings seemed to have a notebook on her lap, which meant she might be a critic. 'Could be the big break. You never know. You never know,' he repeated, as if countering an expression of doubt from me, while at the same time sharing my supposed scepticism. 'OK, OK, here we go. Prepare to be dazzled,' he murmured as the lights went down, rubbing his hands together again.

The set was in place for the first scene: along the edge the stage, in front of a curtain of black gauze, half a dozen small tables had been placed, each equipped with a pair of chairs; to one side there was a counter, with an assortment of liquor bottles and glasses on it. A young man in a white shirt and red braces, his hair thickly oiled and centrally parted, appeared behind the bar, which was approached from the opposite direction by a stout middle-aged gent, in pin-stripes and spats. The stout chap – the banker Elisha J. Whitney – took a tumbler of whisky to a table; two other customers entered, were served, took seats; then entered Billy Crocker, impersonated by Simon Derbyshire, Cerys's boyfriend.

He started nervously: his voice was too quiet, and his accent was like nothing ever heard in New York. An imperfectly audible exchange between Billy and Mr Whitney ensued, but moments later things improved with the arrival of Reno Sweeney, a broad-shouldered, long-legged and large-breasted young woman in a sky-blue satin dress, who crossed the stage with the air of someone who knew that from this moment onward she would be the main focus of attention. Her hair was a black bob in the style of Louise Brooks; her lips were glossy and scarlet; the teeth were of an American-quality whiteness. Up to this point I'd had been tense; I'd been unable to rid myself of the feeling that Sam was somewhere in the hall, watching me. Now my attention was more fully engaged, and the tension weakened. Sean was checking the cast list: 'Katie Lanner,' he whispered in my ear. Katie Lanner started singing, and it was as if the show's volume control had been turned up by fifty per cent; and she wasn't merely loud – the voice

was true as well. The first few lines were aimed at Billy/
Simon, who looked as though he'd been cornered by a
powerfully alluring axe-woman. As soon as she'd sung 'I
get a kick out of you' in his direction once, Reno/Katie
disregarded him and sang for the audience instead, as if
doing a cabaret turn. It was very accomplished, despite
some nasty noises from the band; when she finished there
was applause, which she did not acknowledge.

The curtain of black gauze went up, disclosing the
foredeck of the SS American, evoked by means of two
curving metal staircases that rose to a balcony onto
which two portholed doors opened; a large red and
black funnel in the background, and a lifebelt hanging
between the doors, did the job of telling us that we were
on board a ship. 'Every expense spared,' Sean remarked.
Moments later, Hope Harcourt – Cerys – was strolling
across the balcony, and the idea of Sam's presence disappeared entirely. She looked lovely: her outfit – pale blue
halter-neck top and wide-legged white satin trousers –
suited her figure, and the hair she'd been given – blonde,
crimped into tight little waves – enhanced the shape
and the guilelessness of her face. Billy/Simon, convinc-
ingly smitten, sang 'Easy to Love' with a sincerity that
more than compensated for the deficiencies of technique,
and Cerys was winningly hesitant as the recipient of his
advances. She was just as good in a scene that perhaps
required more pretence, in which, having failed to rouse
any passion in her fiancé, Evelyn (a tall and very thin
boy with a forelock as floppy as a wet face-flannel), she
presented to us a face that was aghast at the feebleness
of his virility. The boldness of her self-confidence was
surprising, and rather touching.

With Billy/Simon she sang 'It's De-Lovely', and
although not every note was hit with perfect accuracy,

they transmitted a reciprocal attraction that seemed to beguile those who didn't know that this was not entirely a simulation as much as it beguiled those of us who did. Brief applause followed them, but then Reno/ Katie was back and again the voltage increased. When she sang 'Anything Goes', every word would have been audible in the back row. The performance was big, with more than an element of showing off about it, but the panache and precision were impressive, and when the entire cast started dancing it was impossible to resist the idea that they were moving around her like satellites, that everyone on the stage knew that this production had only one star. The choreography was too ambitious for some of the participants, notably one of the sailors, who dropped his mop before almost felling another crew member.

The hapless sailor was the first topic of conversation during the interval. Sean reckoned that you shouldn't put yourself forward for this kind of gig if you couldn't tell your left foot from your right; Eleanor felt sorry for the boy, as did Aileen. 'But wasn't Cerys wonderful?' said Aileen. Eleanor had to confess that she hadn't expected her daughter to be quite so good; she was very proud of her, she said, with a glance at Gerry, inviting him to say the same. 'Could be the start of something. You never know,' said Sean. There was general praise for the foppish Evelyn. Shortly before the bell started to ring for the second half, Katie/Reno was at last mentioned. 'Bit too brassy for my liking,' remarked Gerry. 'But hot, no?' suggested Sean. His father tilted his eyebrows and pursed his lips, as if to say that this was a matter of opinion and he was inclined to disagree, but Eleanor thought she was pretty, and had great gusto. 'Best gusto I've seen for months,' said Sean. We returned to our seats. Preoccupied with the possibility that Sam might at any moment appear in the foyer, I'd barely spoken.

Reno/Katie delivered 'Blow, Gabriel, Blow' with redoubled zest, as if she intended the song – or her singing of it – to lodge itself in the heads of every one of us for weeks thereafter. Stalked by a spotlight, she strutted across the edge of the stage, arms aloft, whipping up the crowd. She was comely, but her self-conviction had now become off-putting. Unwilling to be coerced any longer into watching her, I looked away, and then something immensely strange happened. The spotlight, losing track of Reno/Katie for an instant, passed across the head of the young woman who was playing the role of the Angel Charity, and as the beam of light traversed her face she turned her head towards the audience and averted her eyes so that, for no more than a second, they were directed straight at me. And in that second I had the sensation – the thrilling sensation, I have to admit – of being looked at by Sarah.

Why suddenly I should have seen Sarah, I don't know. This young woman was approximately of Sarah's build and colouring, but before this moment I hadn't been struck by any resemblance, and when, afterwards, I looked at her more closely, I noted a vague similarity in the jaw and in the set of the eyes, but nothing else. Perhaps there was something about her eyes in that instant, when she squinted out of the light, or some other evanescent aspect of her expression; or perhaps there was something in the angle at which she tilted her head, or the way her lips opened; or in the quality of the light, in the colours that flared up as the beam passed over her; perhaps it was something in the pattern of shadows that detonated a memory – whatever the cause might have been, the effect was so acute it was as though I'd fleetingly been somewhere else, and while my eyes were seeing this unknown young woman my brain was reacting to Sarah looking at me. The sharpness of the hallucination was such that it seemed that it could only be the resurrection of a specific incident; I tried to work out what that incident might have been, but within seconds there was almost nothing to work from – I was back in the theatre, fully conscious of what was around me, and the sensation had gone, like a photo that had been developing when the darkroom door was opened, and now had vanished.

I could neither find an answer to this question nor pay enough attention to what was happening on stage to follow perfectly the plot. At one point, in the final scene, I leaned towards Sean to ask him what was going on, to which he replied: 'Search me. Do we care?' Only when Cerys was singing could I concentrate. Her final number – 'All Through the Night', a duet with Billy/Simon – was her best: she'd evidently been saving her voice for the last song, whereas Simon, by now exhausted, could manage only a wobbly croon. At the end of the show the family clapped loudly, led by Sean, who raised his hands above his head to make sure that Cerys could observe the fervour of his congratulations. Cerys, noticing, seemed to blush. Katie Lanner took her acclaim with cool aplomb.

We waited for Cerys and Simon out in the street. Still not convinced that there was no risk of being ambushed by Sam, I persuaded the family that we should cross to the other side of the street, so as not to clog up the pavement. In the shadow of a plane tree, I checked every face of the departing audience; Sam was not among them.

Simon and Cerys emerged from the building arm in arm, accompanied by an older man whom Sean, after thirty seconds of doubt, identified as Elisha J. Whitney – evidently his midriff had been heavily padded. He invited the youngsters to accompany him; Cerys declined, with a facsimile of regret, and he said goodbye to her with a kiss for each cheek, and a hand pressed to her back, low down. His name was Nicholas Grainger, Cerys told us, and he was possibly the most conceited pillock she had ever met. He was convinced that he was merely a tad less gifted and handsome than Laurence Olivier, but his brow was Botoxed, his eyes were dull and tiny, and his teeth were substantially ceramic. Furthermore, he was a revolting old sleazebag, whose hands had a habit of inadvertently coming into contact with the backsides of any passing young females. In rehearsal he'd given Katie a playful and encouraging pat on the bum, and been told that if he ever pulled that stunt again she'd kick his bollocks halfway to Dover, which rather took the wind out of his sails. 'She's got that X-factor, don't you think?' asked Cerys, and so we talked about Katie Lanner, all pretending not to have been overly impressed by her. Too brash, thought Eleanor; too noisy and too obvious, adjudged Gerry. He suspected, too, that Miss Lanner might not be the nicest girl in the world. 'She's nice enough,' said Cerys. Sean wanted to know if Katie had a boyfriend. 'I mean, you don't get many of those to the pound,' he said, cupping his hands to his chest. 'There's a waiting list, and a prat like you doesn't stand a chance of getting on it, believe me,' Cerys told him, swatting his shoulder. Unperturbed, Sean requested that she should let Ms Lanner know that he was available.

We went to a bar in Hampstead, where we ordered two bottles of wine, one of which immediately became Gerry's private property. He didn't contribute much to the discussion of the show; he seconded the praise that Eleanor and Aileen had for Cerys and some of her cast-mates, but it wasn't until Sean had taken up the central role in the conversation that Gerry became animated. Sean had much to say about his bugger of a day, which had been made a bugger by the absence of two of his so-called colleagues. One of them was off sick for about the tenth time this year – 'If this guy sneezes it's a 999 job.' The other one, on holiday at the moment, was an OK bloke for a couple of pints after work but a real liability in the office because, at the end of the day, he just didn't know how the bloody machines work, which is why two different customers had been on the phone to Sean that afternoon, burning his ear off because the OK bloke had given both of them some solid-gold stupid advice. But Sean, rather than dumping the idiot in it, had somehow managed to cover his back for him, while also doing a load of stuff that Mr Sick-Note should have been doing. 'How can you sell it when you don't know what it does?' he appealed to me, as a man who understands the laws of retail.

'Let him sink,' was Gerry's advice. 'If this character can't hack it, it's best for all concerned if he goes elsewhere.' Eleanor, essentially of the same mind as her husband, wanted to know how Sean's boss saw the situation. Sean had things to say about his boss and his boss's attitude to Sean; we heard about the boss's thoughts on the subject of leadership and delegation. Overhearing him, anyone would have thought he was talking about life in a unit of the marines.

I made more than the usual effort to be affable with Sean, feeling a need to do penance for my vision of Sarah, even though she had come to me uninvited, as it were, rather than being sought. After ten minutes of office philosophy, however, I was struggling to simulate engagement, and I was grateful when Simon at last started talking. Eager to make a favourable impression on the parents, he spoke chiefly at Gerry and Eleanor – this was his introduction to his girlfriend's parents. Racehorses were his big thing. He intended, he told them, to specialise in equine medicine. The beasts may look similar, he informed us, but each is a distinct character. A week ago he'd met one that had become enamoured of a goat that had wandered into the paddock one day; now the horse wouldn't go out onto the gallops unless the goat came too.

This was moderately interesting – more interesting than anything Sean had to say, certainly. The goat-besotted horse got a laugh from Eleanor and Gerry, and from Aileen and me. Cerys smiled, but was looking tired; when she blinked, she blinked slowly. Then, while Simon was talking, I looked at Cerys again, and although she was still smiling there was, in her eyes, an unmistakable indication of boredom, and it seemed to me that she was becoming bored with her new boyfriend rather than with what he was telling us. Simon downed a glass of wine; Sean made some remark about a wildlife programme he'd recently seen, and this set Simon off again. The intelligence of pigs was the subject – they are brighter than dogs, it would appear. Cerys, listening to him, smiled; there was fondness in the smile, merely fondness, and a sense of distance too, as if she were already feeling sorry for the distress she would cause when she rejected him. I wanted to be mistaken. I wanted the youngsters to be happy with each other, for a few months more, at least, and so, when Cerys slid closer to him and, easing a hand under his arm, kissed him on the cheek, I persuaded myself that I'd been mistaken, even though I still saw a shadow in her eyes. And shortly after-wards it did seem possible that I had made an error: not in seeing a shadow, but in deciding what it meant.

We all walked to the Tube station: Eleanor with Aileen, Gerry with Simon, Cerys and I lagging behind. The director of the show was trying to put together a produc-tion of *Sunday in the Park with George*, which he hoped to be staging in about a year's time. If it went ahead, there was the chance of a part for her, a small part. 'I'm not sure about it,' she said. I asked what she was unsure about – was it the part? No, she said, she had her doubts about doing another musical. I told her once more that I thought she'd been very good. For a few seconds she didn't reply, and then she halted, evidently to let the others get ahead of us. 'You know what I'm thinking?' she said. 'I'm thinking that I don't think I've got what it takes. Not really.'

Again I told her she'd been excellent, that I'd been tremendously impressed, as had Aileen.

'That's nice of you,' she said. 'But it's such a competitive business. You need something special to stand out. I don't have anything special. I can carry a tune, I know that,' she went on, overriding my attempt at an interruption. 'I can learn the lines. I can do a decent job. But I lack that—'. Raising a hand above her head, she clicked her fingers three or four times.

'I disagree,' I began. 'You were—'

'And I'm not beautiful,' she stated. 'In this line of work a non-beautiful woman requires something special to succeed. I don't have it.'

I told her that she was talented, and very attractive.

'But the crucial thing is,' she said, hooking my arm and walking on, 'I'm not totally convinced that I want to have it. I enjoy doing the show. I've loved doing it. But doing it every week of your life – I don't know if that's me. You need to be driven, and I'm not driven.'

I suspected that Katie Lanner was having a detrimental effect on morale. 'I'm not sure that's true,' I said.

'Which bit isn't true?' she asked.

The others were waiting for us at the entrance to the Tube station. 'Both bits,' I answered. 'You're enjoying it, so keep going. Have fun,' I told her.

'Oh, I'm not giving up,' she said, with a light laugh, as though I had completely misunderstood. She let go of my arm and gave me a smile, but the shadow was still in her eyes. 'I'll keep plugging away,' she assured me.

We all took the same train, but Cerys and Simon got out at Camden Town. As she stepped out of the carriage, Cerys turned and grinned and pumped a fist, in a parody of a tennis player's self-encouragement, and I experienced an intimation, at that moment, of something like paternal affection. This had happened before, with Cerys, but it seemed more acute this time.

'What was that all about?' asked Aileen. I explained.

14

Sam repaired the garden wall and again his work was faultless. So impressed was Aileen that she compiled a list of extra jobs we might ask him to do: a couple of the sash windows needed attention; the utility room would benefit from replastering; some floorboards upstairs were in poor condition; another floor could be sanded and sealed. Sam was, she remarked, the workman you dream of finding.

And it wasn't just that he was so versatile and dependable and not at all expensive – he was so helpful as well. When Aileen – needing to get a parcel posted in a hurry – found that her car wouldn't start, Sam came promptly to the rescue. Having ferried her in the Toyota to and from the post office, he diagnosed the problem with the car, removed the faulty battery, picked up a replacement for her, and fitted it. Then he stayed at work past six, to make up for lost time, as he put it. Hearing Aileen coming back from the supermarket, he left the wall for a few minutes to give her a hand with the carrier bags. Aileen made a remark in passing about a wobbly chair leg – next thing she knew, Sam had fixed it, without being asked. A door upstairs was sticking – Sam took it upon himself to plane and rehang it, while Aileen was out of the house for a couple of hours. He'd noticed the small table I'd made for Aileen in our first year together, and had asked if he could take a closer look at it. He'd admired it very much, and so – she hoped I wouldn't mind – she had told him a little about my father and his work. As for Sam's own story, he'd volunteered some more scraps of information, mostly about his years as a boy in the Midlands and his father's blighted career in manufacturing. Those scraps did not include, however, the facts about his place in the Hendy family.

Sam came to the end of Aileen's list on a Wednesday. He'd sanded and varnished the boards of the upstairs room with such care, it looked like something from the Ideal Home Exhibition. Now all he had to do was to put the finishing touches to the utility room and paint the sash windows. Aileen and I were both working at home that day. Midway through the morning, after Aileen had gone into town on some errand, I went into the kitchen; within a minute Sam appeared, ostensibly to get a glass of water. We'd not had anything you could call a conversation since the day I'd gone up onto the roof with him – just a few words in the morning, as I left for London. Now, as if we were resuming a discussion that we'd not had the chance to finish, he said: 'I really liked Cerys, by the way. Terrific pair of lungs on her.'

My comprehension lagged a few seconds behind my hearing of his words. 'You went to the show?' was eventually my response.

'Well, duh,' he replied, grinning; his mockery had a tinge of malice in it.

'When?'

'Same night as you. I was sitting a dozen rows back.'

'I didn't see you.'

'You looked right at me,' he said.

'I couldn't have.'

He shrugged, holding his hands out, open, to the side. 'What can I say? I was standing up; you were standing up, thirty feet away; you aimed your face in my direction; you didn't see me.'

'No, I didn't,' I said. 'Why didn't you come over?'

'I think you mean: "What the hell were you doing there?"'

'I know what you were doing there.'

'You do?'

'I do,' I stated, with incontrovertible emphasis.

His response was an insouciant 'OK' and a shrug.

'So why didn't you come over?'

'Didn't want to butt in, did I?' At this I couldn't prevent a quarter-smile of grim amusement; he ignored it. 'Went very well, I thought, didn't you? Crowd seemed to appreciate it. Must have been gratifying.'

I agreed that the evening had been a success.

'Mind you,' he went on, 'I thought the girls had a better game than the blokes. Quite a girl, the dark-haired one. And your girl was bloody good and all. Nice voice. Not surprised you like her so much.'

'What are you talking about?' I said.

'What do you mean: what am I talking about? I'm talking about your Cerys. She seems very nice. She's cute. She's got a spark to her. I can see why you like her so much.'

'You're in no position to say something like that,' I told him.

'You saying she's not nice?' he replied, affecting bewilderment.

'No. Of course she's nice. I'm not saying that, as you know full well. I'm saying you're in no position to talk about my liking her. You don't know anything about us.'

As I said this, it crossed my mind that if he'd been in the hall and I'd failed to spot him, he might have followed us to the bar that we'd gone to after the show; for a moment, before sense reasserted itself, it didn't seem impossible that he'd seen me walking with Cerys to the Tube station.

He was shaking his head now, slowly, with the demeanour of a man who had decided to let an insult pass. 'You're forgetting,' he said, in a mollifying tone, 'that I have spent time with your wife. She has told me things about your niece. She has told me that you're very close to her. Both of you. And I'm saying that I can see why.' The tone was still low and smooth, but the last phrase sounded like the commencement of a threat.

Before I could form a response, he asked me: 'You an only child, by any chance?'

The question was so presumptuous that, taken aback, I answered it without thinking. I said that I was.

'So that's one way we're alike,' he said, with an encouraging smile, as though this might be a basis from which we could make progress. Then he wanted to know if either of my parents were still alive. Having been told that they were both dead, he asked: 'Get on with them, did you?'

'Yes, I did. Very well,' I replied, intending to stop the interrogation there.

Immediately he had another question: 'How did they meet?' I told him that I didn't know how they met. 'Really?' he said, puzzled.

'I don't see anything odd in that,' I replied. 'And I can't see that my parents' courtship is any business of yours.'

Sam screwed his eyes shut as though stung by smoke; he opened them wide: the message was that he could hardly believe his own ears. 'I'm sorry?' he said.

'None of my business? The lives of my grandparents are none of my business?' He held his arms out as though cradling the vast truth that my decaying old brain had unaccountably overlooked, and then he said, softly, in the tone of someone coming to a subject that could no longer be deferred, however much the person he's addressing might wish to defer it: 'When are you going to tell Aileen? I know it's hard, but just give me an idea. You don't want me to tell her, do you?' This was said as if he were offering to help me out.

'No,' I said, 'of course I don't.'

'When, then? After I've done here? Would that be easier, if I wasn't around?'

I had never thought that Sam was my son. At most, his being my son had seemed not wholly impossible. By this point, however, I had observed him at close quarters for several days, and had noticed not even a tenuous indication of kinship between us. The probability of my being his father was now only an infinitesimal degree short of zero. 'That would be easier,' I agreed. With a sensation akin to that of missing a step, I went on to say: 'But I can't see what would be gained by telling her.'

His eyebrows crumpled; his mouth came open; with jerky movements of his head he looked around the kitchen, as if suddenly he didn't recognise the room. 'Could you say that again?' he whispered. 'You can't see what would be gained? You can't see what would be gained if you were to tell her the truth? You're my father. I want that to be known. I want it acknowledged. Can't you understand? How can you say nothing would be gained? How can you say that?' His voice was rising, but he appeared to be more distressed than angry.

'Well,' I answered, 'if I speak to Aileen, the one thing we know for a fact is that she'll be upset.'

'At first, yes,' he agreed.

'Very upset. Possibly for a very long time. Do you want that? You say you like her. So do you want me to make her unhappy? Is that what you want?'

'No,' he agreed. His eyes scanned the floor, as if tracing a maze there, before coming to rest in a stare of hopelessness. 'So what do you expect me to do?' he asked, still looking at the floor. 'Just fuck off and forget all about it?'

I was on firm ground again, I thought. 'Sam,' I said, 'I like you. Aileen likes you.' He glanced at me; there was tightness around the eyes and mouth; he seemed to making a great effort to prevent tears from appearing. 'And I'm not just saying that. We do,' I said. And then I took the decisive step forward: 'But I have to tell you – I don't think we're related. In fact, I'm sure we're not,' I stated, and the act of stating it made my belief even more secure.

Slowly he turned to look at me. His face showed the profound incomprehension of a man being addressed in a language of which he speaks not a word.

'I'm sorry,' I said, and sorry was a part of what I felt. 'I am not your father.'

This statement too, to judge from Sam's expression, was bereft of sense. He examined my face, as though I were a mystifying object that he'd just encountered in a museum. 'I'm not hearing this,' he said in a dead voice, more to himself than to me.

'I'm sorry,' I repeated. I was trying to be as soothing as possible, but sounded insincere and unctuous.

'What are you talking about?' he said. 'The certificate, remember? Mother: Sarah. Father: you – in her writing.'

'I know you're Sarah's son,' I replied, which was overstating the case. 'But my name shouldn't be there.'

'What? Like it's a mistake?'

'That's one possibility.'

The response to this was a laugh like a paper bag exploding. 'You hope,' he said.

'No. That's what I believe.'

'Look me in the eye and say that,' he said.

I did so, and I wasn't sure if what I saw in his eyes was loathing or the deepest anguish.

'That's ridiculous. Absolutely fucking ridiculous,' he said. The syllables sounded as though they were being pressed beneath an immense weight of anger.

'No, it's not,' I countered, calmly but immediately, because it seemed to me that if I faltered he would be likelier to erupt. Talking in the sort of voice you'd use on someone who was standing on a ledge forty feet above the street, I told him what I believed: that the appearance of my name on the certificate didn't prove that I was his father – it proved perhaps that Sarah had thought that I was the father of her child. 'I was the most likely candidate,' I told him, 'but likelihood isn't certainty.'

'She was certain,' said Sam, in the same pressurised monotone. 'She told me you were my father.'

'OK. But you can see why she might have said that without being absolutely sure in her own mind? You can see why, with you there, she'd want to say something definite?'

He looked away, frowning with the difficulty of accepting what he understood me to have meant. When he turned back to me, it was with an expression of great distaste. 'She screwed around? That's what you're telling me? She was fucking around so it could have been you or it could have been some other bloke. Or who the fuck knows else. Pick a name out the hat. That's it?'

'That's not how I'd put it,' I answered.

'I know that's not how you'd put it. But that's what you're saying. Yes?'

'All I'm saying is that is that I wasn't the only one she was involved with. There was one other man. I know that for a fact. And I suspect there were others. I'm not making any judgement on her. Don't think that. I'm not that big a hypocrite. But that was the situation. There were others.'

Sam shook his head, slowly, like a policeman being asked to accept a risibly feeble alibi. 'This is unbeliev-able,' he murmured. 'Totally fucking unbelievable.'

'It's not unbelievable, Sam,' I said. 'It's possible. More than possible. I think it's the only explanation. The only explanation I can think of.'

'Only explanation you can think up, you mean,' he said. The tone was contemptuous, but his anger seemed to be dissipating.

'No,' I persisted. 'We're clearly not related. Just look at us,' I said, gesturing from myself to Sam and from Sam to myself again. I may even have made myself shrink a little, to enhance the discrepancy between us. 'She may have thought I was your father, but if she were to see us now, she'd know I'm not. The idea is irreconcilable with reality.'

Sam was regarding me as if he were dealing with someone who wanted him to believe that an object in front of him was an entirely different colour from the colour he was seeing. 'I'll tell you what the reality is,' he said. 'You can't accept what's happened. You don't want to see it, so you're making out you don't see it. That's the reality.' I was about to reply when I heard Aileen's car on the drive. Sam turned, registered the sound with a shrug of the eyebrows, as if dismissing it as a triviality, and carried on talking. 'You know why she never told you about me?' he went on. 'It's simple. She wanted shot of you. She thought you were an arsehole. That's what she told me. A five-star arsehole.' He peered into my eyes, gauging the impact of the insult, but there was no impact. For one thing, Sarah had called me worse things than that. For another, it was too long ago: the shot fell years short of its target.

The car door slammed. 'Sam,' I said, 'we have to—'

'I don't have to anything,' he carried on, apparently intending to maintain the attack regardless of Aileen's return. 'It's not that you don't believe you're my father. That's not it. You don't want me to be your son. That's what it is. I'm not the kind of boy you'd have wanted, am I?' With a sneer he surveyed the kitchen; he looked out at the garden, as if measuring it. 'I know what this is about. Oh yes, I do,' he said, with the weariness of one who, though young, has no more illusions as to the rules of life.

The key was in the door. 'Sam—' I pleaded.

'One thing I was wondering,' he continued, oblivious. 'Why haven't you got any other kids? You didn't want any? Is that it? You couldn't handle it?' The question was asked aggressively, as if I were being asked to explain something reprehensible that I'd done.

I wanted to tell him that it was none of his business, but the front door had closed and a weakness had flooded through me like water crashing down a pipe. In ten seconds everything would start to come apart. Sam glanced at me, gave me a smile that seemed to commiserate, and moved towards the back door. 'You're talking nonsense,' he whispered. 'I can't pretend it's not disappointing, but I hope we can work it out. Let's talk again.' Aileen entered. 'Hi, Mrs Pattison,' he said, as if they were passing each other on the street.

But later that day Aileen came into the study to tell me she'd just had a very strange conversation with Sam. She'd gone out into the garden and come across him crouched by the drain at the side of the house, rinsing his brushes under the tap. They exchanged a few words, and while they were talking Sam started to scratch at the scars on his forearm – to claw at them, as if they were giving him a maddening itch. 'Gives me gyp sometimes,' he said. Aileen asked if anything from the medicine cabinet might help; the offer was gratefully declined. It was Sam's last day at the house; she'd wondered about the scar, and now she decided to ask him about it, expecting a brief answer.

Instead, Sam was suddenly as talkative as he'd been during our Sunday lunch. He'd been burned by an Iraqi kid, he told her – or rather, 'a fucking Iraqi kid', the words being pronounced with venom, as though he were seeing the culprit as he spoke. Never before had she heard Sam in unedited mode. They'd been patrolling past some shops, very slowly, because the crowd was so dense, and then the people flowed away in the space of a few seconds and some shots went off, and the next thing they knew this kid – twelve years old, thirteen maybe – had materialised from behind a donkey and was coming at them, holding a Pepsi bottle with a rag on fire in its neck. The kid 'got dropped', said Sam, but before going down he'd managed to chuck his bottle, and Sam's arm was going up in smoke. So two of his mates were putting his arm out while the others were taking cover and returning fire, and then the captain noticed some activity in a doorway, and in the next instant there was an RPG in the air – 'rocket propelled grenade', Sam explained, in a peculiarly detached voice, as if adding a dash of commentary to someone else's narrative. The RPG missed by yards, but the retaliation was bang on target. 'We really sorted him out,' said Sam, almost smacking his lips at the thought of it. 'That lad got superkilled, I'm telling you. You could have put what was left of him in a shoe box.'

To Aileen it was clear that Sam had wanted to shock her, but that wasn't quite the effect he achieved. The story was horrible, of course, but the teller made as strong an impression as the tale, and she was perplexed by him. Perhaps she was also a little disturbed. Certainly she was troubled by what she witnessed not long afterwards. From our bedroom window she looked down into the garden and saw Sam by the wall that he'd repaired. He was examining a part of it as though he'd found something there that dissatisfied him. With a forefinger he was picking at it over and over again, and then he punched the wall, twice, very quickly. That done, he strolled back to the house, his demeanour that of a man with not a worry in the world. He stopped at the rose bush, bent down to look closely at the blooms, put his nose to a flower, and smiled with closed eyes.

At the end of the day, having loaded his tools into the Toyota, he came to say goodbye to me, in the garden. The knuckles of his right hand were bloodied, but neither he nor I made any reference to the injury. 'That's it. I'm done,' he announced, whisking his hands together. I thanked him for all his good work, and handed over the last of his money. 'Another satisfied customer,' he said. Aileen was in the kitchen and the window was open; she would have been able to hear our voices, but perhaps not every word. Shielding his eyes from the sun, Sam scrutinised the upper reaches of the apple tree. 'Right,' he said, as if passing comment on something he'd observed there, 'what do we do now?'

Taking his lead, I turned my attention to the tree and took a few steps towards it. Sam followed; his manner was perfectly casual. 'I'm not entirely sure,' I told him.

'We need to sort this out,' he said, in a sing-song lilt that signified that his patience was nearing its end.

'We do,' I agreed, as Aileen came out to join us.

'We'll talk tomorrow. Castle Cliffe Gardens,' he stated. 'Twelve o'clock.'

Aileen was carrying a magazine, holding it to her chest like a shield as she walked towards us. She thanked him, effusively, as if he'd done us a generous favour. 'I'll recommend you to friends,' she said. 'If you need the publicity.'

'That would be nice,' said Sam.

Indicating the damaged hand with a nod, Aileen told him that he should go indoors and clean it up. 'Kind of you, Mrs Pattison,' he said, 'but I have to hit the road.' He gave me – but not Aileen – the messy hand to shake, and in parting he said to me: 'See you tomorrow, then.'

So I had to improvise another lie when Aileen asked me what Sam had meant by that. He was going to be in town tomorrow, and I was calling in at North Street, so I'd said I'd buy him lunch, I told her. 'That's nice of you,' she said, hooking a hand around my arm. He was an interesting young man, she commented, but she was glad we had the house to ourselves again.

That night, as we were reading in bed, I noticed that the bottom drawer of the chest of drawers was slightly open. As I was closing the drawer I saw a patch of the carpet – a small patch, no larger than a credit card – where the nap was slightly flattened and very slightly paler than the surrounding carpet, as though a mark had been carefully erased, leaving not a stain but only the evidence of its removal. I opened the drawer – not out of suspicion that something was amiss, but simply to set it straight. It's the drawer in which we keep our photographs, in two stacks of wallets. At first glance, everything was as it should be, but then I saw that one of the wallets had been inserted with its spine facing the opposite way from all the others in its pile. This was something that Aileen would never do.

15

I met Sam at midday, at Castle Cliffe. He was sitting on the bench in the angle of the old wall, in precisely the same posture as when I'd first caught sight of him in Russell Square Gardens – head resting on the top of the bench, face presented to the sky, arms outstretched, with a cigarette in one hand. The way he was sitting annoyed me. I watched him bring the cigarette smoothly to his lips and sip at it. With his eyes closed, he blew the smoke out slowly, looking like a bully who was rather pleased with himself. There was something swaggering about him, if it's possible to swagger while sitting. This conversation, I had already decided, was going to be conclusive. I knew what I had to tell him, and I was not going to be deflected from telling him. Seeing him, I was made doubly determined.

He discarded the cigarette and sat up. The day was warm, and there were several people sitting on the grass in the vicinity of the bench, mostly mothers and child-minders with babies and toddlers, but straight in front of Sam a young woman was sunbathing, alone. Part of her face was hidden by strands of copper-coloured hair. She'd fallen asleep, and Sam was ogling her. I saw him shift on the bench, to give himself a clearer view of her cleavage, a substantial quantity of which was revealed by the neckline of her loose white vest, which she'd rolled up to give her belly the benefit of the sun. Sam leaned forward, elbows on knees, rubbing at his jaw and smiling, as if at the thought of what he might say to her when she woke up. He made no attempt whatever to disguise what he was doing – he was examining the girl so blatantly I could almost see cartoon-style tracks in the air, shooting from his eyes to her chest – and he didn't desist as I came up to the bench, even though he must have detected my presence several seconds before I sat down.

'Hi,' he said, glancing at me, as you'd glance away from a gripping episode of your favourite television programme. 'See her?' he said, pointing clasped hands in the direction of the sleeping sunbather. 'She's the spitting image of a girl I saw once. Same hair. Same shape. Amazing.' He'd been up in the watchtower in Armagh, he told me, with his psychotic birdwatching colleague, when this beautiful girl had appeared, riding a horse. For as long as she was within sight he'd kept his binoculars trained on her. 'Love at first sight, it was. At a range of one hundred yards.' Every day, after that, he'd gone up into the tower hoping he'd see her again, but she'd never reappeared. 'But now,' he said, shaking his head at the uncanniness of it, 'there she is. It's her. What are the odds on that? A girl in Armagh has a double in Guildford. Incredible, no?'

'Indeed,' I replied.

He smiled at me as if to chide me for being envious of his extraordinary good fortune. 'All OK at home?' he asked. 'Wall still standing? Roof not collapsed?'

'Wall still standing, thank you,' I said, and then – as he turned his face away from me – I asked him a question I'd thought I wasn't going to ask: 'What were you doing in our bedroom?'

Staring at the sunbather again, he answered distractedly, as if he'd only half-heard the question: 'Sorry?'

'I said: what were you doing in our bedroom? You had no business being in there.'

He looked me in the eye for a moment, before turning back. 'Don't know what you're talking about,' he said, unemphatically, as though in response to a multiple-choice questionnaire.

'You know exactly what I'm talking about,' I told him.

His gaze was fixed on the sunbather. After a pause of fully five seconds, he repeated, calmly but slightly more slowly: 'I have no idea what you're talking about.'

I scrutinised the side of his face, compelling him to give me his attention. He did not move: his profile was an image of intense and solitary concentration. 'You do,' I continued. 'You were in our bedroom. There's a chest of drawers beside the door and you opened it. You were snooping. You looked through our photos.'

With no change of expression he replied: 'In that case you didn't need to ask the question, did you? You've just answered it yourself.'

'OK,' I said, 'so you admit it. That's something. Now—'

'No,' he interrupted, in a tone of strained patience. 'I haven't admitted anything. I said I didn't know what you were talking about.'

'Sam, you were in that room. I know you were.'

Now he faced me. He regarded me placidly before speaking, and every word that he spoke was uttered distinctly yet softly; between sentences he paused, as though to allow me time to digest what he was saying. 'Dominic,' he said – this was the only time he ever addressed me by name – 'I was not in that room. I have told you I was not in that room. I am sorry you don't believe me. Now, I think we should change the subject.

Otherwise I might start to get annoyed.' He widened his eyes jokily and gave me a smile that was totally impersonal, before resuming his study of the young woman on the grass.

He was lying, I knew. I was not surprised that he had lied initially, but I wished he hadn't been so determined a liar, because I was finding it harder and harder to dismiss the notion that a huge lie was being perpetrated – that Sam, contrary to what I'd assumed from the start, had known all along that he was not my son, and that the Sam Williams on the birth certificate was not the same person as the young man sitting beside me. Once again I was trying to put this idea aside, when Sam – with his eyes still trained on the cleavage – muttered: 'Photos of what?'

'I beg your pardon?' I replied.

'You said there were photos. Photos of what?'

'For God's sake. You know perfectly well. You looked at them.'

'Holiday snaps? Weddings? Family get-togethers? Intimate moments?'

I was too angry – and too nervous of a full-blown confrontation – to answer.

'Well,' he said, as if giving voice to his thought processes rather than talking to me, 'it would make sense.' He took out a cigarette, lit it, and gave a young mother an appreciative check-over as she walked by. 'I mean,' he said, with a glance in the approximate direction of my head, 'you haven't exactly opened up, have you? I've made an effort, but you've just not been playing. I've made allowances, but nonetheless – I've not been getting any warmth off you. Know what I mean? You've given me the big clam treatment. I ask you: "Tell me about my grandparents." And you say: "Piss off. None of your business." In my situation, it'd make sense if I wanted to do a bit of research, wouldn't it? Only natural.'

'Snooping,' I corrected him. 'But you've admitted it. That's progress.'

'I'm not admitting anything,' he responded. 'All I'm saying is it wouldn't be hard to explain. There'd be a good reason for it, in my situation.'

'It's inexcusable,' I told him.

He looked at me as if I'd made an observation that was utterly bizarre, then with a flicker of the eyebrows and a pursing of the lips he signified that I was entitled to my opinion but it was of no concern to him. Having taken a long drag, he examined the cigarette for a few moments, turning his hand this way and that, and then he examined my face, steadily, curiously. 'Let me ask you something,' he said. 'If I'd been born a few years earlier, if it had just been a fling before you met Aileen and now suddenly you found out you had a kid, would you be carrying on like this? Or if I'd been someone not like me. If I'd turned out to be more of a suit and briefcase kind of guy – that would have been different, wouldn't it? I think it would.'

'I'm not carrying on like anything,' I said.

'Answer the question.'

'If you were my son,' I told him, 'the situation would be quite different.'

He seemed to let my reply fly past him. Squinting, he scrutinised my eyes – left then right then left then right – as if to verify that each was telling him the same thing. 'I know what you want,' he resumed. 'What you want, more than anything, is for me to not exist.'

'That's ridiculous.'

'You'd like me to be somewhere a very long way from where you are.' This was said with a very slight hint of pathos – but it sounded to me more like the overture to a practical proposal.

'No,' I said. 'I like you, but—'

'Because I could,' he continued. 'I could go away. I'm not welcome. I can see that. You've made your feelings clear. You don't want to know. But maybe that'll change. Maybe if I'm not in your face so much, you'll start to get used to the idea. If I put some distance between us, but we stayed in touch. How about that? I want you to acknowledge me, in the end. So if I got offside for a while, I'd still want contact. I'd be discreet, but I'd want contact,' he said.

'And what else would you want?' I asked. The words seemed to speak themselves, like a bubble of gas rising to the surface of a tar-pool.

For a few seconds Sam frowned at me, uncomprehending, then he jerked his head back as if the suddenly perceived affront were a physical blow. On the path, to his left, lay two cigarette butts. He scowled at them, by which I was to understand that what perplexed him now was why I had so traduced him. Gently he teased the butts together with the toe of a boot, then he placed a foot over them and slowly ground them into the tarmac.

'Sam,' I said, appeasingly, 'there's no need for you to go anywhere. We can have this resolved within the week.'

He applied himself to grinding the shreds of paper and tobacco into finer particles. When that had been done to his satisfaction, he said: 'And how would that be?'

'We have a test done.'

His eyes scanned the sky, as if a sound had come from there and he couldn't locate its source. 'Say again?' he said.

'We do a test. I've made enquiries. It's a straightforward business. A swab from each of us, that's all that's required.

Two minutes, in and out. We go to a clinic, have the swabs done, they're sent off to a lab, and five days later we have the result. We'll know exactly where we stand. There's a basic test and there's a court-approved test—'

'What's the fucking courts got to do with it?' he growled.

'It just means the highest standard of test. So there's no doubt. It's a bit more expensive. The basic test is about three hundred and the court-approved is four hundred, so there's not much in it.'

Sam had taken a fresh cigarette. 'Fuck that,' he muttered, out of the side of his mouth.

'I'd pay for it, obviously.'

'Obviously,' he parroted.

I was watching him closely, gauging the likelihood of an outburst of temper, asking him tacitly to turn round and face me. He did not turn round, and there seemed little risk, imminently, of trouble. He took his time with the cigarette. His demeanour as he smoked was humili-ated rather than angry: he might have been running in his mind a conversation with his boss, in which he'd been told he was going to be demoted and have his pay cut by half. Eventually, having finished the cigarette and mashed the butt into the remains of the others, he said, as morosely as any teenager: 'Want me to do a lie-detector first? Might save you a few quid.'

I told him that I wasn't saying that he was lying. Pleased that I had managed to say it with sincerity, I repeated the assurance: 'I know you're not lying, Sam. I know you believe what you're telling me,' I said, though by now it was hard to accept that this could be so. At best, I thought, he might be wishing that he could still believe it.

'Nice of you to say so,' he muttered.

I said nothing. I didn't even look at him. I was prepared to wait until he was ready to say more. But it began to seem, as he lit yet another cigarette, that he might stay silent for the rest of the afternoon, so I said: 'It's what we have to do.'

There was no response. He blew a long breath of smoke, and seemed to be counting the birds in the sky.

'I can't see any sense in delaying,' I said, 'so I suggest some time next week. Would next week be all right? If not, the week after would be fine for me. You say. Whenever is good for you.'

I didn't have the impression that he was weighing up his options: he had accepted that there was no alternative, it appeared. Nonetheless, it was with some relief that I heard him answer, so quietly that I wasn't immediately sure what he'd said: 'Suits me.'

'Do you want to choose a day now?' I asked him.

'No,' he replied flatly.

'In that case, I'll give you a call tomorrow and we'll make a date.'

'Sure,' he said. Now his gaze had moved back to the sunbather, but there was no appetite in his eyes. He might have been looking at a stretch of unoccupied grass.

'Look, Sam,' I said, 'if it's positive, if it turns out that you're my son, I'll do the right thing. I'll tell Aileen, of course. But more than that – I'll see that you're provided for. If you're my son, I'll make sure you're OK.' There was no response to this proposal – not even a twitch of an eye. The breeze in his ears was all that Sam seemed to be hearing. I had no reason to stay with him any longer, but I didn't want the conversation to end with his ignoring me. So I asked him: 'Do you have a lot of work lined up?'

He gave me a wry smile and answered: 'Am I staying in the area, you mean?'

'No,' I said. 'That's not what I meant.'

'Don't you worry about me,' he said. 'I can get work whenever I want.'

Taking this to mean that he didn't have any work, I told him that I knew of someone who needed some paving done.

'Sure,' he said, 'give them my number. Thanks.'

My suspicions had been dislodged by Sam's apparent indifference at my mention of payment, and now they were carried away, for a time, as if a wave had come in and pulled them out to sea – but not far, not out of sight. He'd said 'Thanks' in the voice of someone bereaved, in response to words that were well-meant but inadequate. Suddenly it was not his potential for violence that was uppermost in my mind, nor the possibility that he was dangerously devious – the image of his filthy old caravan appeared to me, and I felt some concern for him. I asked him what he would do if the result of the test were negative.

'It won't be,' he replied, with placid certainty.

'But,' I persisted, 'what if it is? Are you prepared for that?'

He squinted into the vacant middle distance, and now annoyance was seeping into his face. 'Will I sod off and leave you alone – is that what you're asking?' he said.

'No,' I replied.

'I think it is. Can't think of any other way of taking it,' he said, with a slight increase in the pitch of hostility.

'What I meant was: how will you take it?' I told him. 'If it turns out that I'm not your father, it'll be a setback for you, I know that. Will you carry on looking for him?'

'It is you,' said Sam. 'So it's a pointless fucking question.' He leaned his head back against the bench once more; he clamped a hand to his brow and the other hand over it; sighing, he stared wearily into the sky before looking at his watch and then at me, as if to ask if I could give him any good reason why he should continue to keep me company.

The sunbather had been awake for a minute or two, and now was talking into her phone as she ransacked her bag. Sam stood up and shook my hand, looking at me directly for the first time since I'd raised the subject of the test. 'You needn't worry yourself,' he said. 'I've been thinking of re-enlisting. That's probably what I'll do.' He smiled at me, as though to apologise for having had some fun with me, for not having told me this right at the start.

But the idea, I was sure, was that I was to feel guilty that his life was in such a state that he was reconsidering going back into the army. 'You said once was enough,' I reminded him.

'Did I?' he said, mock-puzzled. 'Well, perhaps more than enough is what I need.'

'You said to me that only a madman would sign up for another tour.'

'So? In that case I'm mad,' he said, giving me a deranged stare.

'No, Sam, you're not mad.'

'OK – bored, then. Is that better? I'm fucking bored out of my skull,' he said, as though I were to blame for his boredom. The stare was now authentically intense, and alarming. 'This isn't being alive,' he said, flailing an arm in a gesture that took in everyone around us. 'This is being asleep. When some fucker is trying to stop you being alive, that's when you're really alive. When you wake up in the morning and you don't know if you're going to see tomorrow – that's what it's about. I'm telling you, I've been more alive than you'll ever be.'

'Nonsense,' I told him. 'You can't say that. You don't know.'

'I was in your house. I know. Believe me, I know. I've lived more than you ever will, and you know it.'

'You're talking nonsense, Sam.'

'Ever been shot at?'

'Of course not.'

'OK then,' he said, with a curt and forceful nod, which brought to mind the sight of Terry Fenway falling back after Sam had cracked his face. 'I'll tell you something else as well,' he went on, glancing at the sunbather, who had stood up and was brushing flecks of grass from her skirt. 'You meet a better class of person in the army. People you'd trust with your life. Straight up. That's not just words. Trust with your fucking life.'

'I'm sure that's true,' I said.

'I tell you, you can keep all this,' he sneered, throwing out both hands in a casting-off gesture. 'This is death,' he said, looking around the park; his eye alighted on me momentarily, as just another aspect of the environment. 'Fuck all of it.'

Sympathy had evaporated again, and all my doubts had returned, as forcefully as ever. I said to him: 'You're saying I'm your father, but I have to ask you: is that the way you would talk to your father?'

In lieu of an answer, he shook his head as if the question were too feeble to merit the effort of a response. The sunbather, chatting on her phone, strolled away; Sam's gaze travelled from her feet to her waist and slowly back down. 'If you'll excuse me,' he said, and he walked off, following the young woman. Five yards away he stopped. 'Thursday,' he called. 'Thursday is good for me. Any time. Set it up and I'll be there. Call me when you've fixed it. I'll be there,' he said, pointing a finger-gun at me and closing one eye to take aim.

The next day I made an appointment at my GP's surgery,

for 9 a.m. the following Thursday. As soon as I'd done that I called Sam; I left a message on his voicemail – I gave him the time and place of the appointment, and said I'd ring him again tomorrow. Three times I left a message for him in the course of the week. The Thursday arrived. At nine o'clock I was standing outside the surgery, having already been there for twenty minutes. I'd told Aileen that my ears were blocked up and I wanted the doctor to take a look. Given Sam's punctiliousness when he was working on the house, I was more or less certain what was happening when there was still no sign of him at five past the hour. At half past I called him, and left another message. On Friday, when I rang again, his number was defunct. On the Monday I drove to the field where his caravan had been parked. I wasn't surprised to find that it was no longer there.

16

A week or so after Sam had vanished, I dropped in at North Street. I hadn't been there in the interim, and it seemed to me, from the moment I walked in, that the staff were regarding me slightly differently than before – and there could be only one explanation for that. Agnieszka's manner had unequivocally, if subtly, changed. She was a somewhat nervy young woman, often with a suggestion of barely suppressed panic in her eyes. Now, however, there was an uneasy watchfulness to her expression, as if I'd done something that was making her wary of me. And when Geoff said 'Hello', it was as though he'd recently seen me behave unreasonably and had consequently adjusted his opinion of me.

Usually, when we meet in Geoff's office, we have a couple of minutes of small talk. Most weekends he goes kayaking, and that's generally worth an anecdote or two. On this occasion, however, the talk was strictly business. It was fairly clear, as I watched Geoff stirring his coffee, that Sam had spoken to Agnieszka, and Agnieszka in turn had told Geoff that she'd heard that Mr Pattison had a son – a son whom he refused to acknowledge. Remembering the comment Sam had made about Agnieszka, I was sure that this is what had happened. If Geoff had seen Sam talking to her, I thought, surely he'd have warned her that this man was to be treated with great caution? So, presumably, Sam had noticed her at work but had spoken to her outside. Perhaps he'd followed her home?

Something had to be done, so I asked Geoff if there'd been any further trouble with the character who'd made a scene with the two women – the young man who'd wanted to get in contact with me. Geoff's response – a too-brisk shake of the head, averted eyes – confirmed that I had grounds for concern. 'Well,' I said, 'I've had trouble from him.' I told Geoff that this character was a stalker, that he'd got it into his head that we were related and had been making a pest of himself. 'We're not related,' I told him, with the air of a man obliged to counter a self-evident absurdity. 'He's mentally unbalanced. And if he shows his face here again, I want you to ring me, right away. Even if he's on his best behaviour. Call me.' Geoff promised he would; and the next time I returned to North Street I could tell from the attitude of the more relaxed Agnieszka that the message had been passed on.

I was relieved to be rid of Sam. But I was also disappointed that he had disappeared, because by running away he had eliminated the possibility that he had not known that what he'd been telling me was untrue. I didn't want him to be a liar, but he was a liar, and I couldn't understand why he'd maintained the lie so strenuously. How had he thought it would end? That I would simply accept him at his word and take him in? That I would pay him to stay away? Had he just wanted to make a mess of my life, for some incomprehensible reason? And I began to wonder if the connection between himself and Sarah might be as much a fiction as was his connection with me. The certificate, after all, was merely a piece of paper. Thousands of people in this country have documents that don't mean a thing. It was intolerable, not knowing who he was. I had to know more, but talking to Sam again, even if it were possible, wouldn't provide any answers.

The phone book, I was astonished to find, contained more than twenty private investigation companies. PDE Solutions (Professional, Discreet and Effective) was the one I selected. The box advert assured the potential client that 'All our Operatives have a Military or Police Background', but I chose PDE chiefly because the advert wasn't illustrated with a drawing of a magnifying glass or a telescope or a shifty trenchcoated individual leaning against a wall, and they were based in a village where there was no risk of my being spotted by someone I knew. I had concocted a story to explain why I needed infor-mation on the late Sarah Williams and her son. I had rehearsed this story so often that I'd managed to convince myself that it sounded plausible. On my way up the stairs to the office I was running through the knottier aspects of the tale. Within two minutes of meeting Mr Innes, the boss of PDE Solutions, I had abandoned the pretence and reverted to the truth, or an approximation of it.

The office, and Mr Innes, were not quite what I had expected. I'd pictured brown carpeting, Venetian blinds that no longer functioned properly, old filing cabinets, fluorescent lights, an unhealthy-looking individual in a cheap suit, behind a messy desk. In reality, access to Mr Innes was through a reception area as smart as an expen-sive dentist's, staffed by a pretty young woman whose cool graciousness could not have more perfectly embodied the words 'Professional' and 'Discreet'. She led me into the presence of Mr Innes, who was sitting behind a black glass desk, at work on a top-of-the-range Mac. Alongside the computer there were two phones, a lamp, and not much else. A vast monochrome photograph of snow-topped mountains occupied much of the wall behind the desk. As for Mr Innes himself, he might have been an upmarket dentist – a dentist who played a lot of rugby, maybe. He was about forty years of age, five feet eight or thereabouts, with crew-cut blond hair and incisive blue eyes, and he was burly, but with no fat about the face or middle. The suit was certainly not cheap, the shirt was pristine white, and the tie – deep blue, silk – had not been bought from a chain store. Having given me a handshake that impressed upon me that I was dealing with a man of probity and decisiveness, he invited me to sit in either of two sumptuous black leather armchairs, which stood on opposite sides of a smoked glass coffee table; he took the other.

'Now, explain the situation to me, in as much detail as you like,' he began. The voice – precise, relaxed, certain of its authority – was also suggestive of a medical man. On the phone I'd said only that I was interested in finding out more about a particular person's background. Now I gave him the outline of events: this young man had appeared, purporting to be my son; he had claimed that his mother was a woman with whom I had been involved many years ago (I omitted the precise circumstances of the alleged conception); he had produced a birth certificate that had been altered; he had agreed to take a test, and then incriminated himself by running away.

Mr Innes had placed a notebook on the table, but as yet he hadn't opened it. 'You're married, Mr Pattison?' he asked. In his eyes I could see that a diagnosis was being made.

'I am,' I answered.

'And your wife doesn't know about this situation?'

'She doesn't,' I said. 'I can't see there's anything to be gained by telling her. Not yet.'

Our conversation was suspended as the receptionist entered, bringing chunky little white cups of coffee and glasses of mineral water. 'I understand,' Mr Innes resumed as the door closed, and I suspect that one thing he understood was that this client was being less than wholly honest. 'Let me summarise,' he went on. 'You believe this young man to be an imposter.'

'Or deluded.'

'Or deluded. Either way, you don't wish to have anything to do with him. He has now broken off contact with you and would seem to have taken steps to ensure that you cannot make contact with him. Yes?' I confirmed that this was indeed how things stood. Mr Innes took a sip of coffee, placed the cup back on its saucer precisely, as though moving a chess piece, then leaned towards me, hands lightly clasped. 'In that case, Mr Pattison,' he said, 'my advice would be to leave it at that. This is what I say to many of the people who come here, believe it or not. "Go home and forget about it" – that's what I tell them. Most of them don't go home and forget about it. And later they wish they had taken my advice.' A softening of the gaze and a small chewing motion of the jaw hinted at the depths of regret these people had experienced. 'This man was a nuisance. He's unsettled you. Now he's gone. You want him to be gone. So leave it. It might take months, it might take years, but in time he'll fade away. Let him go,' he said, but his face said that he could see that in this instance, once again, his better judgement would count for nothing.

I told him that I didn't want him to find Mr Williams – not at the moment, anyway. I didn't want to speak to him, because I found it hard to believe a word he said. But I needed to know how much of what he'd told me was true. It might turn out that his account of himself was a fantasy from start to finish. I wanted to know if he was Sarah Williams' son, and I wanted to know more about Sarah. I assumed she'd had friends. He'd told me that he'd spent time with her, so had she introduced him to any of these friends? Had she mentioned his father to any of them? 'I have to know more,' I told him, as if defining my stance in a business negotiation.

Mr Innes picked up the notebook. Taking from his jacket pocket a Mont Blanc pen, he began to detail his charges, which were impressively high. A plan of action was formulated, and I paid him a sum up front, in cash. We agreed to speak a week later.

Mr and Mrs Hendy were soon found, living in Acock's Green, and an operative named Max – formerly a sergeant in the Metropolitan Police – was duly dispatched to the Midlands. Max was a man people find it easy to talk to, said Mr Innes, and the Hendys proved to be a friendly and talkative couple, but with an air of woe about them, which appeared to be largely attributable to their having more or less lost contact with their adopted son. There had been no falling out – it was just that his life didn't include them any more. Well, it wasn't quite true that there hadn't been a falling-out – they'd had a big row the first time they'd seen him after he'd come back from Iraq, but they'd patched it up right away. He phoned them every three or four months, but they didn't know his number. Since he'd come out of the army they hadn't seen much of him. It was almost a year since he'd last visited. Mrs Hendy thought that the army had changed him. He'd never been what you'd call a chatty boy, but after the army there was a sense that he'd become closed off, she said. And the way he'd lost his temper, that time they'd had a row – he'd always had a tendency to flare up, but this was something different, like he'd completely lost control. Last time he'd been home, he'd not told them much about what he'd been doing – his attitude seemed to be that there was no point talking about it because they couldn't understand.

He hadn't talked much at all, in fact, and certainly hadn't said a word about wanting to find his real mother or father. When he was fifteen or sixteen he'd asked about them a few times, and they'd told him all they knew about his mother – which amounted to barely anything more than that her name was Sarah Williams, and that she'd given birth to him in Canterbury. Nothing was known about the father, not even his name. The Hendys were surprised to hear that he'd gone looking for Sarah, but only mildly surprised, because they really didn't know what was going on in his mind nowadays, if they ever had. Max had the impression that Mr and Mrs Hendy's social circle was small, or non-existent. He was with them for a whole afternoon, and they told him a lot about themselves. Nothing they told him clashed with what Sam had told me: Mr Hendy's CV matched Sam's account and in every corner of the house there was evidence of his DIY skills. It even turned out that Mrs Hendy did indeed have relatives in Ireland, on the west coast, near Donegal. Everything tallied with what Sam had told me. Max brought back a copy of a photo of the Hendys' adoptive son; their Sam was my Sam.

When Max returned from Birmingham, a former RUC officer called Mr Cochrane – a man of such tenacity, said Mr Innes, that he liked to boast that you could drop a golf ball off the top of Mount Everest and he'd find it for you – was assigned the task of researching Sarah's story. Sam had never told me precisely where she'd been living. The nearest sizeable town was Tunbridge Wells, that's all I knew, but I did know where she was buried, and that was enough for Mr Cochrane, who traced a route from the grave to the undertakers, and from there to the old railway carriages. Now home to a weatherbeaten old hippy from Aberdeen, the carriages stood at the end of a long track, and were so secluded that there could have been a terrorist training camp down there and nobody in the vicinity would have known anything about it. The nearest cottage was at a straight-line distance of three hundred yards, and thick woodland occupied most of that space. Mr Cochrane made enquiries at the cottage, and knocked on every door in the neighbouring hamlet. It appeared that Sarah had been regarded as something of a crank, albeit a picturesque crank. 'Scatty' and 'batty' were among the adjectives that Mr Cochrane heard; she was a hermit, someone said; 'an eccentric', said someone else. One old chap had talked to her a month or so before she died; it had been raining heavily and he'd come across her walking along the road, about a mile from home, so he'd given her a lift. 'Did she mention her son at all?' asked Geoff. She had not. To every interviewee Mr Cochrane showed the photograph of Sam that his colleague had obtained from the Hendys. One man had seen someone of similar appearance in the village; another thought they recognised him, but couldn't be positive; neither of them, however, had seen Sarah with him. Nobody had ever heard of a son, let alone heard of the father of a son.

Mr Cochrane turned his attention to the local cat club, four miles away. Sarah was remembered by the club secretary, Mrs Villiers, not as a crank but as 'a character', a 'first-rate breeder', a 'very independent lady'. Of her family and her life story, however, Mrs Villiers knew absolutely nothing. With Miss Williams one discussed only cat-related matters, Mrs Villiers explained; she was the sort of person, she said, who regarded personal questions as an impertinence. Mrs Villiers had visited Sarah's property on a number of occasions; she had never seen anyone except Sarah there, and there were no family photos on display – pictures of cats, yes; people, no. The Hendys' photo of Sam was accorded a glance, for the sake of politeness; he was not recognised. When I knew Sarah, she would rarely spend an evening alone; her address book had no blank pages. Yet even the tenacious Mr Cochrane couldn't find anyone who had regarded the older Sarah as anything other than an acquaintance, at best.

He did, however, manage to find Sarah's mother, in a home full of people you'd have taken to be dead if it weren't for the drooling, as he put it. Delicate as a chrysalis, Mrs Williams spent most of her waking hours propped up in a chair in a large overheated room with a selection of fellow residents, gaping with them at a television that was turned up so loud that conversation would have been impossible, had any of the inmates been capable of conversation. Mrs Williams was wheeled into her bedroom for her interview with Mr Cochrane, which was conducted with a nurse as intermediary. The old lady seemed to think at first that her visitor was telling her that he was her grandson. This misunderstanding was cleared up, but then, having finally understood that Mr Cochrane was a policeman, more or less, she took from somewhere the idea that he'd come to tell her that her daughter was in trouble. As tactfully as was compatible with bawling at her, he managed to impress upon her the sad fact that her daughter was deceased. Once that information had been absorbed, Mrs Williams refused to talk to him, as he'd been responsible for breaking the news of Sarah's death. After five minutes of vacant staring she fell asleep, so abruptly and with so deep a sigh that Mr

Cochrane thought that the last spark of life had at last gone out.

A fortnight after I'd hired him, Mr Innes and I discussed the situation. We now knew beyond doubt that Sarah had given birth to a boy she'd named Sam, that this child had eventually been adopted by the Hendys, and that this Sam had grown up to be the man who was claiming to be my son. 'If we're to move things along, we need to talk to Mr Williams,' Mr Innes concluded. He was confident of finding him quickly. I thought I was satisfied with what had been verified; as for the missing portion of Sam's story, I had strong evidence, even if it were negative evidence – he had refused a test, and thus he was not mine. I was even beginning to believe that it might, in time, be possible to get Sam out of my mind. I thanked Mr Innes and his team for their efforts and told him that I'd be in touch, convinced that I never would.

While this was going on, Aileen was trying to persuade me that we should take a break together. It had been almost two years since we'd last been away for more than a weekend. She reminded me of a holiday we'd taken in Perugia, a few years after we'd married. It had been a wonderful week, she said, and we'd sworn that one day we'd go back. We decided to go to Perugia; within a day Aileen had located and rented an apartment close to the centre of the town.

17

We flew to Pisa, picked up a car at the airport, and by mid-afternoon we were at the apartment, which was perfect, as I'd expected it to be. Aileen has always been the holiday planner, and she's unerringly successful in her choices. If an advertiser says his property is ten minutes' walk from the centre of town, she doesn't believe it until she's checked a map; if it's in a spot that's rural but easily accessible, she'll suspect that a motorway runs right past it; if there's a pool, she has to know precisely how large it is. Our apartment in Perugia occupied most of the upper storey of a modern villa, and it had a pool, a small saltwater pool, which the half-dozen photographs on the villa's website had in no way misrepresented. The rooms, too, were as they'd been shown: spacious and bright, with large windows in the living room that gave a fine view of the city walls and an assortment of churches and towers. The walls, as Aileen had verified, were a kilometre away. The gradient of the road we had to walk up to reach them, however, was a little steeper than anticipated.

Within an hour of unpacking we were labouring up the hill towards one of the old city gates. We had a map that our host had given us, but Aileen barely glanced at it – having been here two decades previously, she knew exactly where she was. From the gate a road descended to a crossroads and another ancient wall. 'If we turn right here we'll come to the university; straight on for the cathedral,' she said, and of course she was right. Passing the cathedral, she reminded me that we'd seen a concert in the piazza one night – a folk group had been playing, with an accordionist who had long grey hair but couldn't have been older than thirty, and a young woman who danced like a whirling dervish through every song. I vaguely recalled musicians leaping about on a stage late at night. At the end of the main street we crossed another piazza and stopped at a terrace which gave a view of a valley that ran away to the horizon; I recognised Assisi, but Aileen could put a name to every town we could see. She pointed out a museum to the side of a street below us – we'd been there and found it boring, apparently. The botanical gardens were beyond it – 'Remember?' she asked me. I remembered that there were botanical gardens, but as to whether they were north, south, east or west of us, I couldn't have said.

All week, wherever we went, Aileen knew precisely what she was about to see: go into this church and a painting of Saint Such-and-such is on the left; up this side-street there's a nice café; this alley is a short cut. 'I envy you,' she joked, 'seeing everything for the first time all over again.' But she didn't envy me – having so precise a mental image of the city didn't dull her enjoyment of it in the slightest. And, as she knew, it wasn't quite the case that I was seeing everything afresh: much of the city had an aura of familiarity, at least, and parts of it – random parts, it seemed – caused moments of recollection, of varying degrees of acuteness.

Aileen observed that I seemed to be enjoying myself. 'I haven't seen you this perky for ages,' she remarked, showing me the picture she'd just taken, in which I was smiling at some statue as if it had just been unveiled solely for my appreciation. I was enjoying myself, very much. Wherever I looked, things struck me strongly – more strongly, it seemed to me, than they had done twenty years earlier. Had I been as impressed by this place then as I was being impressed now, I reasoned to myself, I could not possibly have forgotten so much. I felt that the quality of my experience of the place was more intense now. The sight of things seemed strangely rich: one afternoon I found myself watching the pattern of cloud-shadows moving across the hills – not just looking, but watching, as if a story were unfolding and I wanted to know how it would end. Another day, a portion of pitted stone wall in sunlight was as engrossing as the grain of a piece of wood had been to me when I was younger. Complicated reflections on shop windows; a tattered flag against a perfect blue sky; a huge flagon of dark green olive oil – I was stopped by them all, like a photographer on the lookout for good images.

But it wasn't only what I saw that seemed to have a renewed urgency – every sense seemed enhanced. When Aileen returned to the city's art gallery (the only feature of the place that had changed greatly in the intervening years, she informed me), I sat on the flight of stone steps that faced the cathedral, and sat in the sunlight with my eyes closed, listening, and the mixture of sounds that I heard – voices near and far-off, loud and quiet, male and female; the whine of a scooter; the clatter of metal shutters; the clapping of pigeons' wings – had such an intricacy, it was like a piece of music. It was invigorating to walk into the coolness of a café, to step into the aroma of it and the noise of a dozen conversations clashing. As I stood on the terrace near the end of the main street, looking over the valley, my hand stroked the stone of the balustrade – the once-rough stone that had been made waxy by the contact of hundreds of thousands of hands over hundreds of years – as if testing the finish of something that I had made. As we get older, we become detached from our own experience. It's as if we're always observing ourselves, as if we're adding a commentary to what's going on – 'This is pleasurable', the mind tells itself, or 'This reminds me of . . . ', instead of having that pleasure purely, without a frame around it, as it were. But during these seven days in Italy, there were several moments, sustained moments, in which there was no frame around what I was experiencing. And of course the chief reason for this must have been Sam – or rather, the removal of Sam from my life. He was done with me and I was done with him. With great speed he was receding from me, which is why I was seeing things as they must appear to a man who has just come out of prison.

On our first night we'd intended to go back to the restaurant that Aileen said had been our favourite before. Certain of the address, she took us down a flight of steps and a steep side-road, only to find the premises occupied by a clothes shop. We crossed town to see if another restaurant that we'd liked was still in operation. It was, and we ate there several times in the course of the week: the food was good, the waiters did their jobs politely and without fuss, and the location was perfect – in a tiny courtyard, entered under a skewed stone arch that had no wall above it, enclosed by rugged old buildings. On our last night we ate there again, and sat at our usual table, close to the foot of some heavily worn steps that rose to a thick nail-studded door.

At the next table sat a German family: grandparents, parents, and three kids, all under ten, who spent much of the evening jumping off the steps. They were ebulliently happy children, if too noisy for Aileen's comfort. We chatted, after a fashion, with the parents, who were both taking language courses at the university. The eldest of the children was called Rainer, and his speaking voice was a semi-shout in the soprano range, which elicited from Aileen the smile of a woman with an incipient migraine. Rainer wanted to tell us, in English, what they'd been doing that day. They'd been to Gubbio, and gone up the mountain in a sort of basket that you had to stand in. 'I was flying in the air,' said Rainer, putting his arms out like wings. We had been there too, I told him. 'It is great. Exciting,' he screeched at Aileen. His siblings verified loudly that it had been very exciting. All three children were nice-looking, with large grey eyes and long lashes and a fetching dash of tan across the cheeks, and the parents were affectionate with them, as were the grand-parents – there was a lot of hair-ruffling going on, and much encouragement as each of the kids tried to draw, on napkins, a sketch of the *funivia* at Gubbio. As his family was leaving, Rainer's sister presented me with her napkin, showing three stick-children with heads like Halloween pumpkins, ascending a rock in tiny baskets hung from a wire.

Aileen and I resumed a conversation that had been impossible to continue with the children in close attend-ance. 'We must do this more often,' she had said. With many people such a remark would be merely another way of saying: 'This is nice.' Coming from Aileen, however, it was the opening of a definite proposal. Aileen's mother had died at the age of sixty-four; her mother's mother had died at the age of sixty-four; her great-grandmother had died at the age of sixty-four. The nearest Aileen ever came to being superstitious was in her notion that she wasn't going to live longer than they had. She'd make a joke of it: 'Five years to the deadline,' she'd say, as if she'd signed a contract for that duration, but at times she really did seem to think that she was destined to enjoy less than the average allocation of time. 'We're getting on,' she said, pouring a full glass for each of us, as if to signal that we were about to commence a weighty discussion. 'We should think about what we're going to do,' she said. She thought that in the next year or two I should consider scaling back my involvement in the business. There were things we both wanted to do: she wanted to take piano lessons; I was always complaining that I didn't have enough time for the books I wanted to read; we should see some more places. With our savings and investments, we'd be secure even if we both lived to be ninety, Aileen said; she even scribbled figures on a napkin to show that she wasn't being over-optimistic. By the time we left the restaurant we'd agreed that, at the very least, we'd go to Petra some time soon.

It was a warm night and I wasn't sleepy, so I went for a swim in the pool. Over the city hung a long thin reef of cloud, as bright as milk underneath the half-moon, fading to deep blue-grey where it slanted behind the roofs. Hundreds of stars spattered the sky and the small yellow lights of dozens of windows glittered on the hills. Every few minutes a car would traverse the slopes, raking the olive trees with its headlights, making them flare up and sink quickly back into shadow. Bats were darting around the water, once or twice passing within a yard of my head. I felt that our life might be changing, for the better. There would be many more weeks as enjoyable as the one that was now coming to an end. In the morning, having woken before six, I took one last dip. Standing in the cool water, I watched the sunlight trickling down the slopes, edging towards the lumps of gunmetal-coloured mist that lay in the hollows of the fields. A dog barked somewhere in the distance, intermittently, for minutes on end. In the mood I was in, its yapping was not an irritant, but instead was like the clanging of a church bell: it was the sound of the awakening day; it measured the expanse of mild, still air that the hills enclosed; it underscored the silence of the morning. I could not have been more content.

A little over a week after we'd returned to England, I came home to find Aileen sitting in the living room, reading a magazine. I fell into the armchair opposite hers. I was tired, having been in a meeting most of the afternoon, talking about the idea of opening another branch, in Bath. 'How did it go?' she asked. There was no sign that anything unusual had occurred, but as I was giving her a summary of what had been discussed she lifted an envelope from the arm of the chair and handed it to me.

There was no stamp on the envelope; our address and Aileen's name were written in capitals, with a cheap ballpoint. 'Read it,' she said, as if it were something that might amuse me. Inside was a single piece of paper, ruled; the message too was written in capitals, with DEAR MRS PATTISON underlined. I AM THE SON OF A WOMAN CALLED SARAH WILLIAMS WHO TRAGICLY DIED LAST YEAR, it began. FOR MANY REASONS THAT I WONT GO INTO I WAS NOT BROUGHT UP BY HER AND SADLY I DIDNT GET TO KNOW HER UNTILL THE LAST YEARS OF HER LIFE. I WAS BORN IN 1981 AND BEFORE THAT MR PATTISON HAD A RELATIONSHIP WITH MY MOTHER. I HAVE MY BIRTH CERTIFICATE WHICH SAYS THAT MY FATHER IS YOUR HUSBAND. I TOLD HIM THIS IS A FACT BUT HE DOES NOT ACCEPT THAT THE SITUATION IS WHAT IT IS. I AM NOT AFTER MONEY OR ANYTHING LIKE THAT MRS PATTISON. I JUST WANT THE TRUTH TO BE KNOWN.

THIS IS NOT GOOD NEWS FOR YOU I KNOW. YOUR GOING TO BE UPSET BY IT BUT IN THE LONG RUN IT IS ALWAYS BEST IF PEOPLE ARE HONEST I THINK. There was no signature.

'Do you know who this is from?' asked Aileen, squinting as though looking into the sun, which is what she does when she's keeping herself on a tight rein.

'I do,' I answered.

'Who is he?'

'Someone who's been pestering me,' I said.

'Tell me more.'

'A fantasist.'

'A fantasist equipped with a birth certificate that has your name on it?' she asked, placing the magazine on the table beside her chair, as though to indicate that the conversation was now becoming extremely interesting and required her complete attention.

'He doesn't have a birth certificate with my name on it,' I said.

'You know that for a fact?'

'He has a certificate on which he's written my name. It's a fake.'

'You've seen it? This certificate – you've actually seen it?'

'Yes. He's written my name on it with a ball-point.'

'Therefore: you've met this individual?'

'I have,' I replied.

'Where?' she asked, rubbing the skin between her eyebrows as if to tamp down her incredulity.

'Tottenham Court Road.'

'This man just appeared at the shop, out of the blue, clutching a birth certificate with your name on it?'

'With my name added to it, that's right.'

'And when was this?'

'A few weeks ago. May.'

'This man appears, claiming to be your son, and you don't think to tell me?'

'I thought about it, and I decided not to.'

'And why did you decide that?'

'What would have been the point? Why trouble you with it?'

'Because I'm your wife?' she suggested. With an upright forefinger she drummed lightly on her lips, frowning. She put out a hand to receive the note, and I gave it to her. 'So, what did you do? Apart from not tell me, that is.'

'I told him it was total nonsense.'

'And his response was what?'

'That he's my son. Nothing I said made any difference. It was like arguing with a Jehovah's Witness.'

After an unamused small smile, she said: 'So he's mad, is he?'

'Certainly not thinking straight.'

'So what happened next? You told him that you couldn't agree with his point of view, and then he went away?'

'Well, no – obviously not,' I said, gesturing at the note.

'And why do you think he's done this?' she asked.

'To make trouble. He didn't get what he wanted from me. As he saw it, I'd let him down. So he decided to get his own back.'

Aileen has this gesture that I've seen her employ in meetings, when people have spent too long on irrelevancies or shown themselves to be under-prepared for the discussion. First she puts the fingertips of both hands to her brow, and massages the furrows for a few seconds; then she slowly drags her fingers over her lowered eyelids, all the way down to her chin, and when she opens her eyes again her face has become the embodiment of serene attentiveness. She did this now, and then she looked straight at me, and at that moment I knew I was doomed. 'But if it's total nonsense, what trouble could there be?' she said. 'If you're just some random man he's decided should be his father, how could this note cause trouble? Surely there's no point in doing this if there's absolutely no chance that he might be right, if you can just say: "I've never heard of this woman." You see what I'm getting at? And more to the point, if he's simply a lunatic with a story that makes no sense, why wouldn't you tell me?'

'His story doesn't make any sense. It's not possible,' I persisted, as if merely by reiterating my innocence I might somehow prevail. 'I'm not his father.'

'Not possible because you never knew this woman? Or do you mean "It's not possible" as in someone coming home and finding a bus has crashed into the front of the house and the only thing he can think of saying is "It's not possible"? Is it the first one or the second one?' she asked, jabbing a finger onto the left arm of the chair and then onto the right. Her eyes hadn't left mine since she'd wiped her face with her hands, and the look in them had remained steady; now, however, she blinked, trying to quell her dismay. 'It's number two, isn't it? It's the bus crash. Of course it is. You were involved with this woman. That has to be the case.'

Sam was in my mind and I loathed him. I wanted harm to come to him, and I couldn't recall ever wishing harm on anyone before. He was a liar and I was a better person than him, and I would prove to myself that I was a better person than him by telling the truth. The moment had come: it was like seeing a huge wave rearing over you, and turning into it in the hope that it will carry you back to the shore instead of pushing you under. 'Yes,' I said, 'I knew her.'

'This is a euphemism, yes? You had sex with her.'

'I did,' I said. 'Once or twice.'

Disregarding the qualifying phrase, Aileen picked up the note again and scanned it. 'Born 1981,' she read out. 'So we were living in Chatham Road and you were seeing this Williams woman.'

'Yes. But not when he thinks I was. The dates don't match.'

'At the moment that's not quite the issue, Dominic. The issue isn't his perception of events – it's mine. We were living in Chatham Road and you were seeing this woman, correct?'

'Well—' I began, and never did a single syllable sound so pusillanimous.

'Who was she?'

'She was somebody I met.'

'That goes without saying, doesn't it? Where did you meet her?'

'She was a customer.'

'What age?'

'Mid-twenties.'

'OK. Good-looking as well? Charming? Witty? Intelligent?'

'Not especially.'

'Not especially what? Not especially intelligent? I assume she pleased the eye. They generally do.'

'I suppose so.'

'You suppose? Suppose? You were there. At very close quarters. Tell me.'

'She must have been attractive, yes,' I said.

'Don't be coy, Dominic,' said Aileen. The tone was like that of a therapist talking to someone many years her junior, but in her smile there was, I thought, a hint of pity – perhaps for me, perhaps for both of us. 'Tell me more,' she went on. 'I'm intrigued. This Sarah must have been quite a girl. We're talking about 1980. We'd have been, what – four years in? A bit ahead of schedule for a seven-year itch. So what was she like? Tell me. I'd like to know. Really, I would.'

'Aileen,' I said. 'There's no point in this. It was years and years ago. I can barely remember her.'

'I find that hard to believe.'

'It's true. I can't remember her clearly. It's so far in the past, and—'

'Not to me she isn't. Until this afternoon I'd never heard of her, and now she's here. She's the present, as far as I'm concerned. She's the foreground. Very much so. And I want to know why you did it.' Getting no immediate answer, she tried to help me out. 'Was it my fault? It's usually the woman's fault when the man has an affair, I know.'

'It wasn't an affair.'

'What word would you prefer?'

'I don't know.'

'In that case we'll stick with "affair",' she said, briskly. 'Now, the explanation. I thought I was being supportive. I know you had a tough time, but it was tough for both of us. I was involved, and I thought I was doing my bit. I thought I was helping. The worst came later, as I recall. Before London we had the odd bit of friction, but nothing out of the ordinary, I'd say. We were getting along fine, weren't we? So I'm at a loss here. Wasn't I supportive? Did I do something wrong? Do feel free to interject at any time.'

'Of course you were supportive.'

'But not enough. You needed a bit more.'

'It wasn't you. You couldn't have been better.'

'The evidence seems to indicate that I could. In some way I fell short.'

'No. It wasn't that at all.'

'So what was it, then? She was irresistible. That must be it. You couldn't resist. But if she was that lovely,' she said, cocking her head to one side as the contradiction occurred to her, 'you wouldn't have forgotten her, would you? Or maybe you haven't forgotten her and you think you're sparing my feelings by making out that you have. So tell me – she was a stunner, wasn't she?'

'I've told you. I can't say.'

'Oh come on, Dominic. Don't be bashful. Out with it,' she coaxed, banteringly, as if I were a brother rather than her husband.

'I can't remember, Aileen. I can't remember. Really I can't. And it doesn't matter.'

'It does to me.'

'What matters is now – you and me. And right now I don't know that I can do anything except say I'm sorry. It was idiotic of me and I can't explain it. But it was so long ago. I'm not saying we forget it, or try to – I'm not saying that. We can't – I know that. It was a mistake, a terrible mistake, and I don't know why it happened. I'm sorry. I don't know what else I can say,' I blathered. 'But I can't tell you why it happened. I didn't know what I was doing.'

'Don't be ridiculous. Of course you knew what you were doing. You were having sex.'

'And that's all it was. It wasn't an affair. A few minutes of lunacy, that's all.'

'Sex is quite significant, I'd say. It tends to mean something if human beings are involved.'

'This didn't.'

'It certainly means something now.'

'More than it did at the time, I'd say.'

Looking down at the floor, she shook her head slowly and sighed, as if I'd wearied her by my inability to comprehend a very simple idea. 'Dominic,' she resumed, 'before you met me, you'd had two girlfriends, yes?'

'Yes.'

'Two proper relationships.'

'That's right.'

'And apart from those two, how many other girls had you been to bed with?'

'None.'

'Are you sure about that? Now's the time to own up. Might as well clear the decks.'

'I'm sure. Just two.'

'Right. That's what I thought. From this we can conclude that one-night stands were never your style. You were not a boy who had sex for the sake of it. With you it was always serious.'

'But in this case it wasn't. Really it wasn't,' I said. 'I don't know what I can tell you. It happened, but it wasn't me. I wasn't myself.'

'And who might you have been, then?' she asked. 'The crown prince of Nepal?' The jibe was delivered with an expressionless face, but in a voice that had a punch of bitterness. 'Anyway,' she resumed, 'this young man – you say he's not yours. Are you certain of that?'

'One hundred per cent. The dates don't tally. He was born too late.'

'Well, there's a fair amount of leeway when it comes to dates.'

'They don't work, believe me.'

'Believing you isn't quite as straightforward a business as it used to be.'

'The dates are medically impossible.'

'You told him this, I assume?'

'I did, but that wasn't enough for him. So I arranged to have a DNA test, to prove it, to put an end to it. But he didn't turn up. Which tells you—'

'And when was this?'

'Weeks ago.'

'Four weeks, fourteen weeks?'

'Not long after the show. Round about that time.'

'My God,' she murmured, 'what a rich and varied life you've been leading.' I started to apologise again; she interrupted with: 'So why the note, all of a sudden?'

'Like I said, he's not right in the head,' I answered. Then I added: 'He was a very strange young man.'

For thirty seconds or so she rubbed at her temples, and then her expression began to change. She was gazing across the room at the window, her face slack and her eyes wide, as if she'd just seen someone do something idiotically dangerous and come through it unscathed, and now that the danger was past, it was the idiocy of what this person had done that was making her wonder. 'My God,' she whispered, 'it was him. It was him, wasn't it? This note – it was him.'

I couldn't say anything.

'Sam Hendy,' she said. 'That's who wrote this.' A full minute passed before she could look at me. Tears were coming, but her eyes were incensed, not sorrowful. 'You had him here, in this house—'

'I didn't have him here. He arrived. He conned his way in.'

'You had him here, in our house, and all this was going on, and you didn't say a word?'

'I couldn't say anything.'

'There was this game going on—'

'It wasn't a game for me, I—'

'Whatever you want to call it. This thing was happening, and I was in the centre of it, and I didn't have the faintest idea what was going on. You've been carrying on this performance; you've been lying to me, day in, day out; and I didn't have a clue. It's unbelievable. Can't you comprehend how this makes me feel?'

'Yes, I can. Of course.'

'I'm not sure you can, Dominic. I really am not sure you can. You've humiliated me. You've treated me with contempt.'

'No,' I began, 'that's not—'

'What were you thinking? What on earth were you thinking?'

'I was trying to get rid of him. I thought it best that you didn't know who he was. That was wrong, I see that, but it's what I thought.'

'And what the hell was he thinking? What was he doing here?'

'First and foremost, he was making me squirm. It gave him pleasure to make me squirm. But I think he liked being here as well. He wanted to be part of this kind of life. And he liked you.'

Aileen, now drying her eyes with a tissue, laughed sharply. 'That's nice to know,' she said. 'That makes things a lot better. He liked me. Great.'

'But he did like you. He liked talking to you. He liked you a lot more than he liked me. That's why I'm shocked that he's done this.'

'It must be quite a blow for you,' she muttered, then there was a long silence before she said: 'I don't understand it.'

'Neither do I,' I said. 'I really don't know what was going on in his head. You said yourself there was something wrong with him. But maybe—'

'That's not what I meant,' she said, in a tone that stopped me. She was examining the carpet as if searching through images of all the days that Sam had been in the house. After a while she began to shake her head slowly. 'I don't know how you could have done it,' she said. 'I simply cannot understand.'

'I felt trapped,' I told her. 'I didn't know what else to do.'

She considered my face, withholding empathy from the fool that was her husband. All she said, in a sigh, was: 'God Almighty, Dominic.'

I asked her: 'What do you want to do?'

'I want to wake up and find that none of this has happened,' she said, giving me a look in which there was no anger – just immeasurable disappointment. 'I don't know what I want to do,' she said. 'I'll tell you tomorrow.'

'I'll tell you anything you want to know,' I said.

'I've heard enough, Dominic. Enough for now. The details can wait, thanks all the same.' She stood up, and patted her chest lightly as she drew three or four quick little breaths, as you might do if you were settling yourself after coming close to being clipped by a car. 'Any other offences to be taken into consideration?' she asked. 'Any other meaningless girlfriends lurking in your past?'

'No, of course not.'

'I can't see there's any "of course" about it.'

'No,' I told her again, 'there aren't any.'

She passed the note to me, holding it between thumb and forefinger as if disposing of a soiled tissue. 'Will we be hearing more from this character, do you think?' she said. 'What's your hunch?'

'He's done all the damage he can.'

'I hope that's true.'

'It is,' I assured her. 'He can't do anything more. And he's gone. He's not around any more. His phone is dead; he's left where he was living; he's gone.'

'You knew where he lived?'

'Yes.'

'The surprises just keep on coming,' she said, exhaustedly.

'I'm sorry,' I said again, and she nodded. She looked me in the eyes, seeming to search for an explanation as to why this man could have betrayed her; not a trace of an explanation could be found, though, because the man who'd betrayed her wasn't there any more.

'I need to think, Dominic,' she said, rubbing her eyes. 'I really need to think.'

18

Aileen and I were a close couple for more than thirty years, and in all that time I saw her lose her temper three or four times at most. Even now, having found out about Sarah, she barely raised her voice at me. For several days she barely spoke to me at all. She simply got on with things, and stayed out of my way as much as possible. We ate separately; if I were watching TV, she would find other things to do. The situation seemed to make her tired more than angry; her movements had a deliberateness, as if she were having to concentrate in order to function.

She never again asked me why I'd done what I'd done. But when, after a week or so, we again sat at the kitchen table together, she did remark, when our conversation about work couldn't be made to last any longer: 'It wasn't once or twice, was it?' The question didn't have an accusatory tone, nor did it suggest that she had any great need to know more of the facts: it was said as though she were inviting me, for my own peace of mind more than anything else, to make a statement of the truth. I told her that the relationship – 'affair', she interrupted, softly, as a teacher might correct a student's usage – had lasted for three or four months. 'Four or five' would have been more honest, but I genuinely couldn't have been precise, and the answer appeared to be sufficient for Aileen. Her eyebrows lifted slightly, signifying that this was more or less what she'd expected to hear. Some time passed before she made any comment. 'I had no idea,' she said. Then she asked: 'And when you say the dates don't tally, that's not a lie?' I told her that it was not; having told the lie repeatedly, I had almost come to believe it. 'And the test?' she asked. I promised her that what I'd said about the test was true as well. Nothing more was said on the subject. Standing at the sink after we'd cleared the table, she looked out at the garden, but I could tell that she was not seeing it. Her mouth was tight, expressive of an anger that didn't match perfectly the expression of her eyes, which was almost wistful; I had the idea, not for the last time, that she was imagining how it would have been, had this woman and I done what Aileen and I had failed to do – produced a child.

Afterwards, she went out into the garden, to read for a while. She spent a lot of time in the garden, whenever I was in the house. This was a Sunday afternoon; a fine, mild day. Later, I looked out and saw her dozing in her chair. A magazine lay open on her chest and she had a hand on it. Her hand didn't move and her eyes were closed, so I thought she was asleep, but her eyes opened without a flicker and I realised that she hadn't been sleeping, and that what I had taken to be her face at perfect rest was in fact an expression of aggrieved resignation. 'How are you?' I asked when she came indoors. 'As well as can be expected,' she answered, without pausing on her way to the door.

There was no shouting, but there was the occasional flare-up of bitterness. One evening she got up and switched off the TV in the middle of a programme, turned to face me and said: 'It's a horrible idea, that we got married when you were on the rebound. I'm finding it difficult to accept. Very difficult indeed.' This was said sharply, with a vehement glance directly into my eyes. I told her she didn't have to accept it, because it wasn't what had happened. 'As far as I recall,' she carried on, 'there was never any question of getting married. We were fine as we were. And then you said you wanted to get married. It was your idea.'

'It was,' I said.

'You treated yourself to a fling, and then you decided you'd like to be married after all. Tried the grass on the other side of the fence, and it turned out not to be greener after all. That's about the size of it, isn't it?'

'No.' I insisted. 'It was a long time after, when we got married.'

'Not my idea of a long time,' said Aileen.

The business with Sarah, I said, had been a mistake. Of course the grass wasn't greener; and I'd never thought that it would be. It was a dalliance – that was perhaps the best word for it.

'I prefer "mistake",' said Aileen, with the implication that some mistakes are irreparable.

'I did an idiotic thing,' I continued, 'and I hate myself for it. I hated myself for it at the time—'

'I'm sure, I'm sure,' said Aileen, wearily.

'But it was meaningless. Which isn't to say,' I quickly added, 'that there's no reason to be upset. Of course, I understand. In your position, I'd be upset.'

'Thank you.'

'But it didn't change anything, for me. There's no connection. It just happened and as soon as it had happened I wished that it hadn't.'

'"As soon as" meaning in this instance "after three or four months",' she pointed out.

My response was not immediate. 'She was irrelevant,' I said.

Her expression was that of an examiner at the conclusion of a candidate's extraordinarily incompetent presentation. 'Please, Dominic,' she said. 'When you're in a hole, stop digging.' She turned the television back on.

A day or two later, I found myself recalling my father more vividly than I had done for quite some time. I was standing beside the chair that he'd made, the Nakashima chair. Thinking of nothing, I stroked the slender, glass-smooth ribs of its back, and as I was doing this I began to see my father at work. I saw him, as sure as a surgeon, sliding the block plane over the wood. I even seemed to hear the light hiss of the blade. I saw his hands at work, and I could see him standing in front of a finished piece, inspecting it sternly, as if, rather than something he himself had constructed, it were an artefact that it was his job to judge. And of course I felt the loss of him, as I often did, but there was another element to the mood that now came over me: a regret – weak and transient, but nevertheless distinct – that I'd been unable to follow him in his work. This was absurd. These were the facts: my way of thinking had diverged from my father's; I had made a considered decision to go my own way; I had always known that this decision was correct. And yet, briefly, these certainties were lost, as if dissolved in a miasma of regret that had originated with Sarah and Aileen, then flowed over the memory of my father. I was now imagining that I might have continued to work beside him, if only I had not lacked his aptitude for the craft.

Other scenes began to appear, in which my father and I were together, thirty-five or more years ago – just glimpses of his face, a few gestures, a word or two, like sequences of film reconstituted from some discontinuous frames and scraps of soundtrack. He appeared to be disappointed that I was leaving. He had been disappointed, that was true, but I couldn't trust what I was remembering. Had his voice really fallen in the way I seemed to hear it falling? Had that turn of his head, as he left the room, really been so slow, or did the apparent sadness of that movement belong more to the moment in which it was being remembered than to the moment in which it had happened? Was I even remembering what I thought I was remembering, or were these fragments in fact a composite of episodes that had been about something quite different? What had my father really thought of my leaving him? In later years, when he had seemed so pleased for my success, had his disappointment persisted, unexpressed? I didn't think so, but now, with both parents gone, there was no way of knowing.

Hours were consumed by such maundering, and by anger with Sam and with myself. I detested the person I had been, even though I could no longer apprehend him clearly. At the same time I resented feeling guilty for the actions of a man who today had little more to do with me than Sam Williams did.

Last thing at night, it was often Sam that I was thinking about. Sometimes I chose to think of him, as a sort of puzzle, as a relief from thinking about what I had done. More often he appeared uninvited, usually inside the house and looking at me with fury, or slouching at the table as if he owned the place, or striding towards the open-top BMW, brandishing a wrench like a tomahawk. Sitting in the garden, reading the paper, I would suddenly become nervous and lose my concentration, because I suddenly felt as if he were up on the roof, watching. The effect of this sensation was so marked, on one occasion, that Aileen asked me if I was OK. 'Just a bit dizzy for a second,' I replied, which sufficed; I suspect she thought I was angling for some sympathy. Sometimes when the phone rang I'd feel my pulse accelerate in an instant and it might take minutes for me to calm down. It was never Sam. It could never be Sam, I told myself, because he couldn't possibly reappear after what he'd done; and then I corrected myself – what I meant was that no reasonable person could return after doing such a thing. Sam was not a reasonable person.

Even when I was asleep I couldn't get away from him. One night I dreamed that Aileen had found that he was living in a room upstairs, a room that we hadn't known existed. In another dream Sam and I were walking through a town during a power cut; candles and oil lamps were burning in the houses that we passed; the streets were empty – no one was walking except us, and no one was driving; we didn't talk, and after what felt like hours of walking in silence, I understood that I was going to be punished, perhaps executed, if not by Sam then by the person he was taking me to. From that nightmare I came awake yelling, so loudly that I woke Aileen. She was in our bedroom and I was in the guest room, on the other side of the landing. That had been the arrangement since the evening of the revelation. This wasn't necessarily going to be a permanent banishment – for now she wanted to sleep alone, but she would tell me when the time was right for me to come back, if that day were to come. Previously we'd always both gone to bed at more or less the same time; now Aileen frequently said goodnight a little earlier than our usual hour; and I watched more late-night films on TV than had been my habit. Looked at more films, I should say, rather than watched. Often, when I eventually went to my room, the light would be on in our bedroom.

Sometimes I'd knock and Aileen would be sitting up in bed, reading, or at least holding a book. We'd have a brief talk. 'We'll be OK,' she said to me one night. 'But I can't pretend that we can go back to being exactly as we were before.' She accepted a kiss on the forehead, the first kiss of reconciliation, then I left.

The following morning, a couple of minutes after she'd left the house, I looked out through the window on the landing and saw her sitting in her car, staring through the windscreen as if the reason for going out had been entirely forgotten; she wiped an eye before driving off. That evening she barely spoke while we were eating. 'What's on your mind?' I asked her. 'What do you think is on my mind?' she replied. The silence coagulated around us. After a minute I asked: 'Do you want to talk?' She looked at me as though I were sitting behind glass, like a prisoner in a visiting room. 'Talking is not going to make a blind bit of difference,' she answered.

19

I contacted Mr Innes the following day. Tracing Sam might take some time, I thought, but before the week was out he'd been run to ground. The Hendys had spoken to him recently, but had no idea where he was. However, I had known, approximately, the location of the house with the music room that Sam had helped to build, and that was a sufficient toehold for Mr Innes and his team. I was given to understand that an employee of the local council's department for planning permissions had been helpful in finding the house in question, and once the house had been found the search for Sam was a fairly straightforward procedure: everyone who had worked on the music room was spoken to, and it was discovered that one of the builders had talked to Sam recently, about a job that was coming up soon. He had a phone number for him, which wasn't the number I'd been using. Sam was called, on a pretext plausible enough to extract from him the address at which he was working: he was building a kitchen in a house in High Park Road, Farnham, and would be there for the rest of the week.

As I drove into Farnham, I was asking myself what I hoped to achieve. I must get him to understand the consequences of his actions, I said to myself. And perhaps, once he had learned that a satisfactory amount of wreckage had been created, there would no longer be any point in continuing with the pretence, and he would explain why he had decided to persecute me. I imagined a confession, an apology, but I imagined them in the abstract, rather than coming from Sam. The trip would be futile, at best, I knew a moment later. There would be a huge argument. Something might be said that would make the situation even worse than it was. I was doing this because I had to have the last word, but it was never possible to have the last word, I argued against myself. Turning into High Park Road, I was so preoccupied that I barely avoided a collision with an oncoming car.

Outside the house, a wiry fair-haired young man was throwing lengths of skirting board into a skip. 'I'm looking for Mr Williams,' I said to him, half hoping to hear that Sam was no longer there, but before the young man could reply I saw Sam through the open door, hammering at a wall. His hair was longer than it had been before, and he'd grown a moustache and goatee beard that didn't suit him at all. 'Jack!' the blond lad called out, and Sam turned. He saw me, and was gratifyingly displeased. Slowly he wiped his hands on his overalls; he moved some tools from one part of the work area to another; again he wiped his hands; he spoke to one of his workmates; and at last he came out of the building, walking with his face downturned and rolling his shoulders exaggeratedly, as if shoving his way through an invisible crowd.

'Hello, Jack,' I said.

He squinted at me, with a thin grimace of a smile. 'There's another Sam on site,' he said. 'I'm Jack, to avoid confusion. Because Jack is my middle name, remember? And I look like Jack White, apparently.' He explained who Jack White was.

'We have to talk,' I told him.

'If you insist,' he said, blithely.

'I do,' I answered. The look I gave him – a baleful scowl, I hoped – had no apparent impact.

He glanced at his watch and said: 'I can give you fifteen minutes,' as if he were a man of influence and I'd come to ask him for a favour. 'There's a park behind there,' he said, pointing to the houses opposite. We said not a word to each other as we walked to the park. I felt like a man on his way to a duel, but Sam's attitude was one of bored compliance: he strolled along on the opposite side of the road, inspecting the houses just to give his eyes something to do while he accompanied me on this time-wasting chore.

Once through the gate we were at the foot of a grassy hill. We walked up the slope, and I turned to him and said: 'I want to know what you were thinking of when you sent that note to Aileen. What did you imagine would be the outcome? She is extremely upset. She's the one innocent party in this – the only person who's done nothing wrong. And now you've made her unhappy. Desperately unhappy.'

'Could have been worse, though,' he said.

'Could it?'

'Very easily. If I'd put at the end: "Oh, by the way, I'm the bloke who did the roof." That really would have dumped you in the shit, wouldn't it?'

'As opposed to where I am now?'

'Would have been a lot worse, I'd say. Lot more explaining to do. But I thought: he's got enough on his plate as it is. One step at a time. No point going straight in at full volume. That's what I was thinking.'

'So you were doing me a favour?'

'Well, yeah,' he said, as if this were self-evident.

'I should be grateful that you dumped me in it anony-mously?'

'I've saved you a bit of extra bother,' he said. 'But if you like, I could tell her. If you want everything above board, just say the word.'

'Christ Almighty,' I muttered, clasping my brow. 'You really are an idiot.'

This brought him to a halt. 'Say again?' he requested, peering at me as you might frown, half-smiling, at a child that's just used an insulting phrase that you suspect it doesn't understand.

'She knows it was from you.'

'You told her?'

'No, Sam, I didn't tell her. I didn't have to tell her. She worked it out.'

His expression wasn't exactly that of a man nonplussed; it was more extreme than that – rather as though a nerve below a tooth had suddenly throbbed.

There was some satisfaction in observing this effect. 'She's not a fool, you know,' I went on. 'She's come across two unusual young men recently: the one who was working in the house; and the one who sent her this letter. Did you think it wouldn't occur to her that there was a connection?'

He started walking again. For a few seconds he appeared to be giving the idea some thought, then with a shrug of the eyebrows he let it go. He could have been a man with a bizarre type of amnesia, so abrupt was the transition. As he strode up the hill beside me, he was looking around the park, smiling at the sunlit greenery, at the children on the swings and at their minders, apparently without a care.

'This has become the worst time of her life, thanks to you,' I told him.

'Thanks to you, strictly speaking,' he replied. 'You're the one who—'

'Yes, I don't have to be reminded. I shouldn't have done what I did. I'm not pretending otherwise. But the fact is, she would never have known about it if it weren't for your note.'

'If it wasn't for me, you mean. If I didn't exist. What you're saying is, I don't have any right to know my father. That's what it comes down to.'

'I'm saying you should not have written that note, and I want to know why you did it. It was malicious. Nothing good could possibly have come of it. Why do you think I would want to have anything to do with someone who could do a thing like that?'

'Dumb question. I don't. And you didn't want anything to do with me anyway.'

'OK. Let's put it another way. What was to be gained by making my wife unhappy?' I stood in front of him to ask this, forcing him to stop. He appeared, at last, to give some thought to Aileen.

Unable to look me in the eye, he rubbed his neck roughly before answering. 'Yeah,' he said, 'you might have a point.' He kicked a plastic bottle out of the grass. 'Sorry, OK?' he said, but it was as though he were apologising for a trivial absent-minded oversight. 'Are we carrying on?' he asked, indicating the crest of the hill, having checked the time. Apparently the subject of Aileen's distress was now closed.

'So now we're quits, are we? Is that how you see it?' I demanded.

Folding his arms, he studied the sky above my head, then gave me a stalemated look. 'What else do you want me to say? There's nothing I can say. I'm sorry. I apologise. It wasn't the smartest move. But it's done now. Nothing I can do about that.'

'I'd like you to explain,' I persisted. 'You've admitted you were lying—'

'I what?' he shouted, his face a mask of incredulity.

'You ran off. There was no reason to do that, if you weren't lying. So I want to know what was the reason for it all. Just to mess up my life? Was that all it was?'

Breathing deeply, he stared towards a huge fallen tree trunk that lay about twenty yards from where we were standing; I was being asked to observe how he strove to master his emotions. 'Let's walk,' he said, which seemed to signify that there was, after all, more to say. In a voice that was taut with the stress of self-restraint, he asked: 'You really can't understand that I had a good reason?'

'For writing that note? No, I can't. None at all.'

'For clearing off, I meant.'

'There's only one way of reading it,' I told him. He shook his head in disappointment, but said nothing. 'What's done is done, as you say,' I continued. 'But now that it's done, why don't you just come out and say it? Then we can try to put it behind us.'

'Say what?'

'That it was a story. A pretence. A fixation. Whatever word you prefer.'

His gaze roamed over my face, as if scrutinising his own reflection. 'I can't,' he said, almost in a whisper, and for a moment I thought he was saying that he lacked the courage to confess. But then he stated: 'I haven't been lying.' To me the phrase sounded like words that he'd trained himself to believe.

We were at the remnant of the oak, and there he stopped and looked down at me, frowning at my obtuseness. 'Look,' he said. 'You're my father. That's a fact. You don't want to know. OK. That's another fact. So why should I do a fucking test?' His voice was still low, but his teeth were bared; holding a hand open between our faces, he chopped the other hand into it. 'So the test comes out positive – and if the test works like you say it does, it would have been positive, no question about it. So it comes out positive – what then? All of a sudden your attitude changes? I don't think so. You don't want a son, that's obvious. Or you don't want me as a son. "I'll see you're provided for," that's what you said. That's what you said. Your exact words. I'll never forget them. It's so fucking insulting – don't you get it? Can't you comprehend? I don't want paying off. That's not what I wanted. But things are what they are. You don't want to know me, and I sure as fuck don't want to know you any more. So here's the deal: you leave me alone and I'll leave you alone. OK? That'll suit me just fine. Give me the contract and I'll sign it.'

It took me a few seconds to compose myself: I could barely think straight after this drivel, and I was, I admit, scared of him too. There was nobody within sight of us, and his hands were trembling as if he needed to strike at something to get the tension out of them. Then I said: 'It would have suited me too, but you didn't leave us alone, did you? That's the point. You sent that damned note.'

'I was angry,' he said. 'I was fucking furious.'

'Not all that furious, I'd say. You took your time about it, didn't you?'

'Yeah, well, revenge better cold and all that,' he replied after a pause, with unbearable nonchalance.

'Revenge?' I replied. 'I had doubts about the story you were giving me, completely reasonable doubts, and you're telling me that revenge was called for? Put yourself in my shoes, for a minute, if you can manage such a thing. If you were in my position, wouldn't you wonder what was going on? Of course you would.'

'I wouldn't be in your position,' he answered.

'And what's that supposed to mean?'

'What it means is that I would never have done what you did.'

All I could think of saying was: 'What in God's name are you talking about?'

He twisted his face into a caricature of consternation. 'What am I talking about?' he replied, mimicking my voice. 'What am I talking about? I'm talking about my mother, you dick.' There followed a tirade on my betrayal not only of Aileen but also of Sarah, who, according to Sam, had been fool enough to trust my promises and had been repaid for her naivety by being heartlessly cast aside.

The reality had been completely unlike his version of it, I told him: there had been no promises, from either of us, and each had rejected the other. And it was astonishing that he should have the nerve to lecture me on the subject of my relationships with women, after the things he'd told me about himself.

His response was a look of insolent bemusement, so I had to remind him of what he'd told me about living life to the maximum: 'Picking up women at the club. Remember?'

'Totally different,' he said.

'Is that so?'

'Two reasons,' he went on, jabbing a forefinger upwards to emphasise point number one. 'A: I was off my head at the time, like I told you. And B:' – thrusting out a second finger – 'I never two-timed anybody. I was always straight. They knew what it was about. But you weren't straight. That's the thing. You made promises. You took advantage,' he said. He folded his arms and regarded me with doltish self-righteousness.

'This is ludicrous,' I told him. 'You don't have any idea. What promises? There weren't any promises.'

'You know I'm right,' he replied, training his eyes on mine, unblinking.

Both oppressive and stupid, his gaze was impossible to bear. I stepped away and leaned on the tree trunk; affecting composure, I shook my head as I surveyed the park. 'I know what happened,' I said. 'You don't. I'm not going to discuss it.'

'You took advantage,' he repeated.

'I did not take advantage.'

'You didn't treat her with respect,' he stated tonelessly.

'We were both selfish, we were both thoughtless, we were both culpable.'

'She was younger than you. She was at a disadvantage.'

'She was as much in charge of the situation as I was. It was Sarah who ended it, and she was right to end it. She decided she didn't want to see me again. She took that decision and she stuck to it. It was her decision. I regret what happened, deeply. But Sarah wasn't deceived. Only one person was deceived, and she wasn't Sarah.'

'Her decision, was it?'

'Yes, it was.'

'That simple, eh? Make a decision, move on. Just like that?' His hand made a fluttering gesture, mimicking a wispy object borne away on the breeze, while his eyes narrowed with loathing.

'There's no point in continuing with this,' I said.

'Why do you think you never heard from her?' he continued. 'Why do you think that was?'

'She wanted to be rid of me. You said so yourself.'

'I'll tell you why,' he said, as if I hadn't spoken. 'She couldn't stand it. It was too much for her. That's why. She loved you, and you broke her heart. That's what you did. And she didn't recover, not for years. That's the truth. So don't talk to me about messing up your life, mate – you ruined hers.' Again he crossed his arms and looked at me steadily, tilting his head so that the glowering eyes were partly obscured by his eyebrows.

A woman was coming towards us, throwing a ball for her dog to retrieve; a short distance behind her, a man was striding up the hill with a pink-clad girl on his shoulders. Feeling safer for their presence, I told Sam that he was a truly extraordinary individual.

'Thank you,' he said, modestly accepting a compliment.

'You behave like a pig to my staff; you post disgusting photos through my letterbox; you take it upon yourself to disrupt our lives; yet you somehow think you're in a position to accuse me of having no respect?'

'That's right,' he said, with a small complacent nod, as if, rather than accusing him of grotesque hypocrisy, I'd been paraphrasing a notion of such subtlety that only now was I approaching a comprehension of it. 'And you had no respect for me, either,' he added.

'I can't see what you've done to deserve respect,' I told him.

'Right from the word go, you had no respect,' he said. 'The way you looked at me, the way you spoke to me. I'd hardly opened my mouth and you'd judged me. I could tell. Like a fucking book, your face was. I hadn't done anything, and you'd judged me.'

'I judged you?' I almost shrieked. 'I judged you? That's rich, coming from you, the self-appointed judge and jury. Who the hell do you think you are?'

'Could ask you the same thing. You didn't know me from fucking Adam, but you had me pigeonholed in five seconds flat,' he said loudly, though the man and the girl were near enough to hear him.

'But I did know you from Adam. You'd been intimidating my staff. I knew that much about you.'

'"My staff",' he echoed, with mocking pomposity. 'Just listen to yourself, will you? Lord of the fucking manor and his peasants.'

'They work for my company. Therefore they are my staff. And you'd been intimidating them.'

'Not true.'

'Yes, you had. You were aggressive. My manager at Tottenham Court Road – you threatened him.'

'Yeah, well – that streak of piss would feel threatened by his own fucking shadow,' he said. He smirked, pleased with his own wit. The man and the girl now crossed his line of sight, and he waved to them: 'Hi, Gaz,' he called out, instantaneously assuming a smile of expansive affability. He received a wave from the girl and her father. 'The client,' he explained. 'Nice chap. Very nice chap.' He watched them disappear over the hill, then turned back to me, blinking rapidly as if coming out of a daydream. 'I'm sorry – you were about to say?'

I felt an urge to break something on his head. Instead I repeated that I wanted an explanation from him.

'This is getting very, very boring,' he said, looking at his watch. 'You've had your explanation.'

'No I haven't.'

'Anyway,' he said, 'you've run out of time. The folks need their kitchen built. Got to earn my wages.'

I told him once more that he'd done great harm to Aileen, and I could see no sense in what he'd done.

'We've covered this already. I said sorry. I'll say it again if you like: sorry,' he said, with not a grain of true apology. He stood squarely in front of me and stooped a little to bring his face to the level of mine. 'She'll get over it,' he whispered. 'You'll both get over it. Life goes on.' This banality was imparted as though it were the considered distillation of a lifetime of experience and thought; he started to walk away. It was insufferable, and in a spasm of rage I kicked out at the tree trunk. Sam paused: he looked at me, at my foot, at the spot where I'd kicked the tree, then his gaze travelled slowly back from tree to foot to face, and a smirk appeared. He straightened his back and drew his head back a little, as if the few extra inches were necessary to bring this remarkable scene into perfect focus. 'Well, well, well,' he commented. 'Woken you up, haven't I?' He might have been a sergeant addressing a formerly hapless squaddie who had at last shown some fighting spirit. His arrogance made me speechless; I was enraged with him, and dismayed with myself, for having allowed him to make me so angry. It was exciting too, being this angry – and demeaning. I wanted to be elsewhere, immediately. He took a couple of steps towards me, to pat me on the shoulder. 'I have to go, OK?' he said. 'I'd love to stay and chat some more, but an honest day's work for an honest day's pay, and all that.'

Very calmly, looking him in the eye, I said: 'I hope this is the last time I ever see you.'

'And I hope so too. I really do,' he answered, and he smiled a sad, philosophical smile – the sort of smile with which you might bring a long and once close relationship to an end. Water gleamed for a moment in one of his eyes. 'I should have taken the money. That's what I should have done,' he said, as easily as saying: 'I should have put on a warmer jacket.' He let out a loud crack of a laugh. 'Just joking,' he assured me, delivering a last pat on the shoulder before loping off down the slope. As he went into the shade of the trees at the bottom, he raised a hand to the side of his head, without turning round, as though batting away a fly.

Too agitated to drive, I stayed in the park for a while, walking aimlessly, and in my mind – despite myself – I continued to argue with him. I couldn't go home until I had found proof that his accusation against me was false. No proof was immediately forthcoming. I walked through the town, trying to dredge up evidence in my favour, and after an hour or so I had some. I saw Sarah pummelling the bed in frustration at what she said was her weakness, accusing me of not caring for her as much as she cared for me. It was raining heavily; she was wearing a shirt that had belonged to her father, a blue-striped shirt with tails that reached to her knees. 'I love you,' she said, and what she meant by this was that I owed her something in return. In tears, she told me that she loved me, and I understood that to stop her crying I had to say the same words, but I didn't – not then, nor at any other time. By then I had come to wonder if what she needed above all was for me to be fascinated by her – or merely to tell her that I was.

Her volatility had seemed, at times, unspontaneous. One evening she'd thrown a full glass across the room, but had reached for the farther glass (water) rather than the nearer (wine), and had aimed precisely for the fireplace. Then again, there were times when a sudden change of mood seemed to overcome her. At the door one evening, she hurled herself at me and was as happy as I ever saw her; within the hour, slumped in a corner of the room, she was telling me: 'I can't go on with this – it's pathetic.' In bed she could be frantic, as if the purpose of it were to render herself senseless and I was nothing but the means to oblivion; but I recalled, too, something of the delicacy of her kiss, and the gleefulness of her laugh. And I recalled the revulsion with which she had dismissed me for the last time; she wasn't distraught. She was younger than I was, it was true, but she was a twenty-four-year-old woman, not a teenager – and her age had its advantages as well. I pictured her, absolutely sure of her attractiveness, showing me the photos of herself. But perhaps this first step had been prompted by some signs of interest from me? It seemed likely, but I no longer knew what I'd done. I was sure, however, that Sam's accusation was groundless, and the idea that Sarah would have been bereft at the end of our affair was incredible. And yet, even though I suspected that this was Sam's intention, I felt some responsibility for what had happened to her. Her breakdown, of course, might not have happened: it might have been nothing more than one of Sam's stories. And if it were true, her collapse could not have been my fault, or would have been mine only to a limited extent, unless the child had been mine, which I had never believed. Nonetheless, there was this taint on my mind. It was like a conspiracy theory that you know – when you think about it – is ridiculous, but which you cannot categorically dismiss, once you've heard it.

20

Aileen and I went to Petra, as planned. We were there for five or six hours, and for most of the time we explored the ruins independently of each other. At one point I saw her dabbing her eyes with a handkerchief. She was moved by what she was seeing, she said, but I knew this wasn't the explanation. It was something of a shock, after so many months, to see her upset like that.

Soon after we came back home, I was allowed to return to our bed. This was not a major gesture of renewed intimacy. It was rather that we were going to find out if it might be possible to continue our day-to-day lives as before, at least in form, and our day-to-day lives had previously entailed sleeping together. It proved impossible for us to sleep in the same bed. I'd taken to grinding my teeth, Aileen told me. The snoring was worse as well. So I removed myself to the guest room again. It was not as if we were newlyweds, as Aileen said; many people of our age have a similar arrangement. Aileen felt fresher in the mornings than she had done in years, she told me, more than once.

Our marriage was reduced. It would have been better had the truth not been uncovered. But Aileen had forgiven me, she said. As she once put it, the affair happened three decades ago, and even if you kill someone you usually get released before thirty years are up. And she could see that my reasons for staying silent about Sam were not wholly self-interested; she might even have done the same herself, in such a situation, she said, though we both knew that for Aileen such a situation could never have arisen. I had been judged leniently, but there is necessarily a distance in the act of judgement, and that distance cannot be closed. I was always aware of having been forgiven, of being indebted to her, and I did not, I have to admit, find it easy to live in debt. Nothing in the way Aileen conducted herself, in the way she talked to me or looked at me, was intended to impress upon me the magnanimity she had shown in trying to overlook my lapse, and rarely did I detect in her face or in her manner even as much as a hint of a consciousness of the superiority of her virtue. Two or three times in the course of a year, no more, she referred to what I did. But I was always conscious that our lives were continuing as they did because of her decision not to punish me. The balance of our marriage was changed.

There was something else. Some of my guilt was felt on behalf of a man I no longer was, and had not been for a very long time, but some of it was entirely mine, because Aileen had forgiven me without knowing the extent of my deceit. I had confessed yet had not been wholly honest, and I was still lying. I was renewing the worst offence by revisiting, frequently, the photographs that Sam had given me. Only after several months had passed did I destroy them.

For weeks I was as bad as an alcoholic with his half-bottle of Scotch hidden in the toilet cistern. Whenever the opportunity arose I would go up into the roof and take the pictures down from the cranny in which I'd taken to hiding them – in an angle of the rafters, at the far end of the loft. Sometimes I would stay up there for an hour or more, holding the photos under the glare of the lightbulb, putting the same questions to them over and over again: what had happened, and why had it happened? Often, though, I wasn't asking any questions at all – I was urging the photographs to transmit something more of the life they recorded, something more than the surfaces of these particular moments of my past. When I looked at the photograph of Sarah by the gate, frequently I thought of sex. Being in bed with the woman in this picture had been thrilling, I told myself, but it was as though I were reciting a piece of information, like a label attached to a souvenir. I had desired her too much, and yet when I tried to imagine the body that I'd desired all I could retrieve was a barely perceptible glimmering of sensation – a micro-measure of pleasure, as dilute as a homeopathic dose. Sarah could be funny – I knew this to be true of her, almost as you would know it to be true of a character in a book that you read many years ago. I could call to mind two occasions on which she had made me laugh – only two. In fact, I could barely remember anything that she'd said to me. Our last argument was the most substantial relic; a few disconnected phrases remained from the other days; the rest had gone.

When I looked at the photographs, whatever life they gave off was like the gleam emitted by a torch's bulb as the last of the battery's power gave out. The images became inert in my hands, and I was left, every time, with the most prosaic thoughts repeating themselves in my head, as tenaciously as advertising jingles: Sarah was dead and before long I would be dead too; how many years have passed since then, so quickly. I would return downstairs and Aileen would come home, and then I would become myself again.

I threw the pictures away and was pleased with myself for having done so. I felt better now that they were no longer hidden in the house. I tried not to think about Sarah, and was soon managing, nearly always, to delete the thought of her as soon as it appeared to me. And yet, while I largely succeeded in banishing the image of Sarah from my mind, I was still prey, from time to time, to a kind of nostalgia, but a nostalgia that has nothing real as its object. This is the case even now. The affair with Sarah sometimes enters my mind as something much vaguer than an image, as vague as an aura, and an aura that has nothing to do with the facts as I remember them. I don't know how to describe it. In a way, it's like what you see when a bright white light is abruptly extinguished – shapes and colours that are not the shapes and colours of the objects that were in the light. The affair with Sarah was no great romance; it was squalid, and I regret it profoundly. Nonetheless, the idea of it sometimes brings to me a sense of having once experienced a relationship of unusual depths, of having lost something of value. There are moments in which I wonder if this sense might be the product of submerged memories of things that my waking mind has forgotten. I am as certain as I can be that this is not true. This nostalgia, for want of a better word, is baseless and ridiculous. It is a fiction, yet I cannot rid myself of it.

Throughout the year that followed Sam's appearance, a fume of dissatisfaction would envelop me from time to time. This perhaps is inevitable, at my stage of life. Before Sam, however, I was satisfied with my life, generally; more than most people are, I suspect. Sometimes it felt as if Sam had detached me not just from Aileen but from myself. At work my mind wandered. It wanders still. Occasionally I find myself thinking about Sam, or about Sarah. More often, I'm thinking of nothing – I simply become unfocused, and find it difficult to hold on to any train of thought. I feel older than I should, as though the events of that summer have added a decade to me. I have bouts of boredom, which never used to happen before, not at work. And when I look up from my desk, I sometimes catch sight of my reflection in the glass wall opposite, and it's like looking at a photograph that you might see in a magazine article on the sterility of modern life. I have glanced at my reflection and been struck by the dismal comedy of it – all that well-ordered space, all those well-designed objects, with one ageing male face in the midst of it, making a mess of the arrangement.

The TV company sent me a DVD of the interview with Otis Mizrahi. I watched it with Aileen. 'You come across well,' she said, and it's true that they'd done a good job with me: the camera angles flattered me and the editing made me eloquent. But the programme presented me as someone whose career had followed precisely the course I had chosen for it: as a young man I had decided that I must bring the best of modern design to the attention of the British public, and I had achieved this ambition, with not inconsiderable commercial success. This falsehood was not solely the creation of the programme makers – I had been complicit in it. It would have been truer to say that what I'd wanted to do more than anything else was to design and make furniture but I had failed at that, and had become a salesman because it had seemed to be the next best thing. As for the commercial success, good fortune and good advice, much of it from Aileen, had been as significant as my supposed flair and vision, but flair and vision were the key terms in the programme's vocabulary, and I'd been happy to play the part. Listening to myself talking to Otis, watching myself as my hands shaped in air the perfect contours of my favourite lamp, I asked myself how this person should be described. 'Smug' wasn't quite the right adjective, but perhaps that was only because of the worry that Sam had put into me. Had the programme been made a couple of months sooner, 'smug' might very well have fitted perfectly. As it was, this was certainly a man who was too comfortable in his life, and a man it would not be difficult to dislike. I threw the DVD away, at the same time as the pictures of Sarah.

I dreaded Sam's return. When the phone rang, it would often occur to me that it might be Sam, and the idea was like a claw to the chest. But in effect he was always with us. Several times I walked into a room and found Aileen standing there, looking around like a detective revisiting the scene of a crime, picturing in her mind the exact disposition of what she'd found. From time to time I'd catch her looking at me in a way that reminded me of the way I had sometimes looked at Sam: she seemed to be trying to find points of similarity between the man in front of her and the man she had known as her husband. Sometimes, she said, she could see Sam sitting at the table, or she could hear him talking to her, or it was as though he'd left the room only a minute earlier. The house had been sullied by him, and by what he repre-sented. It was no great surprise when she said to me one night: 'I'm not sure if I can stay here.' By this, it turned out, she meant that she no longer felt at home not only with the house but also with me. She had forgiven me, she insisted, but forgiveness was not enough. 'I can never trust you completely,' she said, 'and if you can't trust someone completely, you don't trust them at all.' She knew that she would always live with the memory of what I'd done; some days, she could think of little else. It was like water getting into the tiny crevices of a rock and freezing there, and melting and freezing over and over again, until the rock falls apart.

We moved to a house that has a separate flat at garden level, and that's where I live. Eleanor was told that neither of us had felt right in the other house, and we'd decided that we should give each other a bit more space. There was some surprise at this, but not too much – no more than Eleanor's surprise that Aileen had married me in the first place.

Three or four evenings a week we eat together, most weeks. I stay to watch TV. We go out together, to the cinema or for walks. We're still on good terms, having shared a long past – even if, for Aileen, it wasn't shared quite as fully as she had thought for many years. She's not spoken Sam's name since we moved; as far as I can tell, she's obliterated him.

Business has been slack lately, and the opening of the new branch in Bath has been suspended indefinitely. The situation in London isn't too bad, though. I'm working as many hours as before; I need to be in the office; I enjoy it. Aileen has cut down her work to one or two days a week. She has been travelling: she's been to Prague, alone, and a couple of months ago she was in Peru with a gang of intrepid seniors. She has plans to travel to Costa Rica, Madagascar and New Mexico, and Eleanor is giving some thought to joining her, if she goes to Madagascar. So far, Aileen has not told her what happened with Sam; her view is nothing would be gained by telling her. I disagree. The secrecy must be very difficult for her to maintain: never before has she had to keep a significant occurrence in her life hidden from her sister, and perhaps nothing in all the years of our marriage was more significant than this. There's a chance that Aileen, fatigued after a day's hiking through the Madagascan jungle, might one evening tell her sister the full story. After that, I'm sure Eleanor and Gerry would want to keep me at arm's length. For me, that would be no great loss. But Cerys too might consequently decide to keep her distance, and that would be a different matter. Cerys stayed with Aileen last week. The current boyfriend, Derek, is a lighting technician, whose eye she caught when she was doing *Sunday in the Park with George*. She was very good in it, but she tells us she has given up the idea of being an actress, and has decided to become a primary school teacher. She seems very happy.

Aileen too is happy, or much happier than she was a year ago. She has taken up the piano as well: she has a lesson twice a week, and practises for an hour or more in the evening. She has discovered something of an aptitude. Already she's playing Mozart and Bach – simple pieces, but Mozart and Bach nonetheless. She regrets having delayed for so long. The piano is in a room over my bathroom, but I can hear her clearly wherever I am in the flat. Occasionally I go upstairs to listen to her play, but she plays better, she says, when she doesn't have an audience. It's saddening, often, to hear her playing when I'm downstairs. The sadness of it almost smothers me, and I have to go for a walk or a drive.

In my mind I see Sam Williams every day. Usually he appears to me as an aggressive young man, swearing ceaselessly, leering at girls in the park, brandishing a cigarette like a blade, but I've also recalled him at his best, talking about the Baikal Teal at Minsmere, or showing me the work he had done. And I have imagined, frequently, how it might have been to have had a son.

The ground has been cleared for him, so to speak. A place has been made available – not for Sam, but for a son. After seeing Cerys, I have sometimes entertained this daydream: a young man makes contact and proves to me that he is who Sam claimed to be, and everything works out well. This is ridiculous too – as ridiculous as envying Cerys her youth, which is something else I've taken to doing. My hypothetical son is an absurdity, but nevertheless I have imagined him almost as precisely as I imagined having a child during the years when being a father was something that might have happened. In fact, once or twice I have even envisaged a life with Sam himself in it – but fleetingly, as an idea that's beyond the realms of reality. I remind myself of how terrible he could be, and the fantasy explodes.

One day, not long after I'd moved into the flat, I encountered him again, not far from North Street. I had dropped in to see how things were going with the new manager. Geoff had recently left for a job in London, taking Agnieszka with him, which was an unexpected development. I stayed for a couple of hours, then went for a coffee. While I was in the café the sky darkened; I decided to get back to the car quickly. Head down against the drizzle, I hurried along the street, turned left, in the direction of the car park, and saw a couple sauntering towards me, under a huge red umbrella. The woman caught my attention first: she was slim and tall, with thick shoulder-length hair that was a fifty-fifty mix of black and grey; her clothes – loose black slacks, soft grey roll-neck top, charcoal overcoat that reached almost to the ground – looked expensive. The man was wearing smart jeans with a white shirt and well-cut navy blue jacket; his face was at first obscured by the umbrella, but when they were about twenty yards from me the woman tilted

the umbrella back to check the state of the sky, and I saw
that her companion was Sam Williams. He was talking
to her, looking into her face, laughing; then, sensing that
someone was in their way, he glanced up and saw me and
recognised me immediately.

His initial intention, I think, was to walk straight by,
but he saw something in me that showed him that I wasn't
going to let him pass – although I'm sure I wouldn't have
stopped him had he not seen me. 'Mr Pattison!' he called
out, as though no surprise could possibly have pleased
him more. A matching facial expression was displayed; it
would have fooled anybody. His friend was smiling at me:
she was a rather good-looking woman, with a strikingly
straight nose and a full-lipped mouth; her face suggested
a warm and outgoing character, but there was something
about her eyes that seemed indicative of nervousness, or
a tendency to anxiety; the make-up was extensive, I could
tell, but very discreet; she was, I'd say, at least fifteen
years older than Sam.

He put out a hand and I shook it. His grip – firm
and brief – was that of a man who is confident of his
dominance of the situation. 'How are you?' he asked, but
before I could answer he moved on to the introductions.
'This is Mr Pattison,' he told his companion. 'I did
some work for him last year. And this is Marianne.' In
his voice there was no trace of its former coarseness.
It might have been Sam's more prosperous and better-
educated twin.

'How do you do?' said Marianne, giving me a hand that
was nearly weightless; a huge acrylic bracelet, translu-
cent red and flecked with gold flakes, slipped out of her
coat sleeve onto her wrist.

'Pleased to meet you,' I said, before turning to Sam.
'So, Sam, how are you?' I asked, thinking that he might

have given Marianne another name, and consequently be embarrassed. He was not embarrassed.

'I'm fine. Very well indeed. How about yourself? You're looking dapper. Aileen well?'

'Very, thank you.'

'Been away?' he asked. 'You look tanned.'

'Not recently,' I answered. I told him we'd been to Petra.

'I've always wanted to go there,' said Marianne, with a glance to Sam which seemed to mean that he might give some consideration to the idea.

'How's work?' I asked him. 'Busy?'

'Busy enough,' he said. 'Roofing. That's what I'm doing now. Just roofing.'

'He does a good roof,' I said to Marianne.

'I know,' she said, cocking an eyebrow at Sam. The rain was becoming heavier by the minute. Marianne angled the umbrella to give me some of its shelter.

'We're going to Ireland. To live,' said Sam. 'Always raining in Ireland, so they need good roofers. I've got family there.'

'Oh really?' I said, as if this were news to me, and interesting news. I was doing all I could to betray no sign of my delight at hearing that he would soon be gone.

'Yes,' he stated, gazing steadily and calmly into my eyes. 'On the west coast, near Donegal.'

Marianne, sensing in this exchange a hint that something was being said that lay beneath the literal meaning of the words, looked at Sam with a faint puzzlement in her eyes, and Sam gave her a tender smile, as if they were alone. Then he put out his hand again, a paragon of good manners. 'Well,' he said, 'it was nice to see you again. Take care of yourself. Give my regards to your wife.'

'Nice to meet you,' said Marianne, moving off. For a moment she was between myself and Sam. He took her arm; in a few moments he would be gone, and I would never see him again. I could hear myself yelling at him: 'You've ruined my life.' I imagined Marianne's reaction when I told her what her boyfriend had done to me and my wife. But I kept my mouth shut. Sam hadn't ruined my life – that was just a phrase that came to mind. It was the sort of thing a man in this sort of situation might say in a television drama, but it wasn't true. There was a crack in my life, a wide and permanent crack, and Sam had been a cause of it. But my life hadn't been ruined – the latter part of it had been damaged, but I'd had a good sixty years before that. And what would have been gained, if I had told this woman the truth? Sam would have told his version of the story and he'd have been the one she would have believed. He, unruffled, would have listened to what I had to say and then told her the facts of the case, his facts, and I would have lost my temper and looked like a fool.

I'm not certain, however, that these reasons for saying nothing had formed in my mind until some time after Sam and Marianne had left me. It was a glance from Sam that silenced me. In the instant that Marianne stepped forward he looked at me over her shoulder, and the look that he gave me, though it filled such a tiny splice of time, had as much meaning in it, it felt to me, as any conversation we had ever had. There was some amusement in it, and contempt as well. But, prevailing over those, there was also a pain – a pain that I saw as a pain of rejection – and a resolute farewell. His eyes said to me: 'You were wrong. I was your son. I no longer am.' I did not tell Aileen that I'd seen him.

My father lay in bed for the last week of his life, too weak to even turn his head. Delirious for much of the time, he muttered words that were mostly indistinguishable. During those last seven days, though, he would mumble a phrase that sounded like 'but Mark will know'. Sometimes we heard the last word as 'willow'; sometimes we thought he'd said 'pillow'; but nearly always we heard 'Mark'. Again and again we asked him what he was saying, but he couldn't hear us. Neither I nor my mother knew who Mark might have been. Perhaps my father wasn't saying anything. Perhaps his brain, short-circuited by illness, had merely formed a sequence of sounds that pleased it, and had kept the sequence playing. That, in the end, is what my mother and I had come to believe, most of the time. The alternative – that there had been a last message that we had failed to take from him – was too hard to live with. In all likelihood, there was no last message. And yet, whenever I remember my father, I always have to push past the memory of that last week, and that phrase being murmured over and over again. Likewise, I think that for the rest of my life the first thing that I will see whenever I recall Sam Williams will be that final glance, telling me that I had been wrong.

Once in a while I come close to feeling that I can no longer endure not knowing, that I'll have to track him down again. Then I get past the image of his face in that last instant, and I remember him more fully, and I know I don't want to see him again. I did once try to send him a text, but it wouldn't transmit.